About the Author

I am a retired manufacturing engineer, having spent thirty-three magnificent years at Jaguar Land Rover. I now spend my time writing, playing golf at Droitwich Golf Club and watching my beloved Derby County as a season ticket holder. I also dedicate a lot of time walking my Labrador retriever, “Charlie,” who is a very special family dog.

Christchurch or Bust

Charlie Summer

Christchurch or Bust

Vanguard Press

VANGUARD PAPERBACK

A CIP catalogue record for this title is available from the British Library.

ISBN 978 1 80016 805 3

Vanguard Press is an imprint of
Pegasus Elliot Mackenzie Publishers Ltd.
www.pegasuspublishers.com

First Published in 2024

Vanguard Press
Sheraton House Castle Park
Cambridge England

Printed & Bound in Great Britain

This book is dedicated to my beautiful wife, rock and soul mate, Anna Williams. It was her inspiration and selflessness that opened the path to write this novel.

Acknowledgements

Acknowledgement to Ray Hubbard, Janet Hubbard, Sharon Moore, Debbie Hubbard (RIP), Andy Cornes and of course the loveable Penny for the inspirational and unforgettable holiday memories. Also, Miriam Dean for her valued friendship and to the good times spent in the past.

Acknowledgement to Steve Brown, Dean James, Martin Reay, Andy Little, Sebastian Ariel Maringolo, Hayden Brown, Andy Brown, and all the fabulous people at Alhaurin Golf Club. Many thanks for making my Spanish writing experience so inspirational and special.

Acknowledgement to Angela Chabior for her long standing friendship and for sorting the Alhaurin accommodation.

Acknowledgement to John Kenny for his continued support and belief.

Chapter One

It was late afternoon on a warm summer Friday. Rob was sitting at the bottom of his bed, staring at himself in the built-in wardrobe mirror in his bedroom. Today was end of term and Rob should have been sitting there with a huge smile across his face. Instead, it was a look of despair. Worcester Royal Grammar School for Boys had called time on the summer term. Rob could have had six weeks of freedom ahead of him. Being a keen and active sportsman, he should have been looking forward to countless days of ferociously competitive tennis ball cricket on Sammy's car park. Trying to make sense of Barrie Hawker's unplayable leggies. Or a short walk to the 'patch' by the Worcester-Birmingham canal for an equally merciless game of football with his pals. But no. Rob had made a schoolboy error six weeks ago, and it was now coming back to bite him, Rottweiler style.

Eight weeks ago, Rob was going out with a girl called Fiona, a blonde beauty who attended Worcester Girls' Grammar School. Fiona was a very attractive and clever individual, blessed with a sharp intellect, along with the enviable ability to absorb any information that was presented to her. Plus, she had a photographic memory which gave Fiona the tools to hit straight 'A's' in all subjects with little or no effort. But Fiona was more interested in being a rebellious teenager rather than setting herself up for the rest of her life.

Rob's love of sport combined with Fiona's desire to look for a more rebellious lifestyle resulted in the pair drifting apart, so they had called time on their eighteen month relationship. Rob was just too safe for Fiona. He didn't want to experiment with weed. He didn't want to find a remote, secretive place and get wasted on White Lightning cider. He wasn't interested in the council estate gang culture that blew a toothless storm in the suburbs. Rob would rather spend his winter weekends playing local football, and his summer weekends playing local cricket. That was just too boring and ordinary for excitement seeking Fiona.

Six weeks ago, Rob had been summoned to the Spencer household by Fiona's mum, Christine. He was fond of Christine who had been incredibly kind to him during the eighteen months of turmoil with Fiona. Not knowing the purpose of the visit, Rob showed up as an act of courtesy and respect towards Christine.

However, the visit proved to be an awkward affair. Christine explained to Rob that she had booked a caravanning holiday near Christchurch a few weeks previous, and Rob was on the booked attendee list. The ever hopeful Christine saw this as an opportunity to weave her magic, giving her a week to arbitrate and get

Fiona and Rob back together again. Christine liked boring and ordinary boyfriends as it stopped Fiona from creating havoc.

This placed Rob in a precarious position. He had no intentions of reuniting with his ex. But, on the other hand, he didn't want to upset Christine's feelings. After a period of almost desperate pleading from Christine, Rob cracked and agreed to go on the jolly. After all, it was only for a week. If he kept his wits about him, he could keep plenty of distance between him and Fiona, so what could go wrong?

Also considered in Rob's decision making was the fact that Fiona's sister, Jenifer, was also going on the holiday. That was good for Rob. He liked Jenifer and shared a healthy chemistry with her. The downside was that Jenifer's long standing boyfriend, Barry, was also tagging along. Barry was an absolute Liverpool Football Club nutcase. He lived, breathed and talked Liverpool Football Club. At times, his incessant devotion spilled over to such an effect, he could empty a room in record time.

Rob was a fervent Derby County supporter. So clashed with Barry on a regular basis. Rob would jibe Barry for being a plastic, armchair Liverpool supporter, as Barry had never once set foot in the sacred Anfield, whereas Rob was a regular visitor to the Baseball Ground. This level of superiority won the day on most occasions for Rob as Barry had no answer to this angle of attack. This, along with Barry's knowledge of Rob's soft spot for Jenifer, fuelled the fires of borderline dislike between the two.

Rob was finding it ever difficult to lift his frame from the bed and break off the mirror stare. Did he really still want to go? Rob's gaze moved over to the blue Adidas holdall that contained his clothing and toiletries for the week. It looked uninviting. For inspiration, Rob turned his head further to his left, to a poster of Led Zeppelin in concert at full throttle. Rob would rather spend the week listened to *Dazed and Confused* on a constant loop than spend the week in a poxy caravan in the south of England.

In addition, recent communications had soured Rob's mood further. Remote decisions had been made regarding an early departure. Stan, Christine's husband, had decided to leave on Friday evening at six p.m., giving them the whole of the next day to start enjoying their holiday. It felt more like having a year placed on a prison sentence for good behaviour, rather than the thrill and excitement of extra time in the caravan park.

It was four forty-five p.m. and time to move. Rob trudged downstairs with his holiday holdall, each step laboured, as if he was wearing deep sea diver boots, each downward movement an arduous and energy absorbing affair. He was greeted at the bottom of the stairs by his father, who was going to drop Rob off at the Spencer household.

"All ready to go then?" asked a joyous Graham. "Have you packed your toothbrush? Have you packed your Derby shirt? You know you don't go anywhere without it."

"Yep," replied a sombre Rob. "Let's get this over with."

As they went through the front door, Graham looked back at his wife, Jean, with an enormous smile on his face. They were both excited as they were about to enjoy an empty house for a week, a treat rarer than a golden eagle in Cripplegate Park. To their great fortune, both kids were away on holiday at the same time, so it was going to be party, party, party for a week.

The drive to the Spencer residence took just over ten minutes. As Graham's bottle green Mark Three Cortina pulled up, Graham could not contain his joy, as his face broke out into a huge beaming smile, just like a child in a toy shop.

"Have a great time," smirked Graham. "Don't get sunburnt."

Rob just looked across at Graham showing negative emotion on his mortified face.

"Thanks for the lift," said Rob as he jumped out of the car and traipsed wearily towards the blue front door in front of him. Rob gave the jumping stag door knocker a rattle. As per normal, the jumping stag fell to the ground like a lemming jumping off a cliff. The broken door knocker was a temporary fix, another job on Stan's 'to do' list.

The front door burst open. It was the bubbly and welcoming Christine who immediately threw her arms around Rob, giving him an enormous bear hug.

"You came!" exclaimed Christine. "Stan thought you wouldn't show up. That's another pound he owes me. Come in, come in, put your bag down in the front room, by the television."

The house was alive with action and intolerable noise. Stan was fretting about, trying to remember all the caravanning accessories to ensure their holiday was fully equipped. He was dashing between the garden shed and the front door, making a random, untidy pile of accessories in the hallway.

He stood over the pile wittering to himself.

"Awning, awning pegs, airbeds, pots and pans, spare gas bottle, swing-ball, tennis rackets, spare bedding, spare pillows," Stan mumbled, in a spin.

Christine appeared with a hot mug of tea, thrust it in Rob's hand whilst ordering him to sit down and stay out of the way.

Rob took a seat on the comfy leather armchair in the corner and proceeded to try and come to terms with the mayhem in front of him, preparing him for the week ahead.

Stan was still scurrying around holding a variety of caravanning equipment. Christine followed his every step, nagging his every action like a mother hen. Jenifer had appeared from the kitchen. She seemed to be in charge of the food they were to take with them, adding boxes of cornflakes and egg cartons to the growing pile in the hallway.

"Not there, not there!" yelled a frustrated Stan. "That's the equipment pile. Food goes on the food pile. Equipment goes on the equipment pile. You are ruining my system, Jenifer."

Rob was trying his best to make out the system being employed. To any observer, it just looked like a pile of stuff in the hallway.

"Where is the food pile?" begged an angry Jenifer.

"You tell me!" shouted back an equally stressed Stan. "You're in charge of food."

Jenifer looked at Rob in complete disbelief.

"Put the food in the kitchen," replied a helpful Stan. "Leave it on the floor by the fridge, then I will load it after I have loaded the equipment."

"I've just brought it from the kitchen," yelled Jenifer.

"That's a bit of a waste of energy then," quipped Stan.

"I can't put it by the fridge," retorted Jenifer. "I'm taking food out of the fridge for holiday. So I need access."

"I don't know then," replied an inattentive Stan. "Put it somewhere else then. You are an educated girl. You fathom it out."

Jenifer let out a frustrated shriek.

At the front door, the sound of the falling suicidal stag attempted to break into the bedlam. It was Barry.

After replacing the dizzy deer, Barry confidently entered the living room.

"It's holiday time," exclaimed an excited Barry.

He walked across to Rob and fluffed up his mullet.

"All right, rammy?" asked an exuberant Barry. "Looking forward to your holiday?"

"Can't wait," responded a despondent Rob.

"Come on," Barry continued. "No school, the weather forecast looks great, this time tomorrow we will be on the beach."

"Great," replied Rob.

"When do Derby start their pre-season?" asked an eager Barry.

"No idea, mate," replied a disinterested Rob.

"We go on a tour to Denmark for ours, in three weeks," continued an enlightened Barry. "The full squad is going. Maybe we might pick up a few new signings before then? Who knows? The first fixture is at Brondby FC. Did you know they were formed in 1964?"

"No, I didn't," replied a disengaged Rob. "Sorry mate, I'm going outside for a ciggie, I'll catch you in a bit to discuss the tour."

Rob rushed through the kitchen and into the back garden to liberate himself from the pending Liverpool trivia onslaught. It was a stark reminder that Rob needed to be on his toes for the next week. He needed to avoid being cornered for any football history lectures from Barry at all costs. He liked Barry but couldn't bring himself to listen to very lengthy and detailed Liverpool trivia.

"Now, Stan, what can I do to help?" inquired Barry walking towards the kitchen.

"Start loading the equipment into the caravan," instructed Stan. "From the pile in the hallway."

"Consider it done," said Barry, enthusiastically.

Barry made his way to the hallway, picked up a yellow bucket from the pile, then opened the front door. In front of him was a caravan on the driveway, hitched up to Stan's jet black 1971 Ford Zodiac Mk 4, Stan's absolute pride and joy. Stan spent hours tinkering with his beloved car. Cleaning, polishing, servicing, nursing, loving, he even spent time having conversations with the beast. Barry walked to the caravan and opened the entry door. He placed the bucket inside the doorway, then returned to the house for more equipment.

In the kitchen, the food pile was growing. With six hungry mouths to feed, fare taken from home would save money, meaning the frugal Stan could spend less money down south. Stan was known for his reluctance to part with his hard earned cash, to the degree where he would be more than prepared to buy second-hand teabags. Jenifer methodically sought through the fridge, following the strict instructions administered by her father to capitalise on dining opportunities for the caravan.

Barry had been working like a beaver, making light work with the hallway equipment pile, so he returned to the house to take up further instructions. As Stan came from the garden shed laden with even more essential equipment, in his haste he stepped into the kitchen, straight into Jenifer's building food pile, sending provisions to all corners of the kitchen. Eggs were broken. As if her radar was set on 'spillage', no sooner had the broken eggs started to release their contents onto the kitchen floor, the family dog, Penny, was on hand to lick up the mess.

"Penny, out of there," screamed a fuming Stan, clutching a garden spade. "Which brainless idiot put that heap of food there?"

"I don't believe it," shrieked an upset Jenifer. "Why don't you open your eyes and look where you are going, you idiot?"

"Why did you put the food in the doorway?" berated Stan. "Just leave it on the worksurfaces, out of harm's way. This is going to cost me a fortune to replace those broken eggs."

Jenifer looked around the kitchen at the worktops. They were loaded with clothes yet to be packed, an inflatable swan, copious amounts of dirty pots, pans, plates and cutlery that was still waiting for Fiona to start the washing up. Furthermore, any other prized worktop real estate was inhabited by Christine's vast cookbook library.

"Exactly where on the worksurfaces?" begged Jenifer.

Stan stopped in his tracks and took a quick look around.

"It's your issue," responded a flustered Stan. "You're in charge of food, you sort it. And clear up this mess you've made."

"I've made?" screamed Jenifer.

It probably wasn't a good time, but in the melee, Rob entered the kitchen holding an empty mug.

"This is for washing up," said Rob ironically.

Jenifer just stared back at Rob, just as Rob looked over at the mound of washing up desperately seeking attention.

"Do you want me to do the washing up?" asked Rob. "I'm just sat in there doing nothing."

"That would be priceless," replied Jenifer.

One in the bank for Rob, he thought as he turned on the hot water tap.

With the hallway equipment pile now dealt with, Stan wanted to assess the room available in the caravan for last minute but vital accessories. Barry obediently flanked Stan out to the caravan like a Beatles groupie.

As Stan opened the caravan door, he took a startled step back.

"What have you done?" asked a bemused Stan. "Have you ever packed a caravan before, Barry?"

"Nope," replied a hapless Barry. "It's pretty easy though. Look at the good job I have made."

Stan looked at the equipment that was piled randomly in the caravan doorway. Instead of walking the accessories into the far reaches of the caravan, and storing the accessories neatly and balanced, Barry had just piled the accessories in and around the caravan doorway. This made access impossible, plus Stan had countless more items that he needed to pack inside the now part laden caravan.

"I'll just have to take this all out and do it properly myself," said a bemused Stan.

"I can help you," offered a willing Barry.

"I don't think so," snapped Stan. "You couldn't pack a pillowcase."

Item by item, Stan started to remove everything from the blocked doorway onto the front lawn, ready for repacking.

"Going anywhere nice?" asked Paul, the nosey neighbour who just happened to be walking past the house.

"Christchurch," grunted Stan.

"Nice," replied Paul. "The wife and I love it down there. Beautiful part of the world. We used to stop at the King's Arms by the river. Beautiful rooms, great food. You know—"

"Paul, I'm really busy," interrupted Stan. "We are trying to get away this evening and I have all this to do."

"Okay, okay," responded Paul. "Have a nice time."

With his feelings deeply hurt, Barry had returned to the house to seek comfort from his girlfriend. Walking into the kitchen and seeing Rob and Jenifer working together set Barry's hackles up. But not wanting them to see how much Rob's presence next to his princess bothered him, Barry bit his stiff upper lip.

"Need any help in here?" asked a jolly Barry.

"All under control," replied Jenifer.

"Me too," added Rob.

This made Barry feel even more unwanted.

"You can come and help me," came a voice from the garage, where Christine was ferociously unloading the tumble dryer.

Barry willingly wandered into the garage, where he was faced with the picture of Christine with more washing tucked under her arms than she could manage. Garments were dropping to the dirty and dusty floor, resembling a laundry ticker tape parade. Barry stretched forwards, trying to grab as many falling garments as he could. The small pile which was already amassing on the floor had been soiled by the grubby floor, rendering them unfit for use.

"Silly me," gasped Christine as she still tried to grasp more laundry. "We'll just have to cut back on our packing."

Barry helped with the remaining items, rescuing them from their potential oily landing.

"Right, it's time to pack," announced Christine, walking towards the door with her bundle of washing under her arm.

As Christine arrived in the kitchen, she spotted Rob at the sink, washing up the oversized pile of crockery.

"What are you doing, young man?" asked Christine.

"Just doing my bit," replied Rob.

"Fiona was supposed to do that," replied an irate Christine. "Where is she? I haven't seen her in ages."

"Probably smoking behind the garden shed as usual," quipped Jenifer.

"We'll see about that," stated Christine assertively.

Christine stormed into the garden and marched over to the garden shed located in the corner of the well maintained garden. Christine battled through the evergreen tree which protected the back of the shed from spying eyes.

"What do you think you are doing, young lady?" growled Christine upon finding Fiona halfway through a Player's Number Six.

Fiona quickly flicked the cigarette over the fence and waved her hands in front of her face to disperse the smoke.

"You know you shouldn't be smoking," continued Christine in her rage. "Wait until your father hears about this. Why aren't you inside, helping out? We are leaving inside the hour, and we are far from ready. You are never around when there is work to be done. Come on, get inside and start pulling your weight."

Fiona begrudgingly rose from her makeshift smoking stool and followed her mother inside the house. When they reached the kitchen and Fiona spotted Rob, her mood swung even lower.

“What the hell is he doing here?” asked an incensed Fiona. “He’d better not be coming on holiday with us.”

“Surprise!” exclaimed Christine. “I thought you’d be happy with the company for the week. At least you will have a smoking pal.”

“I’m not going,” shouted Fiona.

“You are coming young lady,” snapped Christine. “Whether you like it or not, even if your father and I have to drag you into the car kicking and screaming.”

“I’ll go to Aunty Betty’s,” responded Fiona. “She can look after me whilst you are away.”

“Aunty Betty is in hospital,” responded Christine, “having her in ingrowing toenail sorted.”

“Then I’ll go to Uncle Dave’s,” replied Fiona, in desperation.

“He’s going to Cornwall, camping tomorrow,” retorted Christine, dedicated to foiling any of Fiona’s counter-holiday plans.

“I give up,” said Fiona, throwing her hands in the air petulantly. She stormed off, running to the sanctuary of her bedroom.

“It’s going to be a great week,” said Rob as he winked at Christine.

“She’ll come round. You’ll see,” replied a desperate Christine.

As time crept forward like an unwelcome slug on a prime lettuce, bit by bit, the holiday preparations were addressed. Stan had sorted the caravan packing debacle created by Barry, Rob had finished the washing up,

Christine had finished the packing and Jenifer had gathered the food supplies, transferring them to the caravan.

Stan whizzed around the house for a final inspection, ticking off his pre-holiday preparation checklist as he advanced. Once Stan was satisfied that all was in order, he commanded the troops to get themselves inside the 1971 Ford Zodiac Mk 4.

Christine took the passenger's seat with Penny sitting on her lap. Fiona took the seat between the front passenger and driver on the modified bench seat. Jenifer and Barry snuggled up in the back seat together, with Rob taking the seat behind the driver. All were ready for the off.

Stan jumped into the driver's seat and sat there motionless for a minute, then sparked the Zodiac into life. Checking all around for obstacles, he gently reversed out of the drive.

"This is a bit strange," said a concerned Stan, checking that he had completely released the handbrake. "Something doesn't feel quite right."

Stan gently reversed back another few yards then stopped.

"I'm going to check outside," added a now concerned Stan. "The car just doesn't feel right."

Stan jumped out of the car to investigate. Once he had walked completely around the car and caravan, Stan opened the driver's door.

"Everybody out," exclaimed Stan. "I don't believe it. The ruddy caravan has got a puncture."

The relative holiday joy within the Zodiac soon dropped to one of deep frustration, as the wannabe holiday makers traipsed back into the house, as Stan returned the rig to the driveway.

"Need a helping hand, Stan?" asked an ever eager Barry.

"Sure, why not," replied an exasperated Stan.

Stan walked to the back of the caravan to release the spare wheel from its cradle. However, it wasn't long before Stan's memory was jogged.

"Oh blast," howled Stan.

"What's up?" asked Barry as he ran to the back of the caravan to join Stan.

"My brother Dave has got the spare wheel," replied a dejected Stan. "I gave it to him to repair and refurbish in preparation for our holiday. I was supposed to go and fetch it last night, but there was a Morecombe and Wise special on TV, and I forgot about the spare wheel."

"What are we going to do?" asked Barry.

"I'll have to go round now and collect it," replied Stan. "I'll ring him first, to make sure he hasn't left for Cornwall yet."

Stan jogged back into the house and called his brother. Thankfully, Dave was not leaving until the morning, plus he confirmed that the tyre in question was ready to go.

Following the invigorating phone call, Stan dashed to the back of his beloved Zodiac, unhitched the caravan, and sped off to his brother's house.

Forty minutes later, Stan was back with the spare. With Barry's assistance, it took another twenty minutes to replace the punctured tyre. At last, the holiday crew were soon back in the Zodiac, ready for the off.

"Right, let's go," announced a more than relieved Stan. "We just need to stop at the Texaco for fuel before we hit the motorway."

"Why didn't you get your fuel last night?" nagged Christine.

"Morecombe and Wise, that's why," japed Barry from the back seat.

Jenifer landed a firm slap on Barry's arm.

"Don't be rude," she snapped as Barry cowered into the corner.

Stan backed the rig off the driveway and set off. The petrol station was just a five minute drive around the corner, on the main road. As they approached the fuel station, Stan indicated to pull in. As he drove onto the forecourt there was an almighty crash as the Zodiac jolted to a halt.

"What on earth was that?" asked a concerned Christine.

"No idea," replied Stan. "I'll go and take a look."

As Stan clambered out of the car, the problem became immediately apparent. Stan had forgotten about the caravan that he was towing, and sadly, the extra height of the caravan had collided with the low hanging petrol station canopy, causing the flimsy canopy to buckle.

As Stan was inspecting the damage, an irate forecourt attendant came running over.

"What the hell have you done?" quizzed the animated worker.

"I'm sorry," replied a sheepish Stan. "I just clean forgot about the caravan."

"Forgot about the caravan?" retorted the attendant. "It's thirty feet long or more."

"It's easily done," responded Stan.

Stan got back into the Zodiac and backed the rig onto the main road, much to the annoyance of his fellow motorists. Barry assisted by flagging down motorists to create a gap for Stan.

Next door to the fuel station was a pub, with an ample, empty car park. So, Stan backed the caravan into the car park, unhitched the caravan, then drove the car back to the fuel station to administer his fuel.

As he filled the car, the forecourt attendant was inspecting the canopy damage with a fellow worker. The pair walked over to Stan.

"There's a fair amount of damage, mate," piped up the forecourt attendant. "What are you going to do about it?"

"We are off on holiday now," responded Stan. "Can I sort this out when I get back?"

The two petrol station workers looked at each other.

"We need your name, address and car registration number," said the attendant. "I guess you are in a rush to get away. I'll give you a break, just this once. We can sort this mess out when you get back. At least the damage is not terminal."

"Thank you," replied a relieved Stan.

The petrol nozzle stopped pumping as the fuel brimmed at the top of the tank. Stan opened the driver's door of the car.

"Give me my wallet, dear," said Stan. "I need to pay now."

"I haven't got your wallet," answered Christine in confusion.

Before angrily responding, Stan shut his eyes to try and remember where he last saw his wallet. Sure enough, the picture of his wallet on the bedside cabinet entered his mind.

"Blast," said Stan to himself.

"Blast what?" asked a worried Christine.

"I may have left my wallet at home," admitted an embarrassed Stan.

"What?" snorted Christine. "You are an airhead. Of all things to leave behind. What else have you forgotten?"

"What sort of question is that?" replied a defensive Stan.

"I know you are tight," continued Christine, "but this is a new low for you. To plan on spending no money at all in Christchurch is right up your street."

"Don't be absurd," responded Stan. "I didn't do it on purpose."

"That's what you say now," said Christine. "I reckon this is a deliberate and pre-determined act. You'd rather spend your money on this confounded car."

"You are just being ridiculous now," said a distraught Stan. "I need to go and sort this out."

Stan walked over to the petrol station shop to explain his predicament to the attendant. Considering his plight on the way, Stan didn't hold out much hope of being shown mercy. After all, he'd just driven up to their petrol station, taken away half of their canopy, and now expected them to accept delayed payment for the fuel. Moments later, Stan returned to the car.

"Barry," said an embarrassed Stan. "I need your help. My wallet is at home, on the bedside cabinet. These kind petrol station gentlemen won't let me leave, so you need to run home quickly and fetch my wallet."

"Absolutely," responded an animated and eager to please Barry as he clambered out of the back seat.

Christine wound down the window and shouted at Barry as he was about to disappear behind the wall surrounding the petrol station. Barry stopped in his tracks.

"You will need these," she said, dangling a set of house keys from her fingers.

"Ah yes," responded Barry.

As Barry disappeared, Stan was instructed to park up and wait in the corner of the petrol station.

"We would have been halfway there by now if he'd remembered his wallet," growled Christine, sitting impatiently in the car.

"Hardly," said an argumentative Jenifer. "Maybe on the M5."

"Don't be pedantic," snapped Christine. "You know what I mean. It's like this every time we go away. Next time, if there is a next time, I'm going to write him a big list. His wallet will be top of that list. Mark my words."

"Will oily washing also be on that list?" quipped Rob.

Jenifer administered a firm slap to the back of Rob's shoulder.

"What do you mean?" asked Christine as she quickly spun round to face Rob. "Are you complaining about my washing techniques?"

"I was just having a joke with you," responded a defensive Rob. "Just to lighten the mood. This holiday has certainly not started on the front foot."

"Front foot?" barked Christine. "You wouldn't know a front foot if it kicked you in a sensitive region."

Twenty minutes later, Barry reappeared from behind the wall, carrying a blue Adidas holdall.

Completely out of breath, Barry walked up to the front passenger's window.

"Is this anyone's?" asked Barry. "I found it by the front door next to the potted shrub."

"That'll be mine," admitted a relieved Rob.

Christine reached out and punched Barry on his upper arm.

"Why didn't you pack Rob's luggage you numpty?" asked an angry Christine.

"I've had so much on my plate," responded Barry. "I just made a mistake."

"It's a good job Stan forgot his wallet," added Christine. "Otherwise, Rob would have been in the same undies all week."

"Yuck," growled Fiona from the front seat.

"Can we stop talking about my undies and get going?" demanded Rob.

After Barry had delivered the wallet, Stan and Barry returned from the shop, having at last paid his fuel bill. In no time, Stan re-hitched the caravan and the intrepid group were at last Christchurch bound.

Just as the rig cautiously edged out of the car park onto the main road, a voice piped up from the back seat.

"Are we there yet?" asked a jovial Rob.

"Don't you start," said Stan, pretty much at the end of his tether already.

Chapter Two

Stan guided his rig through the bustling city centre streets of Worcester, heading towards the busy M5. Being school's out day, heavy traffic on the M5 southbound was predicted. This was an annual event at this time of year, with the end of school term lining up with the Birmingham factory fortnight. It seemed that most Midlander's headed south in unison. Great thinking!

As Stan reached the slip road of Junction Seven, the visible traffic on the M5 was moving, but only at around forty miles per hour in both lanes.

"Typical," said a frustrated Stan. "I knew this would happen. That's why I wanted to get away early, to miss this rush. We've got absolutely no chance of getting to Christchurch in the light. Unbelievable."

"If you'd remembered your wallet," replied Christine, "and not crashed into the petrol station, we would have been further south by now."

"Don't be ridiculous," responded Stan. "That barely took fifteen minutes out of the journey."

"More like an hour and fifteen minutes," retorted Christine sternly. "Plus, you should have packed the caravan last night, instead of insisting that you watch Morecombe and Wise on the telly. I could have taped it for you, and you could have watched it later."

"It's never the same watching it on tape," responded Stan.

"Are you kidding me?" raged Christine. "It's the same programme, nothing changes when it gets transferred onto videotape. What do you expect to happen? A different dance routine with Shirley Bassey?"

"You know what I mean," added Stan.

"Actually, no, I don't," responded Christine with her arms folded tightly across her chest. "Tell me."

Knowing that he was on a loser, Stan backed down from the conversation, feverishly checking his wing mirrors as he attempted his first overtake manoeuvre.

All was well as they passed Strensham Services. Traffic was heavy, the speed was slow, but at least they were moving. Stan hated any 'start-stop' situations on the motorway.

When Stan passed the Tewksbury junction, he started to get a feeling that the car was losing power when he pressed the accelerator. This feeling was amplified when Barry wound down his window to get some air into the back of the car. As he did so, an unfamiliar dull drone could be heard coming from the back of the car.

With a gap of around fifty yards available in front of Stan, he decided to test the car's performance by pressing hard on the accelerator. Confirming his fears, the expected acceleration just wasn't there. Stan looked down at the array of dials in front of him. Unfortunately, the engine temperature gauge was on the rise, showing well above normal. He throttled back as a precaution.

"I think we may have an issue with Betsy," announced Stan.

"Oh, what now!" exclaimed Christine folding her arms tightly across her chest once again.

"I haven't got full power when I accelerate," added Stan. "Plus, the engine is running a little warm."

"I really don't know why you keep this contraption," replied Christine. "And Betsy is a ridiculous name for a motor car."

"You leave her be," responded a protective Stan. "She's done nothing to offend you."

"Oh yes she has," replied an animated Christine. "She keeps breaking down on us."

Stan appeared to be on a loser again. His losing streak was now building fast. There appeared to be no way to outwit Christine's forthright and sensible comments.

"We can stop at Cheltenham," said Stan, trying to concoct a plan. "Alan, our next door neighbour, works at Bristol Street Motors, in the parts department. He will help us out."

"Have you seen the time, Dad?" said Jenifer from the back seat. "I suspect the parts department don't have a night shift."

Stan was now starting a losing streak with one of his daughters. Was there no end to this?

"I will find a phone box in Cheltenham," continued Stan. "I will ring Alan and tell him about what has happened. He might be able to tell me what he thinks the problem is. I remember, he is working tomorrow, it's his turn to work a Saturday."

"Saturday!" yelled Christine. "So, we won't be arriving in Christchurch tonight?"

"I suspect not," replied an embarrassed Stan. "I could try and carry on, but I don't think Betsy will make it in this condition."

"Will you stop calling this pile of junk 'Betsy'," ranted Christine. "It's a car, not a person. And not a very reliable car either."

Stan carried on down the M5 cautiously, trying to block out the negativity that was pouring in his direction. It was only another four miles until the Cheltenham junction, and traffic was still moving.

Moments later, Stan's worst fears became a reality, as in the distance, Stan could see an epidemic of brake lights about three hundred yards in front of him. It wasn't long before Betsy came to a halt in a heavily attended traffic jam.

Barry took a look over to his right to get a look at what was going on.

"Nightmare," cried Barry. "Just what we wanted."

"I half expected this," replied a downbeat Stan. "We need to keep moving, Betsy might overheat if we are stationary for too long."

Christine leaned forward and administered a slap to Stan's arm around Fiona, who was sitting next to her. As the blow landed, Penny fell from Christine's lap into the footwell, as her solid and comfy resting place had been unevenly disturbed.

"Now what you've made me do, Stan," complained Christine picking up the hapless pup.

"What was that for?" asked a despondent Stan.

"What have I told you about calling this heap Betsy," responded Christine assertively.

"Oh, come on," responded Stan. "It's only a bit of fun."

"You treat this car better than you treat me," added Christine. "Your relationship with this vehicle is definitely not healthy."

"Here, here!" chanted Jenifer from the back seat.

As quickly as the traffic flow stopped, the two lines of jammed vehicles started to creep forwards. Soon, the speed increased back to a more acceptable thirty miles per hour.

Stan maintained a vigilant watch on Betsy's engine temperature gauge, occasionally winding down his side window to keep an ear on the strange tone coming from the exhaust.

As Stan passed the three hundred yard marker for the Cheltenham junction, he started to feel a little easier.

He wanted to avoid the expensive indignity of being recovered from the motorway. That would require him to spend his cash.

Stan turned nervously onto the A4019, guiding Betsy gently towards Cheltenham. Half a mile down the A4019, Stan spotted a lay-by to the right hand side. The good news was that it was sporting a bright, shiny red phone box. At last, a stroke of luck. Stan indicated and pulled smoothly into the lay-by.

He left the engine running, as he wanted to check out the strange drone coming from his exhaust now they were stationary. The issue soon became obvious, as Stan spotted a fair chunk of his exhaust drooping perilously close to the ground.

Stan returned to Betsy and turned off the engine, to give her a moment's respite.

Now a bit more in the know, Stan checked his pockets for change. He had plenty of ten pence pieces for the planned phone call to his saviour, Alan. Stan sprinted over to the phone box.

Moments later, a dejected Stan returned to the car. He jumped into the driver's seat and let out a huge sigh of frustration.

"Bloody kids!" ranted Stan.

"Language, Stan," replied an angry Christine as she delivered another blow to Stan's arm, once again spilling an unsuspecting Penny to the footwell.

"What's up?" asked Jenifer from the back seat.

"Some kids have smashed the receiver," replied Stan. "It's in about twenty pieces on the phone box floor. Plus, they have stuffed something into the coin slots, so I couldn't use the phone even if the receiver wasn't damaged."

"Just find another one and stop complaining," coached Christine.

"At least this down time has given B… I mean the car time to cool down," added Stan, trying to dodge another one of Christine's Joe Bugner like slaps.

Crossing his fingers, Stan turned the ignition key. His confidence was not one hundred percent in getting an engine re-start. The first crank was fruitless, Betsy was not playing ball. A second turn again proved fruitless.

"Third time lucky," said a hopeful Stan.

The third turn of the key saw Betsy boom into life. Boom being the operative word, as a loud backfire discharged out of the exhaust pipe, causing all holiday passengers to jump out of their skins in fright,

"What was that?" asked Jenifer.

"Nothing really," replied Stan.

"Nothing?" added Jenifer. "I thought I had been shot."

"She sometimes backfires after a short stop," responded a calming Stan.

With daylight now giving way to dusk, Stan checked the road for oncoming traffic. With the road clear, he pulled out of the lay-by.

"Keep your eyes peeled for a phone box," asked Stan. "I want to call Alan before he retires for the night."

As they approached the outskirts of Cheltenham, Christine spotted a phone box ahead, with enough room to park up with the caravan. This time, luck was on Stan's side, when he discovered a fully functional phone.

To his annoyance, Stan had to use up forty pence to complete his appeal for assistance with Alan. However, it appeared to be worth it. Alan suspected that the exhaust sensors might need looking at, which might explain a loss of power. Plus, the dangling section of exhaust pipe would also contribute to the overall dilemma.

"We need to find somewhere to park up for the night," announced Stan on his return to the car.

"You are joking," complained Jenifer.

"We can't go on," revealed Stan. "We just won't get there without repairing the exhaust system and maybe replacing the exhaust sensors."

The morale inside the car dropped dramatically. The plan to leave a day early to maximise the holiday had flopped.

Stan started the engine on the second attempt as Betsy spurted into half-life. With the Zodiac sounding more like a tractor, the holiday gang made their way towards Cheltenham city centre, to try and find a suitable resting place for the night.

Stan drove around and around the centre for ages, trying to find a suitable pull in that could cater for the car and caravan combination. After a forty minute search, in the gloom, Stan spotted a temporary fence around what appeared to be a large area of muddy wasteland.

"This will do," said a confident Stan. "Right, we will sleep in the caravan. Barry and Rob, you sleep in the car tonight. Christine will sort out some sleeping bags and pillows. It's not so cold tonight, so you should be okay."

"Great," said a sarcastic and despondent Barry. "Do I really have to sleep with this sheepie. He probably baa's in the night."

Rob looked across at Barry with a look of disdain.

The crew gradually removed themselves from Betsy. Christine unlocked the caravan, on a search for a kettle and teabags. Access into the caravan was hampered, as Stan's packing of 'totally necessary accessories and equipment' filled the caravan living space.

"How can we function with all of this on the floor?" demanded an irate Christine.

"Let's move it all to the bedroom," suggested Stan. "It doesn't matter if the caravan is not balanced, we aren't on the move. I can put the stabiliser legs down, to stop the caravan from rocking. Come on, if we all help, we can get it done in no time."

Christine led the clean-up, directing Jenifer, Barry, and Rob's every move. Fiona had gone walkies. Her nicotine level had plunged, so she needed a quick-fix cigarette. Stan had rushed out to find another phone box, so that he could inform Alan that they had found a suitable parking space, giving him the approximate location, so that he could rendezvous with them in the morning.

It didn't take long to rearrange the caravan living areas. The pull out beds were now accessible, enough to make a temporary dwelling just for the night.

"I'll put the kettle on," announced Christine as the group sat down for a well-earned rest around the dining table.

"What are we going to do about dinner?" asked Barry. "We haven't eaten tonight."

"I've got sandwiches that I made up for the journey," replied Jenifer.

"That'll do nicely," replied a thankful Barry.

The caravaners sat around the table for over an hour, sharing jokes and making fun of Stan's collision with the petrol station. Stan suggested that they turned in for the night. Alan was due at eight in the morning, and Stan wanted to be ready to roll as soon as the car was sorted.

As planned, Stan, Christine, Jenifer, and Fiona slept in the caravan, whilst Rob hunkered down in the front seat of Betsy and Barry in the back. Both had sleeping bags and pillows, but their bed for the night was cramped and uncomfortable. Furthermore, Penny had taken to Barry, so she was trying to settle down on him in the back seat.

Within ten minutes of his head hitting his pillow, Barry dropped off into a deep slumber. After a further fifteen minutes the barrage started, as he began to omit substantial snores and grunts. Rob thought he was bunking with a wild boar with the flu. The dulcet, high volume tones provided an inhospitable atmosphere for Rob, in which to even consider shutting his eyes. It was going to be a long night.

Eventually, about an hour and a half before dawn, Rob managed to nod off. However, as the first light of dawn had barely illuminated Betsy's paintwork, Barry and Rob were abruptly raised from their slumber by a demented, barking Penny. She was yapping at the shape of a tall person making their way over to the car.

As the figure rattled their knuckles on the driver's side window, Rob sat up and wound down the window.

"You can't park here!" boomed the figure. "You are blocking the entrance to our building site. You need to move your car, right now!"

"Okay," replied a wary Rob. "But it's not my car. I'll go and get the owner, he's asleep in the caravan."

"You best had," responded the stern builder.

Rob scrambled his jeans on inside the sleeping bag, quickly opened the car door and ran back to the caravan. Whilst Rob knocked the caravan door, a frenzied Penny was growling and barking incessantly from the parcel shelf in the car.

Jenifer opened the door.

"Get your dad, quickly," said a distraught Rob.

"What's happened?" asked Jenifer.

"This," replied Rob, pointing at the gathering group of vexed builders.

"Crikey," said Jenifer, disappearing back into the caravan to fetch her father.

Moments later, looking like he had been dragged through a hedge backwards, Stan appeared at the caravan door.

"What's all this then?" asked a confused Stan.

"You are blocking our site entrance, mate," said the burly builder.

"Sorry, I had no idea," responded an apologetic Stan. "It was dark when we arrived here last night, I didn't realise it was a building site entrance."

"You do know there are actual camp sites in the Cheltenham area?" quipped the builder. "They have showers, pitches and all that sort of thing."

"I guess so," replied Stan. "It's just that our car has exhaust problems, so we had to pull over in an emergency. I don't make a habit of this."

"I bet you don't," responded the sarcastic builder. "But in any case, you need to move all this, right now. We are on a tight schedule."

"Right you are," replied Stan.

Quickly, Stan and Christine lifted up the caravan stabiliser's legs and speedily returned the living area to some form of normality in readiness for the impromptu eviction.

Stan jumped into his beloved car and cranked the engine. Betsy refused to play ball and failed to fire into life, not even half-life. Stan tried again, nothing. After six failed attempts Stan got out of the car.

"Sorry, chaps, I can't start the car," uttered an embarrassed Stan. "Can you help give me a push?"

The collected group of builders scanned the locality for a suitable place to push the stricken vehicle.

"Over there?" suggested one of the builders. "In the bus stop?"

"We can't park there," demanded Stan. "I might get a ticket from the police."

"At this time of day?" replied one of the builders. "And it's a Saturday. You won't see the police until well after breakfast around here."

After a short debate, Stan resigned to temporarily parking the car in the bus stop. As the caravan was not obstructing the entrance fully, it remained where it was.

Once the wire fence acting as a makeshift gate was released, a line of Transit vans filtered onto the building site.

"I'm going to have a walk into town," announced Rob. "I need to find a tobacconist. I'm running low on ciggies."

"I'll come too," said Fiona, to Rob's complete surprise. "We can take Penny for a trot."

Once Rob, Fiona and Penny had disappeared from view, Stan popped the car bonnet, to try and fathom out why his pride and joy wouldn't play ball. Just as Stan had placed his head deep inside the engine compartment, the silence was broken by a loud honk on a bus horn. This caused Stan to crash his head into the bonnet as he jumped in fright. Holding his head, Stan peered around the side of the bonnet. To his dismay, an agitated bus driver had pulled up aggressively close to Betsy in disgust. Stan walked up to the bus to remonstrate with the driver.

"You can't park there," growled the irate bus driver.

"I'm not parked here," replied an apologetic Stan.

"Yes, you are!" shouted the bus driver. "Unless your car is a mirage? Last time I checked, Cheltenham is nowhere near a desert."

"Very funny," retorted Stan. "But we've actually broken down. My car won't start, and we are waiting for a friend to come and assist."

"Not my problem, mate," responded an arrogant bus driver. "But what is my problem, is the fact that I can't use my bus stop."

Stan looked inside the empty bus, then gazed at the empty bus stop.

"Why exactly do you need to use the bus stop?" asked a puzzled Stan.

"Because I'm driving a bus," replied the bus driver.

"But there's nobody here," said Stan stating the obvious. "Why pull in if there's no passengers to be picked up?"

"It's my job," responded the bus driver.

"Again, there's nobody to pick up," added Stan.

"Do you want me to involve the police?" threatened the bus driver.

"Absolutely not," pleaded Stan. "I just need you to show some compassion."

Stan felt a hand on his right hand shoulder; it was his neighbour, Alan.

"What's all this then?" asked Alan.

"This plonker has parked up in my bus stop," yelled the frustrated bus driver.

"Broken down," interrupted Stan, pointing his index finger in the air.

"There's nobody waiting," stated Alan. "What's your issue?"

"He's stopping me from doing my job," responded the bus driver. "I can't offer my full service with that car in the way."

"But there's nobody here," said a dismayed Alan.

"It's the principle," uttered the bus driver as he indicated to pull away.

Alan looked at Stan in disbelief as the bus driver guided his bus back onto the road, gesticulating with his arms as he left.

"Well, I never," said Alan in total bewilderment. "Let's have a look at Betsy then."

Alan and Stan took a more detailed look at the stricken vehicle. After four further attempts to start the engine, they stopped meddling to protect the battery life of the vehicle.

"I'll have to arrange a tow truck," admitted Alan. "Problem is, they don't start their shift until nine in the morning at weekends. We'll just have to wait."

Fiona and Rob returned from their dog walking and cigarette purchasing adventure. All signs were good, at least they were both in one piece, with neither of them sporting wounds or black eyes. So, the outing must have been a relatively peaceful affair.

"Everything okay, lovebirds?" asked Christine in matchmaker mode.

"Fabulous, thanks," replied Rob nervously.

"Don't call us that," snapped Fiona. "He's not my boyfriend, got it!"

"I didn't mean it like that," explained Christine, laughing.

"I know what you are trying to do," responded Fiona with a mean look on her face. "Just stop it right now."

After Christine's attempted matchmaking, everyone collected around the caravan. Christine and Jenifer mustered up a round of bacon sandwiches and piping hot tea from the caravan kitchen whilst they waited for the tow truck to arrive.

An hour had passed when a police Panda car pulled up behind Betsy. An officer got out of the car, put on his helmet, and walked up to Betsy to investigate. Stan rushed across the quiet road to confront the police officer.

"Is this your car, sir?" asked the officer.

"Yes, it is," replied an embarrassed Stan.

"Well, you can't park here," added the disgruntled officer.

"I'm not actually parked as such," pleaded Stan. "We've broken down on our way to Christchurch."

"Christchurch?" questioned the surprised police officer. "Wouldn't you be better off using the M5? It's far quicker."

"We were on the M5," explained Stan. "But the car started to play up, so we came off. My friend over there in the blue shirt works for Ford, at Bristol Street. We are waiting for a tow truck. They will be here just after nine."

"I see," responded the policeman. "A predicament. Okay, just this once I won't give you a ticket. But get this contraption out of here as soon as you can. I don't have broken down rust buckets on my patch."

"It's not a rust bucket," pleaded Stan, nursing his damaged feelings.

"I've seen better," said the police officer as he returned to his clean, shiny Panda car.

At nine thirty, the tow truck arrived on scene.

"Where have you lot been?" asked Alan.

"We had to have a brew first," explained the tow truck driver.

"Typical," replied a disgusted Alan.

Twenty minutes later, Betsy was shackled up to the tow truck, and soon on her way to the safety of the workshop for a thorough seeing to.

Stan sat in the passenger seat of the recovery vehicle. He needed to be present at the dealership, as there was a high likelihood that he would be parting with some of his beloved cash. He felt the need to be present to ensure that only essential work was undertaken.

Once Betsy was offloaded and pushed into the dealership workshop, Stan relocated to the plush customer reception area, where he grabbed a coffee from the available machine, but only because he noticed it was on free vend.

Stan then began his vigil, pacing up and down like an expectant father. He wanted his pride and joy back to full working order, but he didn't want to spend a small fortune in doing so.

Thirty minutes later, Alan opened the door to customer reception, flanked by an overalled technician.

"We've got good news and bad news," announced Alan. "Two sensors need replacing, and the back section of your exhaust has gone for a burton."

"That's just bad news," responded Stan.

"The good news is that we have the sensors in stock," continued Alan.

"And the bad news?" quizzed a nervous Stan.

"The exhaust back section," explained Alan. "This is a classic, we don't carry stock for classic cars."

"So, I'm done for?" asked Stan sheepishly.

"Not exactly," said a reassuring Alan. "Jim here can fabricate a temporary system from a standard exhaust. It should be good enough to get you to Christchurch and back."

"Should?" asked a very anxious Stan.

"It will, sorry," continued Alan. "Slip of the tongue. We guarantee all of our work. However, as it's a 'special', it's going to cost a little more, and it's Saturday."

"Come on, Alan," begged Stan. "It's me you are talking to. Just think about all the times I have picked you up from the pub and mowed your lawn when you and Sandra were on holiday. Then, there's the time I disturbed burglars before they had chance to break into your house."

"I get it, I get it," said Alan, taking a step back from Stan's onslaught. "I know how much you like to spend your money. I tell you what. I'll do the sensors and exhaust, but just charge you labour on the sensors, I'll just charge you for parts for the exhaust."

"Any more wiggle room?" asked a tight Stan.

"I tell you what Stan," responded an irritated Alan. "We'll push your car out of the workshop, and you can go and find someone else who can do the job at the price you are prepared to pay, on a Saturday."

Backed into a lonely corner, Stan finally cracked.

"Okay," replied Stan. "As you say, no labour for the exhaust."

Stan offered out his hand to shake on the deal. Alan quickly accepted the handshake. The repair deal had been struck.

As the mechanics started work on Betsy, a despondent Stan walked outside for a breath of fresh air. He also wanted to check the amount of cash he was holding in his wallet, which appeared to be taking a hard hit very soon.

Six long hours later, Betsy appeared at the open doors of the workshop entrance, purring like a kitten. Stan was overjoyed. He drove Betsy up and down the dealership car park three times, just to make sure all was in order.

After Stan had resentfully paid the bill, Alan accompanied him back to his vehicle. Stan looked down at his watch.

"Alan," said Stan. "Looking at the time and how tired and stressed I am feeling, I don't think we will get anywhere near Christchurch tonight. Do you think I can pick up the caravan and come back here?"

"What on earth for?" asked a confused Alan.

"If we can stop here tonight, we will be out of the way," replied a cocky Stan.

"Are you kidding me?" responded Alan in disbelief. "For goodness sake. Unless you haven't noticed, this is a place of work, a car dealership."

"Just this once," begged Stan, desperate to avoid spending money on a proper local camp site.

"I just don't believe you sometimes, Stan," said a vexed Alan.

"Please," continued Stan. "Just this once, I'll park right out of the way."

Alan walked away from Stan to consider the pro's and con's.

"Just this once," replied Alan. "But never again."

"Thanks, mate," responded Stan as he hugged his neighbour tightly. "Christine will be delighted."

Stan sparked Betsy into life, setting off to collect his family and caravan from their building site ordeal.

Fifteen minutes later, Stan backed up to the caravan ready to hitch up. Christine walked across to the car.

"Where on earth have you been?" screamed Christine through the open window. "You've been gone for hours."

"I had no choice," said a defensive Stan. "We needed to get the car fixed. It's all done now. We can go to our site for the night now. Just get everyone collected up, as quick as you can."

"You are saying we aren't going to Christchurch now?" asked a bemused Christine.

"It's far too late," responded Stan firmly. "It's been one of those days. I'm far too tired to drive now, so we're going to stay in Cheltenham for another night."

"You had better have booked us into a nice place," demanded Christine.

Stan just smiled back at Christine.

It took a further fifteen minutes before Stan was able to pull away from the building site. Ironically, as they pulled away, all of the builders had congregated by the site entrance to loving wave them off. Fortunately, Christine saw the funny side and affectionately waved back.

However, twenty minutes later, Christine's mood was about to take a turn for the worse.

As Stan steered Betsy into the gates of Bristol Street Motors, Cheltenham, Christine assumed Stan had unfinished business with Alan.

"Are you going to be long in there?" asked Christine politely. "I want to get to the site so we can settle in."

Stan gripped the steering wheel as if his life depended on it as he delivered his news.

"This is the site for tonight," said Stan with his head lowered.

"Are you joking?" snapped Jenifer from the back seat. "This is where Alan works, isn't it?"

"Yes, it is," responded Stan. "But he's been kind enough to accommodate us for the night, just because it is too late to drive to Christchurch tonight."

"We are talking about Christchurch, Dorset," added Barry from the back seat. "Not Christchurch, New Zealand?"

Jenifer once again delivered a punch to Barry's upper arm.

"Don't be rude to my dad," growled Jenifer. "Of course he knows where Christchurch is."

"So why aren't we driving there now?" continued Barry. "It's probably only just over three hours' drive."

"Stan is tired," interrupted Christine. "He's had a stressful day. He needs a rest."

"I'll drive then," suggested Barry.

"I'm not letting you anywhere near Betsy," said an adamant Stan.

Stan's use of Betsy's name earnt him another slap on the arm from Christine, which also sent poor Penny spiralling back into the footwell with a yelp.

"Let's make the best of it here tonight," said Stan. "Then, in the morning, if we make an early start, we could be in Christchurch by lunchtime. Just in time for a nice holiday barbecue."

"Make the best of it here?" quizzed Barry. "I don't need to buy a family saloon at the moment."

Jenifer administered another now familiar punch to Barry's arm.

Stan manoeuvred the car to a far corner of the dealership, out of sight of potential dealership customers.

"Same sleeping arrangements tonight?" quizzed Barry.

"Absolutely," replied Christine. "There's going to be no funny business on this trip. I'll make sure of that."

Rob could hardly wait. Another night with a pig farm impersonating Barry, along with the expected discharge of doggy noise from an over exuberant yappy lap dog, not wanting silence to fall over Betsy during the night.

Chapter Three

The evening on the dealership forecourt started reasonably well. Christine had managed to muster up some kind of stew for dinner. Desperately digging around his bowl, Stan was trying to find anything that looked like meat, but he was struggling.

"What exactly is in this?" asked Stan.

"Vegetable stew," snapped Christine. "It's all we have in the caravan fridge. I wanted to go shopping when we got to Christchurch, but that's clearly off plan at the moment."

"I knew I shouldn't have put Jenifer in charge of food," complained Stan. "I'm not even a vegetarian."

"Stop complaining, Dad," replied an upset Jenifer. "I took what was in our fridge at home. How can I take anything that's not there? Sometimes there's no pleasing you."

The bickering continued as the final fragments of light departed from a clear, darkening blue sky. After the makeshift stew had been devoured, Christine suggested that the group should partake in some of the games available in the caravan. However, a fractious game of Monopoly would only inflame an already tetchy atmosphere. So, the group collectively, but politely declined.

Rob snapped the lead on Penny, taking her for a walk around the dealership, not only to drool over the new cars on offer, but to try and extract energy from a potential source of noise later. If he tired her out, there was less chance of having to deal with a noisy and petulant pup later.

The night went as expected for Rob. Once the evening pleasantries had wrapped up, within minutes of them squashing themselves into the car, Barry was transmitting snores that started to make the side windows rattle. Even Penny, who was curled up on Barry's torso, looked up with disdain at the deafening freak show.

Enough was enough. Rob slid out of his sleeping bag and carefully opened the passenger door. It was ciggie time. As the door opened, Penny spotted the opportunity, as she bounded between the seats and scampered hurriedly out of the door.

Rob lit up his Gold Leaf cigarette and took a long draw.

"What are you doing out here?" came a voice from the dark.

Rob walked over to the shadows created by the dealership workshop canopy, to try and identify his companion. It was Fiona.

"Hi," said Rob. "I just can't sleep. It's so cramped in there, and Barry is snoring like a walrus."

Fiona sniggered.

"When he sleeps over," replied Fiona, "he uses the settee. I can hear him snoring from upstairs, so I guess you are going through a proper ordeal with him just behind you in the back seat."

"Tell me about it," responded an exhausted Rob.

"So, how's it been going?" asked Fiona. "Everything okay? Have you got a new girlfriend yet?"

"Things are good," responded Rob, totally surprised at Fiona's friendly attitude and apparent concern. "I've had exams, so I've been blitzing the revision. I haven't even been playing cricket, my dad won't allow it. He says my future is more important. So, he's banned me from playing. He's even contacted the captain and told him not to pick me."

"He means well though," replied Fiona. "At least he's not on your case twenty-four-seven like my dad is. His incessant nagging about my schoolwork is driving a wedge between us. It just encourages me to rebel even more. I'm going to do just enough to get through. I've got no intentions of being a 'career girl'. I just want to marry a rich guy and enjoy life."

"You are capable of so much more, you know," responded Rob.

"Don't you start," snapped Fiona.

"I'm not starting anything," added Rob. "I just know what you are capable of. At the end of the day, it's your life and you make the decisions right for you."

"Exactly," responded Fiona with a smile on her face.

"Anyhow," continued Rob, "I hope you are okay with me tagging along this week. Your mum was very insistent and persuasive."

"I'm cool now," replied Fiona exhaling smoke from her cigarette. "Just keep your distance, and don't even think about trying to get back together."

"You've no worries concerning that," responded Rob. "I'm okay with us being mates and smoking buddies this week. No more than that."

"Thank you," said Fiona, stepping forward, placing a tender kiss to Rob's cheek. "I'm glad we've had this chat. I don't feel so awkward now. Let's hope we have a great week away."

Rob and Fiona finished their cigarettes, embraced, then started to walk back to their awaiting beds for the night.

"Oh no!" exclaimed Rob. "Where's Penny?"

"What do you mean?" asked Fiona.

"She came out here with me," added Rob. "I forgot about her when I was chatting to you."

"We'd better find her, quick," said a concerned Fiona.

Rob and Fiona frantically search for Penny. They were confident she was still within the dealership grounds, as the entry gates were closed and secure. Rob told Fiona to go clockwise around the large dealership building, while he headed counter-clockwise. This should cover eventualities.

The pair searched anxiously for Christine's prized pet, but there was no sign. As Rob and Fiona met up at the back of the dealership, there was still no sign of the naughty pup.

To the left of where they stood was a shipping container.

"Let's try over there," suggested Fiona.

The pair walked to the container, discovering the location of the missing pooch. Sat in a plastic receptacle of discharged sump oil, Penny was proudly sat there, covered in engine oil, looking like a dog who had just won Crufts.

"Nightmare!" scowled Fiona. "That dog can't stay out of water, she should have been a fish. I bet she thought that was water in there and jumped in."

"We can't leave her like this," said a fed up Rob. "I'll have a look round and see if I can find a hose pipe. You go back to the caravan. See if you can get some washing up liquid or something like that."

Fiona told Penny to 'stay' and departed on her quest for washing up liquid, whilst Rob walked off in search of a hose pipe.

Five minutes later, Fiona returned to the oily pup who fortunately had heeded the 'stay' command and was still sitting in her greasy resting place.

Soon after, Rob came into view with good news.

"There's a hose pipe over there," said Rob pointing to his right. "I've tried it, and it works. We need to get Penny over there and wash her down."

Not wanting to touch the oily pup, Fiona commanded Penny to 'come'. Penny jumped out of the oil and tagged along as instructed.

At the hose pipe, Rob turned on the water and started to hose down Penny. Once the freezing stream of water hit Penny's fur, this upset Penny who ran off into the darkness.

"I guess someone should have been holding her," said Fiona ironically.

"This just gets worse," replied a frustrated Rob. "Let's go and get her back."

"She won't come now," added Fiona. "Now she knows what's she's in for. She's not stupid."

"Then we need to carry her back here and hold on to her," responded Rob. "So, we need a towel, or something to carry her in. I'm not holding the dog in that state. And I guess neither are you."

"I'll go and get something from the caravan," suggested Fiona. "I'll be back in a jiffy."

As Fiona returned to the caravan in search of a towel, Rob started the second search for the disobedient mutt.

Ten minutes later, Fiona returned with a towel. Rob had found Penny sniffing at fox droppings. The problem being, the oily pooch had a liking for fox droppings and looked like she had been rolling around in the muck, adding a thin coat of fox droppings onto the already present rank coating of sump oil.

"I managed to wake everyone up in the caravan," giggled Fiona.

"How did you manage that?" asked Rob.

"In the dark," continued Fiona, "when I pulled at the towel, some of the washing up fell to the floor. Saucepans. They made a right racket. My dad came at me thinking I was a burglar, until he realised it was me."

"You'll be popular in the morning," remarked Rob.

"Whatever," snarled Fiona. "Right, you pick her up, I'm wearing white."

Rob covered Penny with the towel and picked her up, keeping her at arm's length. Penny was returned to the hose pipe for a clean-up. However, when Penny realised her fate, she started to wriggle in Rob's clutches. Her violent movements caused him to drop her, and she ran off again into the darkness.

"You know what," said a totally perplexed Rob. "This is too much like hard work. Let's put the lead on her and let her sleep outside tonight. We can deal with her in the morning."

"Great idea," replied Fiona. "I'll get the lead."

Fiona and Rob lit up another cigarette, tethered the hapless pooch to the caravan, and retired for the evening.

Rob returned to the Zodiac and opened the door. As expected, he was greeted with a symphony of volumetric snores. Looking around, Rob tried to spot a more appealing resting place as he couldn't face another sleepless night.

Rob walked over to the impressive line of new vehicles on display around the dealership. Maybe, just maybe, one of those vehicles was unlocked, providing Rob with another sleeping option.

Rob tried the car doors one by one. Fortunately, the fifth car he tried had a rear door that had not been locked, and it was a roomy family saloon. Heaven. Rob took off his trainers as a mark of respect for the unblemished interior, then climbed into his noise-free bedroom.

It was a warm and sunny Sunday morning. A gentle breeze caressed the dealership and it's unexpected residents. The creaking of the large metal gates woke Rob from his deep sleep in the family saloon. Not wanting to be discovered, Rob peered nervously towards the gates to see what was going on. It was Alan. He had come down to the dealership early, to make sure Stan and his rabble were off the premises before the dealership opened for business.

Rob covertly jumped from the back seat of the saloon and put on his trainers.

Alan looked over at Rob.

"What do you think you are doing in there?" demanded Alan. "That's a brand new car. You better not have damaged it."

"It's all okay, Alan," replied an apologetic Rob. "I even took my shoes off."

"Good lad," said Alan as he cast his beady eye in the back of the car, looking for any signs of damage.

As Alan was searching, the morning tranquillity was suddenly shattered.

"Oh, my goodness!!" shrieked Christine at the top of her voice. "What on earth has happened to you?"

Christine had discovered her bedraggled looking beloved pooch, tethered to the caravan in shame, covered in oil and fox droppings.

"Fiona, is this your doing?" growled an irate Christine.

"Why's it always me?" came a response from the caravan.

"What have you done to her?" asked a desperate Christine.

Stan jumped out the caravan and looked at the matted mess of fur hitched to the caravan. He smiled cautiously.

"Oh no," bleated Stan, spotting unsightly oil smudges down the side of the caravan, where Penny had been jumping up during the night.

Christine looked at the oil smudges.

"You can come out here and clean up this mess, young lady," demanded Christine. "And just look at my brand new towel. It's completely ruined."

Fiona climbed out of the caravan to face the music. As she looked down at Penny, Fiona couldn't hold back a substantial grin. The usually impeccable pooch looked very much worse for wear.

"Go and clean her up, now," said Stan sternly.

"I'll help," added Rob.

As Rob and Fiona walked off with Penny, Alan came across to a fed up looking Stan.

"Morning, Stan," said Alan politely. "Look, I need you off the dealership grounds within the hour. Sunday's are our busy days. I don't want customers thinking we have a tinker problem when they start turning up. Do I make myself clear?"

"Crystal clear," responded Stan with his head bowed in embarrassment. "As soon as we get this unexpected dog clean up exercise done and dusted, we will be on our way."

"Thanks," replied a relieved Alan. "If my gaffer finds out you were here last night, it might cost me my job."

"I understand," responded Stan.

Christine stood over Rob and Fiona with her arms folded across her chest, supervising the clean-up operation. Jenifer had also turned up to wind up Fiona. Jenifer took every opportunity to get one over on Fiona. Sisterly love was not a driver in their relationship.

Penny looked bedraggled. She was covered from head to foot in washing up suds and dripping wet. Fiona was holding her down as Rob tried to remove as much sump oil as he could.

Every once in a while, Penny would shake herself vigorously, sending oily suds over the onlooking crowd, sending them backwards in fear of the oily offshoots.

Eventually it was pretty much job done. Christine fluffed Penny up using her doggie towel, trying to dry her off as best she could.

"My poor little darling," said Christine as she cuddled her prized pooch.

Stan joined the clean-up gang.

"We need to get going now," said Stan assertively. "If we don't go now, Alan could lose his job."

"That serious?" quizzed Jenifer.

"Yes," responded Stan. "So, everyone, get in the car as quick as you can, we need to get on the road."

Fifteen minutes later, Alan was waving off the holiday troop as they drove out of the dealership. Fortunately, no workers had turned up for work early, so it looked like Alan's job was still intact.

"We need to find a supermarket," said Christine as she started to berate Stan. "There's not much in the way of food left in the caravan. The time consuming distractions on our journey so far have pretty much depleted supplies."

"We can stop in Chippenham," replied Stan. "I think they have a Kwik-Save there."

"You are kidding me?" replied Christine. "Kwik-Save? Are you that desperate to save your precious money?"

"Quality food at quality prices," responded Stan.

"More like tight as a duck's backside," commented Jenifer from the back seat.

“Enough,” shouted Christine, frightening poor Penny half to death, as her owner tried to subdue the attacks on Stan.

For once, the journey continued to Chippenham without incident. Betsy was on her best behaviour, a family row hadn’t erupted, and Barry had refrained from sharing any of his Liverpool trivia.

In light traffic, Stan pulled onto the ample and relatively empty Kwik-Save car park. He drove to the extremities of the car park, parking up facing the exit. With the caravan attached, Stan’s experience told him that he needed to plan for a simple route out of the car park.

“Just essentials,” ordered Stan to Christine. “Don’t you go spending a small fortune in there.”

“You’re coming with me,” ordered Christine. “You kids, stay in the car and look after Pennypoo’s.”

“I’m not stopping here,” complained Jenifer.

“Neither am I,” added Barry.

“Looks like just you and me on paw patrol, Fiona,” said a reluctant Rob.

Stan, Christine, Jenifer and Barry strolled down the sloping car park, whilst Rob lit a cigarette on pooch watch.

Once in the supermarket, Stan stuck to Christine like a leach, watching every item that was placed in the far too big shopping trolley. The games started. If Christine placed any items into the trolley that Stan deemed as 'non-essential', Stan would secretly remove them when Christine's focus was elsewhere.

However, Christine was wise to Stan's tricks, replacing the item back in the trolley when Stan wasn't looking.

Bored with the games, Stan left Christine to it and went for a mooch on his own. To his absolute delight, Stan discovered an absolute bargain in the bakery section. Being a diabetic, Stan had to keep an eye on his diet. So, when he discovered reduced sugar loaves of bread, which happened to be on sale at half price, Stan was ecstatic. He picked up two loaves of reduced sugar bread and carried his prize to the shopping trolley. Christine was sorting through packets of ham, so Stan snuck the bread into the trolley, next to the fresh mackerel. As he did so, Stan picked up the mackerel, inspected it closely, then turned his nose up at it. Stan was not a fan of oily fish. Stan carefully placed the mackerel back in the trolley exactly where he found it, to cover his tracks.

The group spent another half an hour in the supermarket, slowly filling the trolley with essentials, along with a few treats as well.

Stan took charge of the check-out process, with Christine and Jenifer assigned to packing duties. Stan maintained his watchful vigil, making sure items considered to be absolute non-essentials didn't make their way to the packing zone.

"Stan," called Barry. "Take a look at this."

Stan was tangled. Did he remain on check out watch? Or did he chance it, and take a look at Barry's discovery? Thinking it wouldn't harm, Stan sidled over to Barry, who was flicking through some cassette tapes displayed on the sale rack.

"I thought you might like these," said Barry. "Especially as they are on sale."

"Who have they got?" asked Stan, alternating his attention between the till and the sale rack.

"Peter's and Lee," declared Barry. "They are pretty popular."

"You've got me over here for Peter's and Lee," gasped Stan. "What a total waste of time. For all I know, Christine might be packing fig rolls as I'm not there on guard."

"Nothing wrong with a fig roll, lovely," added Barry.

"Non-essential," uttered Stan. "Definitely in the non-essential category."

"Come on, Stan," replied Barry. "Let your hair down. After all, we are supposed to be on holiday."

"Fig rolls are a Christmas treat," replied a vexed Stan. "Not a holiday treat."

"Boy," added Barry. "You are tight."

Annoyed by his wasted time with Barry, Stan rushed back to the checkout, to try and regain control over the unsupervised spending spree.

"All done," announced Christine. "Let's get these back to the car. I bet we'll find Rob and Fiona having a cuddle. They are spending so much quality time together already. It's only a matter of time before they are back together."

"Don't hold your breath," muttered Jenifer in disbelief.

Stan opened the boot of the Zodiac, making space for the overflowing shopping bags. As the shopping transfer was underway, Stan was trying to spot his prized reduced sugar bread. So that he could brag about his discovery and more importantly, his savings. More and more shopping filled the boot and no sign of the bread yet. When the final tin of baked beans was placed in the boot, Stan was transfixed with worry.

"Where is my special, cut price, reduced sugar bread?" asked a distraught Stan.

"What reduced sugar bread?" asked Christine. "We don't have any reduced sugar bread?"

"We do," insisted Stan. "I found it, in the bakery, it was in the sale at half price."

"Well, it's not here now," responded Christine, sorting through the shopping in the boot.

"It has to be," argued Stan. "I put it in the trolley myself. Next to the fresh mackerel."

"Fresh mackerel?" asked Christine in total surprise. "We haven't bought any fresh mackerel. Who eats fresh mackerel? It's disgusting."

"You did buy fresh mackerel," insisted Stan. "I saw it in our trolley, when I put the bread in the trolley."

"I can assure you, Stan," said Christine, raising her voice, "we don't have any pesky mackerel. Are you sure you put it in the right trolley?"

Stan took a step back in horror. Reliving his bread into trolley moment, he did recall two trollies being around at the time. Had he made a blatant schoolboy error? Had Stan made a blunder with his trolley selection?

"Bugger!" exclaimed Stan.

"Language," yelled Christine as she delivered an accurate right jab to Stan's upper arm.

"I think I've made a boo boo," added Stan. "I may have put the bread in the wrong trolley."

"Do you think so?" said a sarcastic Jenifer.

In a blind panic, Stan rushed back into the supermarket to try and retrieve the situation.

Fifteen long minutes later, a dejected looking Stan appeared in the supermarket entrance. Stan dawdled up to the car to deliver his news, and by the look of his body language, it appeared to be bad news.

"Unbelievable," said a miserable Stan.

"What's happened now?" asked a concerned Christine.

"I found my bread," continued Stan. "It was in a woman's trolley, next to some fresh mackerel. So, I picked up the two loaves of reduced sugar bread."

"Where are they now?" quizzed Christine.

"The woman wouldn't give them up," explained Stan. "She grabbed them. Then we started to wrestle with them in the middle of the milk aisle. We tugged to and fro, but the bags gave way and the bread shot all over the place. Ruined."

"You idiot," berated Christine. "Did you go and get some replacements?"

"I tried," said Stan. "But they've sold out. I guess reduced sugar bread is popular around here."

"Oh, bless," responded a sympathetic Christine, administering another right jab to Stan's arm.

"What was that for?" exclaimed Stan in distress.

"For fighting with a woman," replied Christine. "And losing by the sounds of it. Now come on, let's get out of this confounded place."

The car park had filled up since they had arrived, making Stan's intended 'straight forward' exit somewhat trickier. It looked like Stan was faced with a slalom course of vehicles to negotiate in order to make his way to the exit.

Stan inched his rig forwards, the gap between the parked cars and the wall barely big enough to squeeze through.

"I'll get out and guide you," suggested Barry as he opened the back door.

Barry was out waving his arms exuberantly, even before Stan had been given the opportunity to refuse his kind offer.

Inch by inch, Barry guided Stan towards the exit. Stan had to reverse the rig now and then to better align himself with the target gaps. With just one more vehicle between Stan and freedom, Barry waved Stan forward cautiously. As Stan thought he was clear of danger, the tail end of the caravan clipped the final parked car, causing it to sway gently from side to side.

"Stan!!" screamed Christine. "You've hit him."

"Don't worry," responded a flustered Stan. "It was just a minor glance."

Barry opened the back door of the Zodiac.

"You hit that car Stan," announced Barry in a flap. "His front offside wing."

"Just get in, get in," demanded Stan.

With Barry inside the car, Stan sped off as best he could through the supermarket exit.

"You can't leave now, Stanley," berated Christine with her arms folded across her chest. "Stop now, and go back and sort that out, I insist."

"Look," answered Stan. "It was a glancing blow, probably didn't even break the paint. It was a bit of a heap in any case."

"That's not the point," replied Christine angrily. "It's the principle. You wouldn't like it done to you."

"It's too far to go back now," insisted Stan, turning onto the busy main road. "We need to get on our way, we've wasted enough time in that supermarket already."

"We'll stop on the way back home," announced Christine.

Barry, Jenifer, and Rob started to giggle in the back seat. As if that car would still be parked there in a week's time.

Christine had seemed to back off Stan following the car park issue. Peace at last had returned to the vehicle. As they continued their journey, the Chippenham buildings gave way to a more scenic countryside vista.

"Oh, great," stated Stan. "A fuel station. We need some petrol. Betsy seems to be thirsty this week. It must be the extra weight of the caravan."

Christine reached round Fiona and punched Stan in the ribs.

"I'm warning you, Stanley," growled Christine. "One more time. If you mention that name again, I'm going home."

Jenifer leaned forward on the back seat, anticipating seeing her dad mutter the taboo name to test her mother's limits.

But instead, Stan had better ideas.

"Sorry, dear," uttered Stan. "It won't happen again."

Stan switched on his left indicator in preparation for the fuel stop. Manoeuvring onto the forecourt, Stan's progress was suddenly halted with a loud crashing sound.

"Not again!" shouted Christine covering her face with her hands in total embarrassment.

Stan's head dropped to the steering wheel in disbelief.

Barry quickly jumped out of the back seat to investigate.

"Yep," declared Barry. "He's gone and done it again."

"How could you?" begged Christine. "You've only just mentioned the extra weight of the caravan. It's not like you forgot you were towing. I've always said to Mary. This caravan is too tall. It's at least two feet taller than their Sprite."

"Ours has got extra headroom," replied Stan defensively. "Essential when caravanning."

"Extra headroom?" barked Christine. "You are five foot seven. Why do you need extra headroom?"

"In case my brother, Dave, and his family comes to visit," responded Stan. "He's a six footer."

"He will be in Cornwall by now," replied an agitated Christine. "Why would he come to visit us in Christchurch?"

"You never know," said Stan, trying to justify his thinking.

By now, the forecourt attendant had made her way over to Stan's car. She looked up at the damage and started to tut under her breath.

"Who's a silly billy?" said the attendant.

"I'm so sorry," replied Stan getting out of the Zodiac. "Is there much damage?"

"It doesn't look great," continued the attendant. "I'll get someone to take a look. We've got a ladder round the back. Un-hitch your van and get your fuel, we can sort this out in a minute."

"Okay," responded Stan. "By the way, what's your name?"

"Danielle," came the reply.

As instructed, Stan un-hitched the caravan, filled up Betsy, re-hitched the caravan and parked up well away from the canopy.

When Stan returned to the scene of the crime, there was a gentleman called Tom dressed in dark blue overalls at the top of the ladder inspecting the damage.

Once on terra firma, Tom delivered his verdict.

"About a hundred and fifty quid will make that right," he announced.

"A hundred and fifty quid!" gasped Stan. "Never."

"You've made a right mess of our canopy," insisted Tom.

"Let me take a look," replied an unconvinced Stan. "Hold the ladder for me."

Stan scampered up the ladder to take a look for himself.

"I don't believe it," said Christine, looking over from the parked up Zodiac. "He's only going up the ladder himself now."

Everyone in the car quickly looked over at Stan, all smiling broadly.

Stan climbed down the ladder and faced his opposition.

"I can sort that," declared Stan. "I work in a tool room, that's my job. If you can lend me some tools, I can make that look like new."

Danielle and Tom looked at each other in disbelief.

"Are you serious?" asked Danielle.

"Totally," replied Stan. "I'll make a start right now."

Stan walked casually over to Betsy to inform the awaiting group that there may be a slight delay to their onward journey.

Christine couldn't believe what was happening. It was Sunday afternoon, they were just outside Chippenham, they had been on the road for what seemed an eternity, and their final destination appeared to be an impossible dream at this moment in time.

For the next six hours, they watched on as Stan scampered up and down the ladder like a worker ant. Barry and Rob were instructed to share the ladder holding duties, as none of the petrol station employees wanted anything to do with Stan's repairs.

In fairness, bit by bit, the corner of the canopy started to take shape. Stan was a good toolmaker and his skills shone through.

After endless cups of tea, never ending trips up and down the ladder and non-stop hammer bashes, Stan announced that the job was complete.

Stan went into the shop to fetch Danielle, so that she could sign off the repairs.

Danielle slowly clambered up the ladder to inspect Stan's work. To her great surprise, Stan had made an excellent job of the repair. To be fair, it looked better now than it did before Stan crunched his caravan into it.

"I'll just get Tom to have a look as well," said Danielle. "I need a second opinion."

Moments later, the blue overalls appeared, and Tom climbed the ladder to take a look.

Once Tom had validated the repairs, Danielle shook Stan's hand in delight. the deal was done, the repair was suitable. It had been a very strange afternoon.

Looking at his watch, Stan approached Danielle.

"I wonder?" asked Stan.

"You wonder what?" asked Danielle. "You don't want a job here, do you?"

"No thank you," continued Stan. "The thing is, it's later than I thought, and I must admit that the repair took longer than I expected. Is it okay for us to stay on your forecourt tonight? Just for one night. I hate driving in the dark, plus I am really tired from running up and down that ladder."

Seeing that Stan was exhausted, and appreciating his predicament, after a moment's thought, Danielle agreed to Stan's heartfelt request.

Feeling pleased with himself, Stan walked over to the Zodiac to deliver the good news.

Christine wound down her window in anticipation for the off.

"Come on, love," said a smiling Christine. "Let's get going, we've got a fair way still to go."

Stan braced himself.

"Actually dear," mumbled Stan. "We are going to stay here tonight. I'm just too tired to drive."

“What?” screamed Christine, as Penny once again tumbled out of control into the footwell.

It looked like it was going to be another long night for the travellers.

Chapter Four

Stan was mumbling to himself as he rummaged around the cramped caravan kitchen area. He was still nursing the bruising he took when battling for his half price reduced sugar bread. Stan was not one to hold a grudge, but he had a habit of holding on to adversity a bit too long.

"Will you stop moping, Stanley," demanded Christine, who was well versed in Stan's moody behaviours. "After all, we are supposed to be on holiday."

Stan looked out of the netted window above the sink, across at the garage forecourt.

"That's a laugh," replied Stan. "At this rate, we'll never get to Christchurch."

"Don't be daft," responded an upbeat Christine. "Tomorrow is another day. We'll set off early. Who knows, we could finally be lighting that barbecue by early evening."

Stan didn't reply. He was still deep in his bread-loss sulk.

Rob and Fiona had gone outside for a cigarette break. This attracted the attentions of Danielle, who walked across to remonstrate, demanding that Rob and Fiona walk down the main road to the bus stop, fifty yards away. Smoking at a petrol station wasn't the best of ideas.

At the bus stop, the pair lit up their life easing sticks of fire.

"This trip is starting to get a little crazy," said Rob, breaking the silence.

"It's always crazy in our house," replied Fiona. "At least we aren't rowing yet. It's normally the rows that send me to the back of the garden shed back home. To my happy place."

"Your people are okay," replied Rob. "They were kind enough to let Barry and me tag along this week. It could be worse. It could be just you and your sister fighting in the back seat. At least Barry and I are distracting you pair from continual verbal warfare."

"There is that, I suppose," responded Fiona. "Plus, I have a smoking buddy."

Rob and Fiona's conversation was suddenly interrupted, as a single decker emerald green bus pulled up at the bus stop. The front entry doors swung open with a small hiss.

"Are you getting on?" requested the driver.

"No," replied Rob. "We are just having a smoke. The people at the petrol station told us to come here, away from the pumps."

"Well, you can't sit there," continued the bus driver. "It's bus company property, erected for bus company customers."

"We'll only be here for five minutes," added Fiona. "And we will take our cigarette butts with us."

"I don't care," replied the bus driver. "Like I said, it's private property."

"It's just a bus stop," pleaded Rob. "We are not actually damaging anything. What's the harm?"

"It's the principle," added the jobsworth bus driver. "Now, if you don't move along, I'm going to involve the police. They will move you along, and maybe prosecute you for trespassing."

"Involve the police?" laughed Fiona. "Surely, they've got bigger things on their plate? And prosecute us for trespassing at a bus stop? That's laughable."

"It's not a joking matter, young lady," responded the bus driver whose frustration was growing. "I know how your sort operate."

"Our sort?" questioned Rob. "What do you mean by that?"

"You know, your sort," replied the bus driver. "Long haired Jonnie's like you. Smoking, lounging about, causing damage wherever you go. I bet you, as soon as I am out of your sight, you will start writing graffiti on the bus stop. Or try and kick over the sign. Or try to set fire to the wooden bench."

"And you can tell all of that by watching us have a ciggie?" requested Rob. "I think you have been reading too many crime novels. That's an outrageous suggestion to make. Look, mate, all we are doing is having a cigarette away from the petrol pumps. Nothing more, nothing less."

"I've finished," whispered Fiona in Rob's ear.

"Me too," whispered Rob back to Fiona.

Rob and Fiona discarded their finished cigarettes to the floor, smothered them with their footwear and started to walk off back to the sanctuary of the petrol station.

"Come back here, you little perishers!" shouted the irate bus driver. "I haven't finished with you. That's blatant littering. You can't do that. I'll get hold of the police to prosecute you for littering and trespassing. You wait and see."

Fiona turned and walked back to the bus stop to retrieve the cigarette butts. She looked up at the bus driver and poked her tongue out at him.

"Bloody kids," shouted the bus driver as the bus doors closed firmly, hissing again as they did so.

"Nice friendly locals," sniggered Fiona as they walked down the main road.

"I don't know how he finds time to drive the bus," added Rob. "What with all the community advice he gives out."

Light was now starting to fade. Christine and Jenifer had been busy cooking some of the Kwik-Save fare. It was spag-bol on the menu tonight. Barry had cleared the living area of the caravan, so at least the whole team could sit around the table and enjoy a meal together.

The meal went off without a hitch. No arguments broke out. Stan seemed to be over bread-gate, Barry resisted sharing any football trivia, and Rob and Fiona appeared to be in the middle of an amicable truce.

"Same sleeping arrangements," announced Christine. "You two lads in the Zodiac."

Rob rolled his eyes. A third night of vibrating door windows was just too much to take. But there were no other options to take. Where else was there to sleep in the middle of nowhere?

Fortunately, Christine had taken possession of Penny. Her oily encounter at the dealership was enough to put her on close watch with Penny. At least it was one less source of noise in the night for Rob.

As there were no streetlights, the car was a very dark and spooky place to sleep. Fifteen minutes into the night, Barry had dropped into his usual deep sleep. Five minutes later, the traditional nose pipe orchestra sparked into life. The deep, rich baritone snore was audible during inhale, the higher pitch wheeze was present from the point of exhale. A melody fit for the Sunday top twenty show if accompanied by a decent drummer and bass player.

After tolerating ten minutes of the snorting symphony, Rob had reached the limits of his noise tolerance. Grabbing his sleeping bag, he jumped out of the car on a quest for a suitable haven for the night.

Rob then had a light bulb moment. It was a warm, dry evening. The wind was light. Maybe the bus stop could be a suitable refuge for the night?

Rob trotted the fifty yards in the pitch black to the bus stop. Laying his sleeping bag on the wooden slatted bench, it became immediately apparent that Rob would be able to stretch out in the bus shelter. Job done.

Rob managed to get a good few hours snore-free sleep in. As dawn broke, Rob's slumber was disturbed by a familiar hissing sound. Opening his eyes, Rob was faced with the sight of the irate bus driver he had encountered the following evening.

"Not you again!" barked the angry bus driver. "You can't sleep there! It's bus company property."

"You are kidding me," replied Rob as he lit his first light cigarette.

"And put that cigarette out," berated the bus driver. "It's a no smoking bus stop."

Rob looked around him for a 'no smoking' sign.

"Where is the 'no smoking' sign then?" asked Rob.

"It's company policy," replied the bus driver. "No smoking allowed at any bus stops."

"How would I know that if there are no signs?" asked Rob.

"Don't get smart with me, laddie," retorted the bus driver.

"I'm not trying to be smart," responded Rob, attempting to genuinely defend himself. "If there are no signs, how am I supposed to know? Being an out of towner?"

"There are free booklets in the central bus station information centre in Salisbury," argued the bus driver. "On the back of the booklet is our smoking policy."

"Have you got one with you?" asked Rob.

"Don't be stupid," responded the bus driver. "I told you where they are."

"But I've never been to Salisbury," declared Rob. "And I wouldn't have a clue where the central bus station is. Let alone the information centre."

"Then maybe you should have planned your trip a little better," declared the bus driver.

"We are only here by chance," replied Rob. "We had an event whilst we stopped for fuel yesterday."

"What sort of event?" asked a wary bus driver.

"If I told you any more, I'd have to shoot you," joked Rob with a broad smile on his face, trying to protect Stan's unfortunate collision.

The bus driver looked back at Rob with a look of terror on his face. The doors of the bus slammed shut with a hiss, and he drove off in haste, revving the bus engine like his life depended on it.

"How strange," said Rob to himself.

As Rob continued to drag on his Gold Leaf cigarette, he noticed Fiona walking towards him, assuming she was in need of a morning nicotine fix.

"Morning, camper," said Rob. "Did you sleep well?"

"Not really," replied Fiona. "My mum snores like a rhinoceros at times. What are you doing out here with your sleeping bag?"

"I slept here," replied Rob. "You're not the only one who has a snoring sleeping partner."

"Ah, yes, good old Barry. Nightmare," smiled Fiona lighting her cigarette.

As Fiona and Rob exchanged small talk, they both decided to light another cigarette. As they did so, to their left, a police Panda car came hurtling towards them with the blue light flashing vigorously on the roof, the shrill of a siren filling the country air.

In addition, to their right, two more police cars and a large white van came into sight from around the bend in the road. All three vehicles were lit up and discharging tuneless sirens.

"Something's going down," said a surprised Rob.

To their astonishment, the police vehicles came to a skidding halt, blocking the road and surrounding the bus shelter. Several uniformed police officers jumped out of their vehicles with batons drawn.

"You two," barked the lead police officer. "On the ground, now. Hands behind your back."

An alarmed Fiona and Rob immediately did as they were asked, diving to the floor, face down, holding their hands behind their back.

A second and third police officer stepped forward and placed handcuffs on the wrists of Rob and Fiona. As the police officers helped Rob and Fiona to their feet, a maroon coloured saloon vehicle pulled up behind the convoy of police vehicles.

As a figure jumped out of the maroon car and walked towards the melee, Rob almost immediately recognised the figure. It was the bus driver.

"So," demanded the lead police officer, "where is the gun?"

"Gun?" replied Rob in total amazement. "We haven't got a gun."

"We've received reports of a gun," continued the lead police officer. "A member of the public has called it in."

Rob started to reflect on his earlier conversation with the bus driver.

"Was it that bus driver who called it in?" asked Rob nodding his head in the direction of the bus driver, who had now joined the group.

"I'm not at liberty to reveal my sources," responded the lead police officer formally.

"That's him," shouted the bus driver. "He's the one with the gun. He threatened to shoot me."

"Absolute nonsense," replied Rob. "It was just a figure of speech. I was just sharing banter with you. And you know it."

"Shooting people is not to be joked about," added the lead police officer.

"Look," said Rob. "I was having an argument with this bloke just now. He started to get nosey, so I joked with him to shut him up."

"What exactly did you say?" questioned the lead police officer.

"Something like 'if I tell you any more, I might have to shoot you'," responded Rob. "It's a common phrase back home. It's often used in jest. I didn't mean anything violent or dangerous. Like I said, it's just a figure of speech."

Seeing the melee of vehicles from the caravan, Stan, Christine, Jenifer, and Barry, with Penny tagging along, arrived on scene.

"What's going on?" demanded Christine. "What's happening."

"We've had a report of a firearm," stated the lead police officer. "Now, stand back or I'll arrest you all."

"Arrest us for what exactly?" asked Barry.

"Contamination of a crime scene," responded the lead police officer.

"But there hasn't been a crime," added Fiona. "It's just this jobsworth bus driver trying to spice up his boring life."

"How dare you!" growled the bus driver, stepping forward to confront Fiona.

Another police officer moved forward and apprehended the bus driver.

"Look," said Christine trying to maintain normality. "We've have had a pretty stressful week already. We are supposed to be on holiday, but we've had car and caravan trouble. We are on our way to Christchurch. We are reasonable, normal, churchgoing folk. We don't have any guns. The bus driver must be mistaken."

"Enough," shouted the lead police officer. "There is only one way to clear this up. Search them. Search them all. But not here, it's a public road. Right, everyone, go back to the petrol station."

Rob and Fiona were led to the petrol station, still wearing their handcuffs. Stan, Christine, Barry, Jenifer and Penny followed in single file.

Once on the forecourt, one by one, the holidaymakers were frisked by the police officers. Some officers entered the caravan to search for potential firearms, leaving no corner unchecked.

Forty minutes later, the officers appeared in the caravan doorway.

"All clean in here, Sarge," called over the officer.

The lead officer gathered the holidaymakers in a small group around him.

"Right," said the lead police officer. "It appears that you are true to your word. We searched you all, the caravan and the ground surrounding the bus stop, and there are no weapons to be found."

"Like I said," interrupted Rob. "Just a figure of speech."

"Silence!" boomed the lead police officer. "Let this be a lesson to you. And you, young man, maybe you should reconsider your vocabulary? It might save you from another brush with the law. Now, on your way."

It was music to Stan's ears. "Christchurch here we come."

The police officers started to disperse back to their vehicles. The lead police officer beckoned the bus driver over to him with a waggle of his index finger.

"They must have hidden the gun somewhere," stated the bus driver.

"Shut up!" boomed the lead police officer as he placed his arm on the bus driver's shoulder. "Now let's discuss the matter of wasting police time, shall we?"

Overhearing the conversation, Rob and Fiona looked at each other and smiled.

"Fancy a fag in the bus shelter?" asked Rob.

"Absolutely," replied Fiona laughing vociferously.

Jenifer made the party bacon sandwiches for breakfast. As it was a warm sunny morning, Christine set up the picnic table outside the caravan for an al fresco breakfast experience, much to the total astonishment of the petrol station customers.

An hour later, Stan had shepherded everyone into the Zodiac for the off. Stan handed a road atlas to Christine.

"You need to get us on the A360," instructed Stan. "We need to head in the direction of Devizes."

"You know what I'm like with maps, Stanley," replied Christine, in a flap.

"Give it here," ordered Barry from the back seat. "I'm really good with maps."

Christine handed the book to Barry, more than happy to discharge her navigation duties.

Stan, with a sense of total relief, looked up at his canopy repair, smiled, and guided Betsy off the petrol station forecourt.

In fairness, Barry turned out to be a good navigator, as, in no time at all, Stan was powering down the A360. Inside Betsy, the mood was upbeat. Comical stories of miserable bus drivers and confused police officers were high on the agenda, as were regular outbursts of mickey-taking laughter.

However, the mood soon took a dive in a downward direction, as Betsy jolted vehemently. At first, the main suspect was a pothole. But as Stan's complaints regarding Betsy's performance grew louder, focus was trained on the myriad of dashboard gauges.

"Oh bugger," said a frustrated Stan.

Christine reached around Fiona to deliver the 'foul language' punishment, landing another slap to Stan's arm.

"But we're losing oil pressure," announced Stan. "Whatever next?"

As Betsy's performance gradually dropped, Stan was looking around feverously for a suitable pull in.

"What about here, Stan?" suggested Christine. "There's plenty of room."

"But this is a tank crossing," stated Stan. "I don't think we can park up here."

Stan was out of options. Betsy coughed, spluttered, and ground to a halt. Fortunately, off the busy main road but blocking the tank crossing.

"This will have to do," said a flustered Stan, getting out of the car to take a look under the bonnet.

"This car is an absolute disgrace," grunted Jenifer from the back seat. "Make sure he sells it when we get home."

"If we get home," joked Rob.

Barry jumped out of the back seat to help Stan with the post-mortem. It wasn't looking good as steam was clearly visible coming from the radiator area.

"Let's wait for her to cool off," suggested Stan. "I don't want to burn my hands in this hot engine bay. I'll get Christine to put the kettle on."

Stan walked around to the passenger's side window and delivered his request for sustenance.

Seeing that Stan looked a little distressed, Christine felt obliged to satisfy his request. With Jenifer's help, Christine made a large pot of tea, arranging the picnic table and chairs outside the caravan.

The group settled down, waiting for the Zodiac to cool down.

Five minutes into their beverage break, a police car skidded to a halt in front of Stan's car.

A police officer purposefully jumped out of his vehicle and marched up to the holiday troop.

"Not you lot again!" bayed the officer in disbelief.

It was the lead officer who had led the extensive weapons search earlier in the morning.

"You can't park here and have a picnic," cried the aggravated official. "It's a tank crossing. The British Army don't stop for civilians if they are out on manoeuvres. Now move this lot, now!"

"It's not that simple," explained a sheepish Stan. "The car has broken down. We've lost oil pressure. Plus, the car has overheated. It just won't go at the moment."

The police officer scratched his head in frustration.

"You can't leave it here," added the police officer. "It's just too dangerous. I'll get on the radio and see what I can muster up."

The police officer then dashed across to his vehicle.

Ten minutes later, a happier looking police officer returned to give his update.

"Apparently," he said, "there is a garage about two miles down the road, that way. He's got a recovery truck and a tractor with a tow hitch. It sounds like we will be able to get you off this tank crossing quite quickly. You will have to sort out the recovery fee with the garage owner."

This news sent a shudder around Stan's body.

"How much does he charge?" asked a nervous Stan.

"No idea," replied the police officer, looking out for any tank activity.

"Maybe we can push the car to the garage?" suggested Stan, with money saving thoughts filling his head.

"Not possible," snapped the officer. "This is a very busy road, plus there are at least two reasonably steep hills between here and the garage."

"Blast!" reeled a pensive Stan.

Christine persuaded the officer to join them in their tea break, giving the officer two fig rolls with his mug of tea. This didn't go unnoticed by a scowling Stan. He was not impressed with Christine's wanton distribution of the sacred treat.

Half an hour later the tractor arrived, belching thick black smoke out of its rusty exhaust pipe situated at the front of the grimy looking vehicle.

"Are you sure that thing will be able to tow the caravan?" asked Barry.

"She's never let me down once," replied the confident tractor driver.

Stan, Barry, Rob and the police officer unhitched the caravan, pushed Betsy a few yards forward, then coupled the caravan up to the chugging tractor.

The police officer turned to the group.

"I'll take you down to the garage in my car," announced the police officer. "One of you stay here with the car."

"I'll do that," snapped Stan, not wanting to be separated from his pride and joy.

As the police car and tractor pulled away from the tank crossing, the recovery truck pulled up.

A grimy looking gentleman jumped out of the recovery truck and walked over to Stan.

"Afternoon," said the driver. "I'm Gareth. You seem to be in a spot of bother."

"You could say that," replied Stan.

"Anyhow," continued Gareth, "there's been a change of plan. The boss's daughter has just turned up. She's managed to drive her car into a fence, so being the boss's daughter, I'm afraid she has to go to the top of the list."

"You are kidding me," responded a frustrated Stan. "When can you look at my car then?"

"I've had a quick look at the damage," continued Gareth. "And I reckon there is around two to three days' work."

"What!" shrieked Stan. "We are supposed to be on holiday in Christchurch this week. Please have mercy. Can you talk to your boss and see if you can start on my repair first?"

"I can try," replied Gareth. "But I already know the answer. That girl is the apple of his eye. He will move heaven and Earth for her."

"If he can move all that," responded Stan in hope, "then he's more than capable of moving her repair timing?"

"We'll see," replied Gareth, "but we need to get this car off the tank crossing now. They might be on manoeuvres today."

Gareth lowered the recovery truck boom and loaded Betsy to the truck.

When Stan and Gareth arrived at the garage, Christine and company were deep in conversation with the garage owner and the police officer.

"Stan!" shouted an upset Christine. "Brian says he can't start on our car for three days. That means we will lose our holiday completely. What are we going to do?"

"Who is Brian?" asked Stan.

A gentleman dressed in a smart jacket stepped forward, offering his hand to Stan.

"Brian's the name, car sales is my game," said the gentleman. "This is my gaff. I hear you're in a spot of bother."

"We are indeed," responded Stan.

Stan explained the perils of their journey to date in great detail to Brian, trying to get some movement up the pecking order. Sadly, Brian wouldn't budge. His daughter just had too much hold on her father.

"There is a camp site around two miles from here," suggested Brian. "You can stop there whilst you wait. At least you can spend some of your holiday in Devizes."

Stan looked at Christine trying to gauge her mood.

"Well, it's a start," responded Stan. "Plus, I've got my toolbox in the boot. Maybe I can have a bash at the repairs myself."

"Don't be ridiculous," barked Christine. "You don't even know what the problem is. We could be here for weeks waiting for you to put things right."

"This has happened before," added Stan, "so, I may have a very good idea what the problem is. Have you got any Ford parts in stock Brian?"

Stan turned to Brian in hope.

"We don't stock Ford parts," replied Brian. "We are a British Leyland stockist."

Just what Stan didn't want to hear.

After almost an hour of further debate and argument, Stan was resigned to having to move on to the nearby camp site and look at fixing Betsy himself.

As an act of goodwill, Brian arranged transport of the Zodiac and the caravan to the nearby camp site. Plus, to Stan's absolute delight, in another act of goodwill, Brian waived the recovery charges.

The sun was still shining brightly as the caravan came to rest. The camp site looked reasonable. There was a toilet bock, a freshwater tap, and a small shop.

Moments later, Betsy rolled up on the back of the recovery truck. She was carefully off loaded and positioned alongside the caravan.

Once the business of thank you's and farewells had been completed, Stan's attention turned to Betsy. She'd had more than enough time to cool off, so Stan was keen to get his hands dirty.

"What do you think?" asked Barry who had wandered over to see if he could assist with the repairs.

"I reckon," said Stan, "with the loss of oil pressure, it may be the oil pump that has packed up. Or the feed rod has given out. One of the two."

"Is it a big job?" asked Barry in anticipation.

"I'm not sure," responded Stan. "If I can get to the oil pump and diagnose the problem, it might take no time at all. Depending on what replacement parts might be needed. I should have all the tools I need with me. Plus, there will be no labour costs."

Barry rolled his eyes.

In preparation, Stan rooted through the Zodiac boot and collected his tools and toolbox.

With his arms whirling frantically, Stan commenced the repairs. Ordering tools from Barry like a surgeon in the middle of a life-saving operation, Stan began to strip down Betsy's power unit. Lining up extracted components in the order they were removed, Stan made reasonably light work of exposing the oil pump from diagnosis.

With the distributor cap removed, Stan accessed the inner workings of the assembly. It soon became evident that the problem lay with the rod that operated the oil pump. The oil pump appeared to be in good order, but it was not functioning. Stan suspected the rogue rod of doom.

Lifting the rod from its housing, Stan displayed it like a trophy to the gathered audience.

"There you go," announced Stan, who was feeling very pleased with himself. "This is the problem. Look at the bottom of the rod. It's worn away, so the oil pump has no drive. This means that no oil was being pumped around the engine."

"You are boring me now, Dad," chirped Jenifer from the throng. "Is it fixable? And quickly?"

"We just need a replacement," replied Stan.

"Have you got one?" asked a hopeful Barry.

"No," responded Stan. "Us Zodiac-'ers don't carry parts like this. I'm sure we can get one from a car parts shop. Maybe from Salisbury? That's a big town and not too far from here."

"City," butted in Fiona whist dragging on a cigarette. "It's got a cathedral, you know."

Stan looked at Fiona in disbelief. He'd never imagined his rebel daughter would hold such cathedral trivia.

"If I give you this as a template," said Stan holding out the damaged rod, "someone can go to Salisbury and fetch a new one."

"How?" quizzed Christine. "The car's broken."

"Hmm," mumbled Stan. "Go and check in the shop. See if a bus service runs to Salisbury. We're not far from the main road."

"I'm on it," exclaimed an eager Barry as he turned to run to the shop.

"Where does it go then?" asked Rob.

"I'll show you," replied Stan, please to see Rob show a modicum of interest.

Stan placed the rod in position and let it rest in the hole that he had removed the rod from. To Stan's disgust, the rod disappeared into the hole, out of view.

"Bugger!" exclaimed Stan.

Christine stepped forward and slapped Stan on his back.

"What have I told you about bad language, Stanley?" said a hen-pecking Christine. "What's happened now?"

"I've lost the rod," admitted a hapless Stan. "I think the retaining washers have perished, so the rod has gone through the engine and into the sump."

"What does that mean in English?" begged Christine. "Is that a bad thing?"

"It is twofold," responded Stan rubbing his back. "It can't stay in the sump, so I need to get it out. Plus, whoever goes to fetch a new one will need it as a template. If they fetch the wrong model, we will never get the engine running."

"So just get it out," demanded Christine, in ignorance of the task in hand.

"It's not as simple as that," explained Stan. "To get at the sump, I will need to take off the front of the engine. Then there is no guarantee that I will be able to fish it out."

"This damn car!" exclaimed Christine.

"Language!" said Stan, Jenifer, and Fiona in unison.

"The sooner you get rid of this car, the better," snarled Christine. "If you'd have bought a decent car, then you wouldn't be spending all this money on repairs."

Barry returned from his visit to the shop slightly out of breath.

"Would you believe it," said Barry with a smile on his face. "The shopkeeper is a Liverpool fan. She was wearing a Liverpool pin badge on her blouse. She knows loads about Liverpool FC, even more than me, I reckon."

"And what about the bus routes?" asked Jenifer, with a touch of jealousy in her voice.

"Oh bugger," replied Barry, "I forgot, we were deep in football conversation. I'll go back and ask."

Jenifer delivered a venomous, jealous rap to Barry's left wrist.

"You stay here," demanded Jenifer. "I'll go. Time is running out, the shops in Salisbury will be shutting soon."

Stan lifted his head from Betsy's engine bay.

"Take your time, Jenifer," said a dejected Stan. "It's going to take me quite a few hours to retrieve this rod. I think you need to find out when the first bus leaves tomorrow morning."

"Okay," said Jenifer calmly. "But I will still see if they have a bus timetable in the shop."

"Are we ever going to get to Christchurch?" asked a dejected Barry.

"Of course we will," responded a reassuring Stan. "Just have faith. Once I have this sorted, we will be on our way. I can't see anything else going wrong."

It was Monday evening. It was day three of the family holiday to Christchurch, and they had managed a mere ninety miles of the planned one hundred and fifty mile trip, in two and a bit days.

Chapter Five

Stan tinkered into the late evening. As the final beams of sunlight disappeared behind the darkening deep green hills in the distance, Stan called time on his work.

"What's the state of play?" asked Barry, who had been Stan's willing helper all evening.

"It's taking a lot longer than I thought," replied a frustrated Stan. "I thought if I stripped off the pulleys, I might be able to access the front cover. However, it's not that straightforward. I just hope I have lined these parts that I have taken off in the right order. If not, we may need to investigate hiring a mobile Zodiac mechanic."

"I have faith in you, Stan," responded Barry as he placed his hand firmly on Stan's shoulder. "What time tomorrow do you think we can set off for the new parts?"

"Well, if I get up at first light," replied Stan, "and if all goes to plan, then maybe two hours' work, and I should be able to access the sump."

"Excellent," responded an upbeat Barry. "Fancy a cuppa? I'll go and see if there is one about."

"With a fig roll," demanded Stan, desperately trying to get in on the fig roll scene.

Barry took the short walk to the caravan on the hunt for a brew. Barry poked his head inside the caravan door.

"Any chance of a brew for Stan?" asked Barry. "He's been working very hard out there in the heat, I think he's earned it."

"I would make a fresh pot," replied Jenifer. "But we are out of milk."

"Do you want me to get some from the camp shop?" offered Barry.

"Yes," snapped Jenifer. "But make sure you don't get flirting with that bimbo in the shop. Come straight back with the milk."

"Of course I will," replied Barry. "I don't know what you are worrying about. You are the apple of my eye, dear."

"Just don't be long," growled Jenifer throwing a pound note at Barry.

Barry picked up the money from the floor and departed on his milk sourcing quest.

When Christine overheard the fact that Stan was packing up for the night, she wandered outside for a progress update.

"How much longer do you think?" asked Christine, full of hope.

"A couple more hours of toil in the morning," responded Stan. "Then I should be in a position to provide the rod, so the parts sourcing party can get on their way."

"And when the parts are here?" requested Christine.

"Let me see," pondered Stan. "Fit the rod. Replace the parts I have taken off. Check the torques. Check the oil, then I will be ready to try and start the engine."

"What's that in time value?" asked Christine vociferously.

Stan paused as he tried to mentally calculate a time value for each part of the repair process.

"If I get the rod out of the sump first try," responded Stan, "and all the parts go back together as they should, then I reckon about five hours work in total."

Christine glared at her wristwatch on her left wrist and completed her own mental arithmetic assessment.

"So, if you get up and washed by eight in the morning," replied Christine, "allowing for two hours fetching the parts from Salisbury, we should be good to go at three in the afternoon."

Stan looked up, holding his index finger to his chin, validating Christine's timing assumptions.

"Give or take," responded Stan.

Christine mentally etched the agreed timing on the nagging side of her brain. Just in case she needed to access it tomorrow, to berate Stan for yet another failure.

Half an hour had passed. Stan had just returned from the shower block looking spick and span.

"So, where's this cup of tea and fig roll then?" asked an ever hopeful Stan.

Jenifer had been sorting the beds in the caravan so had been somewhat occupied and distracted. She looked around for Barry.

"Is he not back yet?" quizzed a furious looking Jenifer. "Right, we'll see about this."

Jenifer stormed out of the caravan in search of her easily led boyfriend.

When Jenifer arrived at the camp site shop doorway, she paused. She was about to burst through the door to potentially remonstrate with her errant boyfriend. But, thinking that the noise and commotion caused by an exuberant entry may split up any shenanigans, Jenifer decided on a 'softly-softly' approach.

Opening the door as quietly as she could, Jenifer crept behind the tower rack of postcards that was situated adjacent to the door. Through the postcards, Jenifer could see her beloved Barry bent over the counter, resting on his elbows, gazing warmly into the attractive looking shop worker's eyes. Jenifer tried to listen into the conversation, but a passing tractor put paid to that.

Unable to control herself any longer, Jenifer jumped from behind her hiding place.

"So where is this milk then, Barry?" snarled Jenifer in a fit of jealousy.

Barry instantly shot bolt upright in embarrassment.

"I was just about to bring it, dear," replied a flustered Barry. "Have you met Natasha?"

"Just give me the milk," demanded an angry Jenifer. "You've been here ages."

"We were just talking football," responded Barry, trying to find a way out of the hole he was digging for himself. "Honestly, Natasha is a football trivia guru, the things she knows."

"You know what I think about football!" scowled Jenifer, grabbing the bottle of milk from Barry's clutches.

"Don't be daft," added Barry. "Come and say hello to Natasha. She's from Russia. Don't you think her English is superb. Natasha is over here to study English as part of her degree. She is studying at Southampton University. She also knows loads about football in Russia."

"You appear to know a lot about Natasha by the sounds of it," replied Jenifer, with a high degree of sarcasm.

"Come on," said an inviting Barry. "Come and have a chat, Natasha is very interesting."

Jenifer cast a quick eye over Natasha. Seeing a slim, attractive, well presented potential competitor, Jenifer shook her head.

"Not on your nellie," responded Jenifer as she stormed out of the shop.

"Go after her," advised Natasha.

"See you later," replied Barry as he turned and ran after his beloved girlfriend.

Jenifer was fleet of foot. Just as Barry reached the shop doorway, Jenifer was already halfway back to the caravan. When Barry arrived at the caravan, Jenifer had already locked herself in the small bedroom of the caravan. As Barry pleaded for Jenifer to open the door and come out, Christine stood and faced Barry. With hands on hips, wearing the most judgemental face that she could, Christine started on Barry.

"Young man!" declared Christine in the sternest of voices. "Do you have to upset my daughter like this? Don't you think we've got enough on our plates as it is? We've been on the road for nearly four days now, faced everything that the holiday goblins could throw at us, and you have to add to it by doing this."

"I haven't done anything though," pleaded Barry, desperate to free himself from suspicion. "All I have done is to be friendly to the locals, nothing more. I love your daughter, and I wouldn't do anything to hurt her."

"So why do you keep running to that shop, at every given opportunity, with your tongue hanging out then?" shouted Jenifer from behind the bedroom door.

"That is just nonsense," declared Barry. "I've only been to the shop twice."

"Four times," added Fiona trying to stir the pot. "I've been counting."

"Keep out of this, Fiona, it's not your fight," snapped Christine assertively. "You two need to sort this out, and now. I'm not taking another step towards Christchurch until you do."

"We aren't going anywhere soon," commented Rob. "At least not until the car is fixed. Just saying."

"You can keep out of this as well," growled Christine in Rob's direction.

Rob looked at Fiona, gesturing for a smoke break. Fiona nodded in approval, so the pair disappeared outside, just to get away from the building tension inside the caravan.

For the next hour, Christine, Jenifer and Barry carried on the heated debate. It was just like a bunch of politicians trying to make the Russians out to be the peace breakers. Stan watched on, dying of thirst and eager to partake in the delights of the sacred fig roll.

After much toing and froing, eventually, a still upset Jenifer appeared from behind the bedroom door. Barry offered a peace-making hug which Jenifer accepted. Christine looked on with a proud look on her face, thinking that the reconciliation was her doing. Just Rob and Fiona to work on now.

"Am I going to get this cup of tea and fig roll?" pleaded a desperate Stan from the lounge settee.

"Don't be lazy," replied Christine firmly. "You've been doing nothing all day, just tinkering with your spanners as usual. You make the tea."

Stan looked to the heavens for inspiration, then begrudgingly put the kettle on.

With no further outbreak of hostilities, the group eventually settled down for the night, Stan and Christine in the 'master' caravan bedroom, Jenifer in the second smaller bedroom, Fiona on the pull out bed in the lounge, and Rob and Barry in the now erected awning, on blow-up mattress'.

No sooner had Rob's head hit the pillow, following his pre-sleep cigarette, the familiar bedtime symphony broke out. Determined to get at least a few hours' sleep, Rob got off his mattress, walked out to Betsy. Finding her unlocked, Rob returned to the awning for his sleeping bag. Once again, Rob was going to enjoy the cramped leather bench seating of the Zodiac to rest his weary head.

As the primary sunbeams of Tuesday morning began to lighten the back seat of the Zodiac, Rob was raised from his slumber by a loud tap on the window. It was Stan dressed in his overalls.

"What are you doing in there?" asked a rather annoyed Stan. "You have a bed in the awning. I didn't give you permission to sleep there."

"I can't sleep next to that row," replied a half asleep Rob.

"What row?" asked a concerned Stan, thinking that the caravan had a new noise problem.

"Barry's snoring," explained Rob. "It's intolerable."

"I don't care," replied Stan abruptly. "This is my car, and I say who goes in her. Got it?"

Rob didn't respond. He'd rather have a few hours peaceful sleep and a telling off from Stan than a sleepless night, listening to the dulcet sounds of something resembling the tone deaf wind section of an infant school orchestra.

"Now you are up," said Stan, "to repay your rent for your night in Betsy, you can help me with the repairs."

"Great," replied Rob.

Stan opened his toolbox, cast his eyes on the removed engine parts, which were still looking neat as they lay on an old bedsheet, and began his dismantling activities.

Rob followed Stan's instructions to the letter, not wanting a second telling off from the frustrated looking Stan.

After nearly two hours of toil, Stan was in a position to retrieve the delinquent rod from the sump. At the bottom of the engine, Stan had managed to open up a narrow slot to access the sump. It was only a small opening, but Stan was confident he could get his hand into the sump to retrieve the rod.

Stan tried and tried, but his toolmaker hands were too broad for the opening. Stan looked at Rob's hands. They looked a lot smaller, so Stan beckoned Rob to join him.

"Put your hand out," asked Stan.

Rob put his hand forward and Stan measured his hand against Rob's, to get an idea of size.

"Perfect," announced Stan. "Now, Rob, put your hand through that opening and see if you can fish out the rod."

Rob did as Stan commanded and forced his hand into the opening. It was a very tight fit, but Rob just about managed to squeeze his hand through and into the sump chamber.

It was a nasty place. Rob's hand was soon immersed in slimy, smelly, slippery oil. Digging around, at first Rob couldn't detect the rod.

"Anything?" asked a desperate Stan.

"Not yet," replied Rob with his arm fully outstretched.

After a short period of time Rob found the errant rod lying at the bottom of the sump, resting in a layer of thick residue oil.

"Got it," proclaimed a proud Rob.

Carefully, Rob backed his hand out of the opening, holding the pesky rod. Rob handed over the rod to Stan. It was still covered in oil, dripping all over the place.

"Now let's see," said Stan as he inspected the rod. "As I said before, the rod is worn, it's just unfortunate that it gave out this week."

Stan presented the rod to Rob to show him the wear damage.

Rob nodded his head in approval.

"Shall I show you where it goes?" asked Stan, trying to educate Rob.

"Go on then," responded Rob, trying to get back into Stan's good books.

Stan turned to face Betsy and placed the rod in its housing at the top of the engine. Unfortunately, as the rod was still covered in oil, this made it slippery. Stan lost control of his grip and once again the rod disappeared from view, shooting back into the engine sump.

"Bugger!" exclaimed Stan with a wry smile on his face. "I've only gone and dropped the damn rod back into the sump."

Stan expected a response from Rob, but when he turned around, Rob wasn't there.

"Where has he gone, I wonder?" said Stan to himself.

Stan checked the awning and poked his head inside the silent caravan. No sign of Rob. Stan then walked around the caravan, just in case he was out of sight having a cigarette, but nothing. Stan returned to Betsy's engine bay to see if his hand would fit in the slot.

Just as Stan bent over the engine, Rob appeared.

"Where have you been?" inquired Stan.

"I've been to clean up," declared Rob. "That oil residue got right under my nails."

"Ah," responded an embarrassed Stan. "You see, we have a slight problem."

"Problem?" asked a nervous Rob.

"Yes," snapped Stan. "That rod has only gone and made its way back to the sump. I need you to get it out again. At least you know what you are doing."

Rob rolled his eyes in total frustration. He then stepped forward and fed his hand into the revolting opening, this time knowing what to expect.

Fortunately, the rod was quickly discovered and recovered.

Rob presented the oil dripping rod to Stan.

"Now don't go and throw this back into the sump, please," demanded Rob.

By now, the remaining holiday makers were up and about. Christine had the kettle on, Jenifer had the bacon on, and Fiona appeared to be setting up for something electrical, as she fed an extension cable out of the caravan bedroom window.

"What on earth are you up to?" asked Barry.

"I'm going to set up the TV out here," announced Fiona. "The reception is better out here."

"But you won't be able to see the screen when the sun is out fully," explained Barry.

"Got that sorted," responded Fiona holding a bath towel.

Barry shook his head in disbelief.

After a hearty breakfast butty, Stan gathered up Rob, Barry and Jenifer.

"This is the part I need," explained Stan, holding up the worn out rod. "Christine has found the address of two car parts shops in the Yellow Pages. This is a map of Salisbury that Natasha gave me."

Stan handed the Salisbury street map to Jenifer.

"I'm not touching that," snarled Jenifer as she took a step back.

Barry reached forward and took the map from Stan.

"I knew you'd be in there straight away," said a jealous Jenifer.

"Enough already," replied Barry trying to keep the peace. "It's only a map."

"Anyhow," continued Stan, "make sure you get the right retaining washers, top and bottom. It's really important."

"Okay," responded Barry. "What time is the next bus?"

"Nine fifteen," replied a reluctant Jenifer.

"Don't forget Penny!" shouted Christine, poking her head out of the caravan. "It will be a nice outing for her."

Rob, Barry and Jenifer looked at each other in disbelief. Having to take the dog with the added responsibility was not high on their wish list. But not wanting to invoke the wrath of Christine, Jenifer walked over to Penny and attached her lead to her collar.

The parts posse then walked towards the site entrance to the bus stop, which they had been told was one hundred yards down the road to the right of the site.

At nine sixteen and thirty seconds, a large green bus came into view and pulled up at the bus stop. The front doors opened with a hiss. As they did so, a familiar figure came into view. It was the bus driver who had reported them for the possession of a firearm. Rob instantly bowed his head and pulled his baseball cap over his face.

Barry stepped forward into the bus.

“Three returns to Salisbury, please,” requested Barry. “Do I have to pay for the dog?”

“No,” growled the bus driver. “That will be two pounds and ten pence.”

Barry dug into his pocket and handed the exact change to the driver.

As the group started to enter the seating area the bus driver sparked into life.

“Hang on a minute,” said the bus driver. “Don’t I know you?”

“I don’t think so,” replied Barry promptly.

“No, not you,” answered the bus driver. “Him, with the hat on.”

Rob looked directly at the bus driver.

“You’re the one with the gun!” declared the bus driver. Off you get. Now.”

“Don’t be unreasonable,” replied Rob. “I didn’t have a gun, the police proved that.”

An uncomfortable nervous fear fell over the passengers already seated on the bus.

“I don’t care,” snapped the bus driver. “You aren’t getting on my bus.”

“Why not?” demanded Jenifer. “He’s done nothing wrong. It was just a huge misunderstanding. Just show some compassion and move on.”

The bus driver paused for thought.

“Just this once,” declared the bus driver. “But I’m warning you, any signs of funny business and I’ll have you thrown off my bus. Do I make myself clear?”

"Crystal," responded Jenifer.

Rob, Barry and Jenifer made their way to the back of the bus and sat on the empty back seat. Jenifer placed Penny on her lap.

"Have they only got one bus driver in the Salisbury area?" quipped Rob.

Barry and Jenifer smiled.

Ten minutes into their bus journey the air suddenly turned rancid. Unbeknown to Rob, Barry and Jenifer, Penny had been routing in the bin the previous evening, and she had managed to detect some discarded cheese. This was an absolute no-no for Penny as cheese upset her stomach. Penny has broken wind and boy did it smell.

"What is that?" asked Barry at high volume. "That stinks."

Jenifer knew immediately, guessing the source of the ghastly odour. Penny had previous cheese form. Penny was capable of clearing out the entire household into the garden, such were the effects of her trumping, and this was no exception.

Opening the small windows in the bus like their lives depended on it, the three travellers tried to disperse the stench as best they could by waving their arms around energetically. But it was having little effect.

By now, the stench had crept forward, affecting the other unsuspecting passengers on the bus, who promptly opened any windows close to them, then held their noses tightly.

Penny let off a second volley of silent but deadly trumps. This one was worse than the first. Passengers were quickly becoming overwhelmed by the pungent stink, as they started to cough and retch.

Eventually, the smell reached the driver who could hardly believe what his nostrils had detected. Looking around and thinking he was passing the pig farm, the driver soon realised that the pig farm was miles away from their current position, so where on earth was the vile smell coming from.

Looking in his mirror and seeing the distress and discomfort his passengers were in, the bus driver immediately pulled the bus over to the side of the road and pressed his hazard warning switch.

The driver then jumped from his seat to investigate.

"The smell is coming from back there," indicated one of the distressed passengers.

The bus driver swivelled round and returned to his seat. Once in reach, he flicked the switch and opened the front doors.

"Everyone out," declared the bus driver. "Go and get some much needed fresh air."

The passengers stampeded out of the front doors clutching their noses. Some had handkerchiefs to their noses.

As Rob, Barry, Jenifer and Penny approached the doors, the awaiting bus driver had already reached his conclusion as to who the perpetrator was.

“That smell is just not human,” stated the bus driver. “It must have come from that.”

The bus driver pointed his accusing finger at the tail wagging pooch.

“I don’t know what’s wrong with her,” said Jenifer as she carried Penny to the sanctuary of fresh air.

“Well,” added the bus driver. “It sure as heck isn’t getting back on the bus.”

Jenifer took a quick look around to see where they were.

“You can’t leave us in the middle of nowhere,” replied an upset Jenifer. “We’ve paid our fare. You should let us all back on and take us to Salisbury.”

“I have no problem taking you and your friends to Salisbury,” responded the confident bus driver. “But I’m not taking that smelly dog another yard.”

As the argument continued, spotting the hazard warning lights, a police car on random patrol pulled up in front of the bus. The officer got out of the vehicle and approached the bus.

“Sergeant Corthine here,” announced the police officer. “What appears to be the problem? You know you are blocking half of the road in a pretty dangerous position on a busy road.”

“I had no choice but to pull over,” declared the bus driver. “That thing is vile.”

The bus driver pointed at an innocent looking Penny.

"You got all of your passengers off because of a lap dog?" asked Sergeant Corthine. "Was it becoming vicious and biting your passengers?"

"No," responded the bus driver. "It stank the bus out. I've driven past pig farms for fifteen years. That dog makes the pig farms smell like Chanel Number Five."

"It can't be that bad, surely?" asked Sergeant Corthine.

"Go and smell for yourself," suggested the bus driver pointing at his bus.

Officer Corthine walked over to the bus, stepped in, and walked a further five paces. He soon turned around and walked briskly out of the bus.

"I see what you mean," declared Sergeant Corthine. "That is rather rank. What have you been feeding that dog?"

"I think she's been at the cheese," admitted Jenifer.

"Then don't give her cheese if this is the effect it has," said a puzzled Sergeant Corthine.

"We don't let her have it," added Jenifer. "I suspect she has been at the bin in the night."

Sergeant Corthine took a step back.

"Hang on a minute," added Sergeant Corthine. "Don't I know you lot?"

"I'm not sure," responded a nervous Jenifer.

Sergeant Corthine took a good look at Rob, Barry and Jenifer.

"It is you!" declared Sergeant Corthine. "The other day. Didn't we get called out to a firearms incident involving you?"

The unrelated passengers gasped and took a step away from the accused.

"We didn't have a firearm," replied Rob. "It was just a big misunderstanding."

"Ah, yes," continued Sergeant Corthine looking at the bus driver. "And it was you who raised the alarm. Am I right?"

"Yep," replied the proud bus driver.

"Didn't I have to reprimand you for wasting police time?" quizzed Sergeant Corthine.

The bus driver looked at his feet, refusing to get drawn into any further discussion.

"And here you are," continued Sergeant Corthine, "giving your pals a lift on your bus. What a small world we live in."

"They're no pals of mine," grunted the bus driver.

"He won't let us back on," pleaded Jenifer. "He wants to abandon us in the middle of nowhere."

"That's poor form," replied Sergeant Corthine. "You can't leave them here."

"Well, I'm not taking that dog," added the bus driver. "It smells worse that my grandfather's socks, and that's really bad."

"I tell you what," said Sergeant Corthine. "You take these nice people to Salisbury, and, out of the kindness of my heart, and to show you there is no ill feelings, I will take the dog in my vehicle to the bus station. I will wait for you there. You bring the dog with you, young lady."

"Sounds like a plan," responded the bus driver. "Just let me check to see if the bus is habitable first."

The bus driver returned to his bus to smell the ambience. He soon returned signalling that all was good.

Barry, Rob and the passengers got on the bus, watching Jenifer getting into the back of the police car holding the troublesome Penny.

Sergeant Corthine operated his right hand indicator to pull out. As he did, once again, Penny dropped one of her stink bombs. The indicator was cancelled as Sergeant Corthine and Jenifer leapt out of the vehicle, leaving Penny to taste her own work.

"That's unnatural," stated Sergeant Corthine. "I've never smelled anything so bad as that in my life."

"It's unbearable," agreed Jenifer as she watched the bus drive off down the road.

"I'll go and open the windows," suggested Sergeant Corthine.

Sergeant Corthine fully opened all windows to his vehicle and tethered Penny to the door armrest, to make sure she couldn't make off.

"How long does this usually last?" asked Sergeant Corthine.

"It varies," responded Jenifer. "Normally, when she's done her business, she gets better quite quickly."

Suddenly hit by thoughts of a back seat gift, Sergeant Corthine rushed to his police car to make sure Penny had not done her business.

Fortunately, all was in order. So, Sergeant Corthine untied Penny and guided her out of the car.

"Maybe you can encourage her to do her business?" suggested Sergeant Corthine. "Walk her around that field behind us."

Sergeant Corthine and Jenifer walked a few yards down the grass verge to a five bar gate. Sergeant Corthine unlatched the gate and led Jenifer and Penny into the field for a constitutional.

Sadly, after a fifteen minute walk, Penny was not playing ball. Looking at his watch, Sergeant Corthine was aware that he had now wasted more than enough time on this community matter.

"Let's risk it and get on our way," said Sergeant Corthine. "I have other important matters to attend to."

"Sure," replied Jenifer.

The pair returned to the police car and set off. All was pleasant for the first fifteen minutes of the journey. But then, despite the fact that the vehicle windows were fully open, another nasty niff enveloped the car.

Jenifer immediately hung her head out of the back window, in an attempt to gulp in fresh air. Sergeant Corthine tried to get his head as close to the flow of fresh air as he dared, still keeping his now watering eyes on the road ahead.

Fortunately, the steady air flow dispersed the stench in no time, plus they were fast approaching Salisbury.

As the police car entered the central bus station, Sergeant Corthine breathed a fresh air sigh of relief. As the car came to a stop, Jenifer spotted Barry and Rob waiting in the bus station. Jenifer picked Penny up from the back seat.

"Oh, no," said a startled Jenifer as she looked at the back seat that was now displaying a 'Penny present'.

Smelling the results of Penny's present, Sergeant Corthine looked over at the back seat, then dropped his chin to his chest.

"I'll clean it up," declared a totally embarrassed Jenifer. "Just wait here, I'll go and try and find something to clear it up."

"Too right you will," grunted Sergeant Corthine. "I'm certainly not doing it.

Sergeant Corthine very quickly jumped out of the vehicle and scowled across at Jenifer. Barry and Rob had spotted the police car and had walked over to greet Jenifer.

"Penny has done her business in the back seat," explained Jenifer. "I need to nip into the bus station. I'm sure they will have something to clean it up in there."

Barry and Rob waited at the police car with Sergeant Corthine. Barry had Penny at his side on a short lead.

Three quarters of an hour later, Jenifer reappeared with some cleaning materials.

"Sorry I've been so long," said a flustered Jenifer. "They didn't have any cleaning equipment in the bus station. Apparently, they clean the buses at the bus depot. So, I had to go into town."

"I don't want your life story," responded a frustrated Sergeant Corthine. "I just want my car clean."

Jenifer glared at Sergeant Corthine and started her cleaning duties.

Ten minutes later, Jenifer announced that her work was done, and presented a new air freshener to Sergeant Corthine.

"Don't darken my door again," said a perturbed Sergeant Corthine as he jumped into a fresh smelling squad car.

"How embarrassing," admitted Jenifer.

"This trip is just getting weirder and weirder," stated Rob. "What are the chances? We keep bumping into the same policeman and the same bus driver. Are we in some sort of experiment? To test our limits? I bet these people are actors and we are being watched."

"Don't be such a prat," responded Barry. "Which way is it to town, Jenifer? We need to get the car parts and get them back to Stan, pronto."

"Follow me," said a confident Jenifer.

Chapter Six

Rob, Barry and Jenifer headed into Salisbury town centre, trying to find the automotive parts shops. Along the way, they stopped and bought a take-away coffee.

"Apparently," said Jenifer looking at the street map, "one of the shops that Dad told us to go to is not far from here. Just off Bell Street."

"Great," replied Barry poking his nose over Jenifer's shoulder to look at the map.

Five minutes later, Barry opened the door to the car parts shop. Rob walked into the shop behind Barry. Jenifer followed, tugging at Penny on her lead.

"Morning," said Barry confidently.

"Good morning," replied the shopkeeper. "And how can I help you on this glorious morning?"

The shopkeeper cast a nervous look at Penny.

"Is she okay in here?" asked Jenifer. "She'll be no trouble, she's very well behaved."

"I should think so," responded the shopkeeper after deliberating on his response.

Barry produced the defective rod from his pocket. It was wrapped up in a tissue.

"Do you stock these?" asked Barry handing the rod to the shopkeeper.

The shopkeeper took the rod from Barry, reached for his spectacles and put them on for a close inspection.

"What vehicle is this from?" asked the shopkeeper.

Barry took a folded piece of paper from his back pocket and glanced at his notes.

"It's from a 1971 Ford Zodiac Mark Four," stated Barry confidently.

The shopkeeper maintained a close inspection of the rod, manoeuvring it to all angles to confirm his assessment.

"Oil pump to distributor," said the shopkeeper. "Let me think. I'm pretty sure I have one of these in the stock room."

As the good news filtered across the counter, bad news began to filter across the other way. Sadly, it appeared that Penny had not got over her cheese issue, as the air grew pungent and unbearable.

"What on earth is that?" growled the shopkeeper placing his fingers over his nose.

"I'm terribly sorry," replied a totally embarrassed Jenifer. "It appears that our dog has a stomach problem. I'll take her outside."

"Why did you bring her in here in the first place?" demanded the shopkeeper angrily.

"I'm sorry, I'm sorry," responded a now flustered Jenifer. "I'll go outside with her."

"You can all go," boomed the shopkeeper. "I've never experienced anything like that in my life. "Now, out, the lot of you."

"But—"" said Barry trying to continue the purchase.

"I said out," shouted the shopkeeper.

"But what about—" Barry said again, trying to retrieve the faulty rod.

"Out, now!" insisted the shopkeeper.

Barry, Jenifer, Rob and Penny reluctantly trudged out of the shop.

"What are we going to do now?" quizzed Barry. "He's got our sample rod. Even if we find another stockist, we don't have anything to show them."

"All we can do is try," suggested Rob. "Or come back here in an hour or so and see if Godzilla has calmed down."

"Good idea," replied Barry. "Also, I fancy a bacon sandwich."

"I don't believe you pair," said an irate Jenifer. "Just go back in there and get our part. He just can't keep hold of it. It belongs to us."

"You go in then," suggested Barry. "If you are so brave."

"I'm looking after Penny, you go," responded a defiant Jenifer.

"I'm not going back in there," replied Barry. "He doesn't like me. He'll just throw me out. What about you, Rob?"

"I don't think it's a good idea going back in straight away," replied Rob. "Let's try that other shop. They might have what we are looking for."

"I guess so," responded Barry looking through the shop window at a mean looking shopkeeper.

After spending a few minutes over the street map, the three plus pup headed off to find the second car spares shop.

After a bacon sandwich pit stop, the group eventually managed to find the second car spares shop.

"Stay outside with that disgraceful dog this time," stated Barry, as her glared forcefully at Jenifer.

Barry and Rob entered the shop. As the front door opened, it triggered a bell on top of the door.

"Good morning," said a welcoming shopkeeper. "What can I do for you?"

"Good morning," answered Barry politely. "I'm after a rod that fits between the oil pump and the distributor, for a 1971 Ford Zodiac Mark Four."

"Sorry," replied the shopkeeper immediately. "I don't stock classic parts. Have you tried 'Wilf's place off Bell Street? He stocks classic car parts, give him a go."

"I think we already have," responded a sheepish Barry. "I think we annoyed him with our dog. She has a tummy problem at the moment, and she stank out his shop."

The shopkeeper smiled and laughed.

"That's unfortunate," responded an entertained shopkeeper. "Maybe go back and try him again? This time, leave the dog outside. I'm sure he will help you. He's not a bad bloke."

Barry looked over at Rob.

"What do you reckon?" asked Barry.

"What choices have we got," replied Rob. "We can't go back empty handed. Maybe, let me try this time? I'll tell him about my Kawasaki. Maybe he might come round?"

"Okay," replied a desperate Barry. "Like you said, we are running out of options. Thanks for all of your help."

"You are welcome," replied the shopkeeper. "And good luck with Wilf."

The holiday makers hurried back to Bell Street, to try and persuade Wilf to assist them in their hour of need.

As they arrived at the shop, the team stopped for a discussion.

"Wait out here," suggested Rob. "I'll go in and try and work on Wilf."

"Okay," replied Barry and Jenifer in unison. "Good luck."

Rob crossed his fingers and entered the arena.

As Rob approached the counter Wilf looked up from his activity on the counter.

"You again!" barked Wilf.

Rob held his hands above his head in an attempted gesture of peace.

"It's just me," said Rob. "No smelly dog this time."

Wilf looked outside the shop and spotted Penny sat calmly next to Jenifer on the pavement. Wilf then looked Rob up and down.

"So, you are still after a distributor rod for a 1971 Ford Zodiac Mark Four, I take it?" asked Wilf, as he slid a shrink wrapped package from behind the till.

"I certainly am, Wilf," responded Rob.

"How do you know my name?" asked a shocked Wilf.

"We've been to another spares shop," replied Rob. "He told us your name. Plus, he said you were a really decent bloke."

"He did, did he?" added Wilf.

"Really," responded Rob as politely as he could. "If I might explain. Our Zodiac engine is in pieces on a camp site in Devizes. We've travelled from Worcester, starting out last Friday."

"Last Friday?" asked an astonished Wilf. "What did you do? Push the car all the way here?"

"It certainly feels like it," responded a jovial Rob. "I appreciate that we got off on the wrong foot, with the dog problem. We didn't even know about her problem until she cleared a bus on the way here. But it's just me in here now, no dog, and I'm a petrol head."

"Petrol head?" asked an intrigued Wilf. "What do you drive?"

"Ride," responded Rob. "I've got a Kawasaki KH250 triple. Green. I've fitted matt black crash bars and I wax the tank every weekend. She's my baby."

"Two stroke Japanese rubbish," responded an unimpressed Wilf. "Give me a British bike every day of the week. Royal Enfield, BSA, Triumph. There are too many of these cheap Japanese imports flooding the market. Mark my words, they will snuff out British bikes if you give them half a chance."

"Maybe," replied Rob. "But if you ride a British motorbike, then you need to spread something on your driveway to absorb all of the oil leaks."

Wilf smiled and laughed.

"Okay," stated Wilf. "You are pulling at my heart strings. You can have the parts. There are two retaining washers in the pack, make sure you fit them to the rod before you fit it to the engine."

"Will do," said a chuffed Rob.

"So, what do you get out of that Japanese toy?" asked Wilf.

"I've had a hundred and five miles per hour on the clock," bragged Rob. "I was on the tank. I know it's only on the clock and they are usually out by a mile. But it felt quick enough."

"Nuts," responded Wilf.

Rob paid for the parts and joined Barry, Jenifer and Penny outside. As he approached them, Rob waved the white paper bag containing the precious parts in front of him.

"Look what I've got," said a proud Rob.

Jenifer stepped up to Rob and kissed him on the cheek, much to the annoyance on Barry.

"Clever chap," said a happy Jenifer. "let's get back to base."

"Let's go," replied Rob. "Are we going to try the bus again? If so, what are we going to do with Penny? Is she still poorly?"

"We'll just have to risk it," responded Jenifer. "We can't afford a taxi, plus she might perform in that. I think a taxi driver is more inclined to abandon us in the middle of nowhere if Penny performs again."

"Good thinking," responded Rob.

Barry, Jenifer, Rob and Penny made their way back to the bus station, hoping that their bus back to the camp site was not driven by their arch enemy.

Fortunately, the bus they caught had a driver not known to them. Plus, Penny seemed to be over her tummy issues and behaved impeccably all the way back to the camp site.

As the Salisbury crew approached the caravan, they spotted a weirdly shaped blanket positioned a few feet from the awning. Jenifer walked up to the blanket and lifted it up. Underneath, Jenifer discovered Fiona, squatting down whilst concentrating intently on the potable television.

"What are you doing out here?" asked a bemused Jenifer.

"Only place I can get a decent signal on the aerial," responded Fiona flippantly.

"Whatever next?" said a bemused Jenifer.

"She's been there the whole time you've been away," shouted Christine through the kitchen window of the caravan. "She's just a lazy beggar. I've had no help with the washing up. No help with the cleaning. She thinks she's on holiday."

"I'm supposed to be!" screamed a vexed Fiona from inside the blanket.

Stan was working on the Zodiac. Spotting that the parts posse had returned, he downed tools and approached the group.

"Did you get the new rod?" asked a desperate Stan.

Rob handed over the precious white paper bag.

"What about the retaining washers?" requested Stan anxiously.

"They are in the pack," replied Rob. "Don't forget to fit them."

"I won't," responded Stan. "I'm not stupid. Now come and see what I have been up to whilst you were away."

Stan guided Rob and Barry across to the Zodiac.

"I've replaced most of the front end," explained Stan. "All I have to do now, is fit the rod and finish the engine rebuild. Then, hopefully, we should be on our way."

Christine made her way over to join the party, looking at her watch as she walked.

"It's pretty much two o'clock now," said Christine. "How long will it take you to fit the part and start the engine?"

Stan looked at the engine with the fingers of his right hand placed on his chin.

"About two hours," replied Stan after a moment's consideration.

"Is it worth me starting to pack up?" asked Christine. "I can take down the awning, pack up the bedding and get the caravan ready for the off."

"Great idea," replied Stan, with a hopeful smile on his face.

"Jenifer, Rob, Fiona," barked Christine. "You come and help me pack. Barry, you help Stan with the car."

"Okie dokie," replied Barry, happy with his assigned duty.

"Fiona!" boomed Christine. "Fiona! Come and help, young lady."

There was no motion visible from under the blanket.

"Leave her," said Jenifer from the moral high ground. "She'll just get in the way."

Christine tutted in frustration and walked into the awning to start her packing duties.

Stan had removed the rod from its packaging. He held it up in front of his eyes for a close inspection, running his fingers down the shaft to make sure the sharp hexagonal profile was in order. He was happy with what he saw.

Stan offered up the rod to the top of the distributor and positioned the rod above the location hole. Stan let go of the rod, dropping it into its working position within the engine. To Stan's horror, yet again, the rod disappeared from view.

"No!" screamed Stan.

Stan was so wrapped up in the euphoria of the moment, he had clean forgotten to fit the retaining washers.

"What's wrong?" asked a worried Barry.

"Don't ask," responded a totally embarrassed Stan.

"I am asking," continued Barry.

"Keep it to yourself," whispered Stan, "but I forgot to fit the retaining washers."

"Idiot!" replied a frustrated Barry.

"Shhh," snapped Stan. "Keep your voice down. I'm going to have to take off the front of the engine again. We need to get the rod out of the sump."

"Again!" complained Barry.

Stan found his oily sheet and once again placed it on the grass next to the Zodiac. Part by part, Stan once more started to strip down the front of the engine, placing removed parts of the sheet in order of removal. Barry helped where he could to try and reduce the time to strip down the Zodiac engine. At least Stan knew what he was doing, having dismantled the engine the previous day.

An hour and a half later, Stan had removed enough parts to expose access to the sump to retrieve the rod.

"Go and fetch Rob," said Stan to Barry. "And keep it low profile."

"Understand," replied Barry saluting at Stan.

Moments later, Barry returned accompanied by Rob.

"What's going on?" asked Rob.

"Shhh," responded an animated Stan. "Keep your voice down. I forgot to fit the retaining washers and the rod has fallen through into the sump again."

"Numpty," replied Rob with a smile on his face.

Rob bent over the engine bay and fed his right hand into the minimal opening.

"Got it!" announced Rob handing the dripping rod back to Stan. "Just get it right this time."

Stan glared back at Rob. Stan didn't have a great sense of humour when his misdeeds were the banter subject matter.

"Let's get this back together again," added Stan. "I've wasted enough time already."

Stan and Barry again set to rebuilding the engine in readiness for the fitting of the recovered rod. Beating their previous time by ten minutes, a proud Stan and Barry were in a position to fit the rod.

Barry was taking no chances. He had recovered the retaining washers from the packaging, making sure that they were fitted this time.

Stan took the retaining washers and placed them at each end of the rod. Stan then lowered the rod assembly to the hole in the top of the distributor. Stan lowered the rod into the hole.

To Stan's utmost disgust, the top washer sprang off the rod, flying past Stan's left ear at a great rate of knots. Then the unthinkable happened. The rod once more disappeared down it's hole, like a rabbit dashing into its burrow. It was gone again. Stan fell to his knees in disbelief.

"How?" sobbed Stan looking to the heavens.

Barry could hardly believe his eyes, turning away to get away from this most frustrating of experiences.

Stan rummaged around the rod packaging to look for the fitting instructions. Barry joined him.

After a few minutes of studying the instructions, Stan slapped his forehead with his right palm.

"Idiot!" scowled a hapless Stan.

Within the fitting instructions, the text 'slide the retaining washer to the rod. When the washer meets the stop, turn the washer a quarter of a turn clockwise. There will be an audible 'click' to confirm that the washer is locked in place.'

"Why, oh why didn't I read the instructions?" bleated Stan.

Barry could hardly believe his eyes and ears. Barry held Stan in high regard. But the experiences of the last three days were starting to skew his opinion of Stan.

"Come on then," said Barry trying to lift spirits. "Let's see if we can beat our last time." Stan looked back at Barry with a vacant expression of dismay.

After a tea and fig roll break, Stan and Barry set about rebuilding the engine. With a delay caused by Stan banging the back of his wrist after slipping off an oily spanner, the pair took another two hours to rebuild the engine.

It was now six o'clock. Christine was now suspicious that all was not good. Having been promised a four o'clock departure, the time had come to go and pester Stan and find out what had been going on.

"Why are we still here?" asked an expectant Christine. "You said we would be ready for the off at four. It's now six o'clock and we still appear to be on the camp site."

"We ran into a few problems," responded Stan, beavering away with his head still under the bonnet of the Zodiac.

"Problems?" asked Christine. "What sort of problems?"

"Washer problems," snapped Stan.

Barry and Rob looked at each other and smiled.

"How much longer?" asked Christine.

"Maybe another hour," replied a hopeful Stan.

Christine looked at her watch again.

"How long will it take us to get to Christchurch from here?" asked Christine.

"Maybe an hour and a half," guessed Stan.

Christine again looked at her watch, trying to estimate an approximate arrival time in Christchurch.

"It's too late to set off tonight," announced Christine to the annoyance of the onlookers. "We won't get there until after ten, that's just too late. Barry, go and arrange another night here for us with the office. I'll go to the phone box and let the Christchurch site that we have been delayed again. They aren't going to believe me. I'm sure they think I'm mad already."

"Excellent idea," responded Stan. "I've been tampering with this engine all day. I'm totally exhausted, so I don't really want to drive this evening."

The plan was made. The holidaymakers braced themselves for another night in Devizes. Out of sight of Jenifer, Barry skulked off for another rendezvous with the attractive and interesting Natasha.

With Jenifer taking Penny for a walk, Fiona still rooted to the spot devouring mediocre television programmes, Christine unpacking the caravan again and Rob putting up the caravan awning again, Barry had a clear run for an uninterrupted flirt with Natasha.

As he entered the shop, Barry's heart missed a beat as he spotted a lonely looking Natasha standing behind the counter.

"Hi there," said an upbeat Barry. "How are you on this most beautiful of summer's evenings?"

"Fine," replied Natasha flickering her eyelids at Barry.

"How has your day been?" asked Barry, leaning on the counter, trying to look as cool as he could.

"Boring," responded Natasha. "These campers here are boring. They just want bread and milk and have no time for a chat. I think it's because I am foreign, and my skin is a little darker."

"That's a shame," responded Barry, edging ever closer to Natasha. "I've always got time for a chat with you."

"I know," replied Natasha. "You are different to the others. And you have very interesting football stories to tell me. I like my chats with you, they brighten up my day."

As Barry and Natasha became more fixated, they failed to notice that someone else had joined them in the shop. It was a furious looking Jenifer.

"I thought I might find you here!" exclaimed Jenifer. "You never change. You always have an eye for a pretty girl. You are a disgrace of a boyfriend."

Jenifer glared at Natasha and stormed out, slamming the door behind her. The wind from the door displaced a number of postcards to the floor, from their revolving rack.

"What's eating her?" asked a totally surprised Natasha.

"No idea," responded Barry. "She's a bit sensitive and gets a little jealous when she sees me talking to other girls. She will be okay."

"Hadn't you better go after her?" suggested a worried Natasha.

"Nope," replied Barry confidently. "I'll wait for her to cool off first."

Back at the caravan, a tearful Jenifer had already stormed through the living area and thrown herself on the bed in the second bedroom.

"What's wrong?" enquired a concerned Christine clutching a washing up cloth.

"It's him," sobbed Jenifer. "Up to his usual tricks. Flirting with the locals. I don't know why I'm still going out with him. He's always been the same."

"I'm sure there is nothing to it," replied a sympathetic Christine. "He's probably just arranging our extra night stay here tonight."

"Extra night?" exclaimed Jenifer. "Why are we staying here another night? Nobody told me."

"You were walking Penny when we decided," added Christine. "Your father is too tired to drive and it's getting late."

"This week is just turning into one big nightmare!" yelled Jenifer.

Back at the camp site shop, Barry was in mid-flow, telling Natasha about why Liverpool's boot room was a football institute. With Natasha compelled by Barry's story and accent, the tender moment was suddenly rudely interrupted.

With Barry now barely inches away from Natasha, the shop door opened with a muscular looking man filling the door frame.

As Natasha backed away promptly from Barry, the large gentleman walked up to the counter.

"What's all this then?" said the gentlemen in a thick eastern European accent.

"Nothing," said Natasha. "This is Barry. He is staying on the site with his family and girlfriend. He is a massive Liverpool fan."

The gentleman approached Barry with a fierce look on his face.

"Who's this then?" asked a very nervous Barry, intimidated by the size and shape of the threatening looking male.

"This is Sergey," responded Natasha. "He is my boyfriend. He is visiting me."

Trawling as many previous conversations as possible with Natasha in his head, Barry could not recall the mention of a boyfriend.

Barry gulped nervously and offered his hand forward for a handshake. Sergey took Barry's hand and shook it firmly, squeezing Barry's hand with a vice like grip. Barry cowered down in pain.

"Nice to meet you," said Sergey sternly.

"Nice to meet you too," responded a completely intimidated Barry. "Anyway, to business. We need to stay longer. It looks like the car won't be ready until the morning, so we need to stay here for another night. Can you arrange that, Natasha?"

"Sure, no problem," replied Natasha. "Just one more night? Are you sure your beat up old car will be ready in the morning?"

"It's not beat up and old," said Barry defensively.

Sergey reached out and grabbed Barry's wrist firmly.

"If my Natasha says it is old and beat up," growled Sergey aggressively, "then it is old and beat up."

"Absolutely," responded Barry trying to pull his wrist away from Sergey's tight grip.

Natasha wrote the invoice for the requested extra night and handed it to Barry. Without looking at it, Barry tucked it into the pocket of his jeans and pulled away from Sergey's now relaxed grip, nervously.

"Christine will be up to pay later," advised Barry as he rushed out of the shop door.

Barry ran all the way to the caravan like his life depended on it. The unexpected meeting with Sergey had certainly made Barry remember where his loyalties lay.

Leaping into the caravan out of breath, Barry searched around for his now beloved Jenifer.

Seeing Christine's foot poking out from the second bedroom, Barry assumed that Christine and Jenifer were having a heart to heart.

Barry crept into the doorway of the second bedroom.

"I'm so sorry," said Barry. "I absolutely promise it won't happen again. It's just you for me. I won't even go in the shop again whilst we are still here."

Jenifer sat up to consider her response.

Outside, Rob had joined Stan at the Zodiac to try and establish the planned timing for the attempted engine start. Fiona was still buried underneath the blanket watching the portable.

"When do you think you will try and start Betsy?" asked Rob.

"Five minutes," replied Stan confidently. "Just the last few checks."

"Excellent," responded a hopeful Rob.

Stan spent a few more minutes buried inside the engine compartment. Moments later, Stan walked around to the driver's door, opened it, and clambered inside his pride and joy.

"Ready?" asked Stan.

"Go for it," replied Rob with his fingers crossed.

Stan turned the key. Betsy immediately sprang into life with a mighty roar. She was fixed.

Hearing the purring tones of Betsy's engine, Barry, Jenifer and Christine rushed outside to the car.

"I'm just going to take her up the road," announced Stan through the driver's window. "For a test drive. Just to make sure everything is okay."

"Brilliant," replied Christine.

"Do you want to come with me?" asked Stan as he looked across to Barry.

"Absolutely," responded a relieved Barry, pleased to be as far away from Sergey as he could be.

Barry jumped into the Zodiac as Stan gently steered Betsy off the camp site and onto the main road.

"I need to give her some beans," said Stan. "I need to put a bit of pressure on the engine, to make sure the repairs are good."

"I see," said a clueless Barry.

Stan drove a mile or so down the main road. When he spotted a stretch of straight road in front of him, Stan opened up Betsy to test her capabilities.

All was good, Betsy was running like a dream, and her performance seemed better than ever. So, Stan persisted with his speed trial.

As Stan was revelling in the success of his repair skills, and the fact that his pride and joy was running better than ever, in his rear-view mirror, Stan noticed a set of headlamps coming ever nearer at speed. As the headlights closed in, Stan noticed a blue flashing light on the roof of the vehicle.

"Oh, no," declared Stan, taking his foot off the accelerator pedal.

"What's wrong?" asked a concerned Barry. "Is Betsy still playing up?"

"No," replied a downbeat Stan. "I think we are about to have another encounter with the law."

Stan pulled immediately into a convenient lay-by. The lit up police vehicle followed and pulled up behind the Zodiac.

Stan watched in his side mirror as a police officer got out of the vehicle and walked towards them. To Stan's despair it just had to be. It was Sergeant Corthine.

Sergeant Corthine poked his head into the open driver's side window.

"Good evening, Wing Commander," said Sergeant Corthine wittily. "Having trouble taking off?"

Stan bowed his head, making it as difficult as possible for Sergeant Corthine to recognise him.

"Hang on a moment," said Sergeant Corthine baffled by his discovery. "Not you again?"

"Let me explain," said Stan, trying to clear his name. "I've just got the car repaired after a lengthy breakdown. I was just test driving Betsy to make sure the repairs were in order. No more than that. I admit I was speeding, but I needed to make sure the engine would run under load."

"Betsy?" asked a bemused Sergeant Corthine. "What is a Betsy?"

"Sorry, it's my pet name for my car," responded an embarrassed Stan.

"Goodness," replied Sergeant Corthine. "Whatever next. Anyhow, as you have just admitted speeding, I have no choice but to issue you with a speeding ticket. I need you also to take your driving licence, insurance and MOT to the Salisbury police station in the next fourteen days. Understand?"

Stan was angry with himself. In twenty years of driving, this was his first ever offence. He'd not even been given a parking ticket in the past. Seeing this as a possible approach to get out of the ticket, Stan got to work. He explained to Sergeant Corthine about his clean licence, the toils and tribulations of the previous four days, the fact that he would be brutally henpecked when Christine finds out about the speeding ticket, along with the fact that he was on his holidays, Stan held his breath.

Sergeant Corthine walked back to his police car, to buy him some thinking time. After due consideration, Sergeant Corthine returned to give his verdict to Stan.

Stan suddenly had a light bulb moment. Sergeant Corthine was on his own. So who was holding the speed gun? Stan was pretty sure that Sergeant Corthine was a talented police officer, but not that talented.

"How fast exactly was I going?" asked a sneaky Stan. "What was my reading on the speed gun?"

Sergeant Corthine stood in silence. He had been rumbled. He knew that it would be his word against Stan's and Barry's if Stan opted to take the events to court. Two against one was not good odds by Sergeant Corthine's reckoning.

"If you promise that you will be out of Wiltshire tomorrow morning," said a perplexed Sergeant Corthine, "and considering your circumstances, I am prepared to be lenient this once. Plus, there is the fact that I wasn't pointing my speed gun at you, so I can't say with any accuracy what your speed was. So, if I catch you speeding, parking on a yellow line, crossing a solid white line in the centre of the road, or anything else illegal again, I promise, I will throw the book at you."

Thank you so much, sir," said a completely relieved Stan. "I promise I will be a model driver."

"On your way!" demanded Sergeant Corthine.

Stan waited until Sergeant Corthine's patrol car disappeared out of sight. He then cranked over the Zodiac and completed a three point turn, once he had confirmed it was safe to do so.

Stan drove Betsy back to the camp site at record low speed, not daring to break thirty miles an hour, much to the displeasure of Barry.

At the camp site, Stan pulled up alongside the caravan.

Inside, he and Barry shared their encounter with the law with Rob, Christine and Jenifer. Laughter filled the caravan. The humorous conversations focussed on Sergeant Corthine, and the possible conversations he would be having with his colleagues, given the frequency and variety of their meetings.

"Is somebody going to do something with Fiona?" asked Stan. "She's been out there for hours watching that confounded contraption."

"I'll sort this," replied Christine, getting up from her chair.

Christine walked over to the electrical socket and removed the plug. As she did, a loud scream of defiance rang out from under the blanket. It was to be the end of today's transmission.

Chapter Seven

The sun started to show itself over the distant range of hills, filling another Wednesday morning with its joyous light. The night had passed by without a hitch. Rob managed to remain in the awning and sleep through the traditional baritone snoring of Barry. Fiona had eventually given up with her lack of TV protest and had returned to the caravan.

Stan had arrived back at the caravan after paying a visit to the shower block. He was concerned. Whilst readying himself for another day, he was reliving the week's events. Trying to assume the effect of the tribulations on his family and guests, Stan needed to dip his toe in the complicated and dangerous waters of team morale.

Spotting the centrepiece of the bright yellow tea pot adorning the dining table, fully charged with a fresh Christine brew, Stan decided he was to call a team meeting.

It would take quite a while to assemble the team. Barry and Jenifer were still in the shower block. Fiona was still in her pit after her late night protesting. Rob was outside somewhere smoking, and Christine was fussing over the bed linen in the bedroom.

Stan impatiently tapped his foot on the floor, waiting to make his announcement. In order to hurry things up, Stan walked to the bedroom to muster Christine.

"Can you come through to the dining table, please, dear," asked Stan. "I want to have a quick chat with everyone."

"What are we chatting about?" asked a curious Christine. This was indeed strange behaviour for a usually introvert Stan.

"You'll see," responded Stan, keeping his cards close to his chest.

Stan turned around and rattled his knuckles on the second bedroom door, where Fiona was still fast asleep. Stan knocked the door for a second time.

"It's like waking the dead," muttered Stan.

"Leave this to me," said Christine, assertively opening the door to berate her lazy daughter.

Stan watched on as the tug of war battle developed with the bedsheets, Christine coming out victor as she dragged the bedsheet from Fiona's desperate grip.

Seeing a victory, Stan returned to the dining area and looked out of the window. To his delight, at the end of the field, Stan spotted Barry and Jenifer walking back towards the caravan holding hands. Double whammy, thought Stan. Firstly, they were on their way to the caravan, so the team brief could start soon. Secondly, it appeared that Barry and Jenifer had made up after Natasha-gate.

When Barry and Jenifer entered the caravan, and Rob reappeared from his smoke break, Stan made his announcement.

"People," announced Stan. "I want you all to sit down around the dining table please. I want to hold a team meeting with you all."

"Team meeting?" quizzed Rob. "So, we are back at work now? End of holiday?"

"Don't try and be clever," snapped Stan. "I just want to have a chat with everyone."

"What about?" asked Jenifer.

"The holiday," responded Stan dubiously.

"That's a joke," replied Jenifer angrily. "What holiday? We've seen a building site, a car dealership, a petrol station forecourt, and a field in Wiltshire. If that's a holiday, then I'm a monkey's aunty."

The group looked across at Jenifer in unison, trying to fathom out the meaning of a monkey's aunty.

"We all know what's happened so far," continued Stan. "So, I just want your opinions on where we go from here."

"Benidorm!" said Barry, trying to lighten the mood.

Jenifer administered a sharp slap to Barry's arm, in an attempt to quash Barry's attempt at humour.

"Very good," responded Stan in a sarcastic tone. "In reality, all I want to know is this. Do you want to carry on and head for Christchurch? Or do you want to call it a day and head back home? We have been blighted with so much bad luck, it's almost unreal. Just one thing after another. And yes, I hold my hand up. My mechanical repair skills could have been better over the past couple of days."

"I say carry on to Christchurch," stated Barry. He wanted to be off site as soon as humanly possible. Just in case Sergey came looking for another confrontation. "How far is it from here?"

"It's just over fifty miles," responded Stan. "By my reckoning, that will take us just over two hours with a comfort stop."

"By my reckoning," added Barry, "we've travelled eighty miles in four and a bit days. So, I'm confident we could do fifty miles in three days."

Jenifer smacked Barry's arm again, this time with slightly more effort than the previous attempt. This made Barry reach up and rub his arm.

"Will you take this seriously," snarled Jenifer. "Dad's trying to do something here. He's giving us all the opportunity to have our say. At least have the courtesy and respect to give him a chance."

Barry looked down at his trainers in embarrassment.

"Christine," continued Stan. "Any thoughts?"

"You know me, Stan," responded an upbeat Christine. "Always look on the bright side. I say carry on. Surely we've had enough bad luck. I'm confident that we will be in Christchurch within three hours from now. Let's go for it."

“Fantastic,” replied Stan.

“Rob,” said Stan looking directly at Rob. “What are your thoughts?”

“I’m with Christine,” responded Rob. “Let’s crack on. We’ve managed to battle through everything that the holiday gods have thrown at us. So even if things go wrong again, I’m sure we will get through it.”

“Excellent,” responded Stan. “That’s three of us who want to continue, with my vote included.”

“Four if you count me,” added Barry. “Sorry about the Benidorm comment. I actually want to carry on our mystical adventure. But if you do decide to break down again, can you do it next to a decent Wimpy.”

Jenifer was so unimpressed with Barry’s attempt at humour, she couldn’t be bothered to give out any physical punishment.

“Fiona,” continued Stan. “What do you want to do?”

“Go home and watch a TV with a decent signal,” replied an unimpressed Fiona. “Can’t you lot take a hint? Someone is telling us that this holiday shouldn’t have happened. Don’t you lot get it?”

“Okay,” said Stan. “That’s four to one. “Jenifer, what about you?”

Jenifer still wanted a little more time to consider her answer. There was the fact that her boyfriend had been flirting with the natives. The fact that the family dog had embarrassed her so much, she could never get on another bus in Wiltshire. Plus, being in close confined contact with her family was starting to test her nerves. However, Jenifer loved the Dorset coastline and beaches, so her feelings were torn.

"I say carry on," replied Jenifer eventually, much to the delight of her father. "We've got this far, let's go for it."

Stan was delighted. He was desperate to carry on, but he wanted it to be a joint decision, which he had managed to achieve. He was very pleased with himself, especially after his woeful couple of days on the spanners.

"What about me then?" asked a subdued Fiona. "I just want to go back to Worcester. I don't feel part of this, I just want to go home."

"Don't be ridiculous," butted in Christine, seeing her matchmaking opportunity looking like it was under threat. "How do you think you will get home? And you certainly aren't staying at home on your own, young lady. You can't be trusted. You'll be having all night parties with your weird friends."

"I'll go to Aunty Margaret's," responded Fiona. "She will take care of me until you get back. And I can go home on the train."

"They do have a railway station in Salisbury," said Barry confidently. "It's not far from the bus station."

This created a dilemma for Stan. There seemed to be a valid route home for Fiona. Plus, she was a disruptive influence. She wasn't joining in many of the family meals, chats and tea breaks. In addition, Aunty

Margaret was a good guardian choice. Margaret was a no nonsense sister who could handle his unpredictable daughter. However, at the end of the day, this was a family holiday, and Fiona was part of the family.

"I'll tell you what," said Stan after a moment's deliberation. "Jenifer, you go to the shop and see if they have any train timetables. Christine, you go to the phone box and call Margaret. See if she's willing to look after Fiona for a few days. I'm not prepared to make a decision until I know that this is a completely feasible option."

Barry moped his brow in relief, thankful that Stan had assigned Jenifer to the shop detail. The last thing that Barry wanted was another muscular encounter.

Listening in, Fiona smiled for the third time all week. The possibility of being released from this nightmare was deeply joyous.

"I'll start packing up the awning with Rob whilst you pair go out there and investigate," said a jolly Stan. "Barry, you start packing Betsy's boot."

Christine turned her head and scowled at Stan. The mention of 'that' name always provoked some kind of reaction.

As Jenifer and Christine departed on their quests, the camp looked a busy and bustling hive of activity. Bodies were running in all directions, hastily trying to get themselves ready for the off. After Stan's meeting, a spring to everyone's step seemed to be present. Even

Fiona had cheered up, with the chance of early release for good behaviour looking a distinct possibility.

Ten minutes later, Jenifer returned to the caravan and sought out Stan.

"They don't have any train timetables," said Jenifer. "But Natasha is confident that Fiona should be able to get a train today. Natasha thinks it leaves around half past ten this morning."

Barry's ears pricked up with the mention of Natasha. But it was a doubled edged feeling.

"So that is a possibility," replied Stan looking at his watch. "That gives us well over an hour to get to Salisbury railway station. We should be able to make that easily."

Ten minutes later Christine returned.

"Margaret will have Fiona," declared a relieved Christine. "I said I would ring her back when we have decided what to do. Do we have an arrival time for the train in Worcester yet? Margaret said that they can pick Fiona up from the station. So, she needs to know her arrival time."

"We'll have to do that at the station," continued Stan. "Once we know the times."

Fiona was delighted, she was on the cusp of liberty. Christine however was distraught. Her plan to get Rob and Fiona reunited looked to be floundering.

With everyone except Fiona helping out, the pitch was clear and the car was packed in no time. Stan had an hour and ten minutes to drive the twenty-four miles to Salisbury.

After Christine had settled the invoice for the extra night's stay, Stan sparked Betsy into life. They were back on the road at last. The mood in the car was upbeat.

Stan drove to the A360. He had completed some sneaky navigation research whilst Christine was in the camp site shop. Stan didn't want to leave anything to chance. Christine had previous form with getting them lost.

All went well during the drive to Salisbury. There was a bonus along the way, as the holiday troop were treated to the wondrous sight of Stonehenge as they passed it by, Christine trying to take a snap of the mystical stones with her camera on the move.

"Do we have time to stop and take some photos?" asked Jenifer from the back seat.

"No," replied Stan firmly. "We are on plan, and I don't want to be late for the train. Maybe we can come back this way on the way home. We can stop then."

Jenifer didn't respond, just slumped back in her seat, disappointed.

The Zodiac was running like a dream. Stan maintained a hawk eye watch on all the dials in front of him. Plus, he constantly monitored the power output every time he applied the accelerator.

With traffic on their side, Stan arrived at Salisbury train station at almost exactly ten o'clock. He pulled up in the small, empty car park, just to the left of the station entrance.

"I'll go in with Fiona," announced Stan. "You lot stay in here. I won't be long."

"Hurry up then," replied an impatient Christine.

As Stan was rummaging around in the caravan, looking for Fiona's bag, a uniformed traffic warden approached the caravan.

"Morning," said the traffic warden poking his head inside the caravan door. "I'm sorry, sir. You can't camp there, it's for taxi's only. And to the best of my knowledge, you don't look like a taxi."

Stan walked to the caravan doorway and looked down at the white paint on the parking space. Unfortunately, '*TAXI'S ONLY*' was clearly emblazoned on the tarmac.

"I'll only be five minutes," replied Stan looking for sympathy. "I just have to put my daughter on her train, and I will be back. As you can see, I'm towing quite a big caravan. I'm not sure where else I could park up. And by the way, I'm not intending to camp here."

The traffic warden looked the caravan up and down. Sympathising with Stan's predicament, and empathising with Stan's response, the traffic warden used his common sense.

"Just be very quick," responded the traffic warden. "I'll wait here for you."

"Thank you so much for being so understanding," replied Stan. "I'll be as quick as I can."

Stan returned inside the caravan and picked up Fiona's holdall. It was quite heavy.

"Blimey," said Stan to himself. "I wonder what she has got in here."

Stan jumped out of the caravan, holding Fiona's bag with both arms.

"I'm going to have to physically help my daughter on the train if you don't mind," said Stan to the traffic warden. "She will struggle with the weight of this bag."

The traffic warden stepped forward and took the bag from Stan.

"Crikey," declared the traffic warden. "What has she got in there? One of the rocks from Stonehenge?"

Stan smiled.

"Is it okay for me to escort my daughter to the train?" pleaded Stan.

"Just this once," responded the helpful traffic warden.

After she said her farewell's, Fiona rushed inside the station with Stan to look for the ticket office.

The train Fiona needed to catch departed in ten minutes. It had two changes and many stops. It would arrive in Worcester at ten to three in the afternoon.

Once they had bought the ticket, Stan stood next to Fiona and waited for the train.

"Are you sure you want to go home?" asked Stan.

"Yep, positive," responded Fiona. "This trip is just not my thing."

"I guessed that," replied a disappointed Stan. "Just behave yourself when you get to Aunty Margaret's."

"I'll do you proud," responded Fiona.

The pair looked to their right. They could make out the silhouette of the approaching train.

As the train came to a halt, Stan glanced inside the train. It looked very busy.

Stan braced himself and picked up Fiona's holdall. He followed Fiona into the train to find her somewhere to sit. They walked to their left. Unfortunately, the carriage was crammed with no seats available.

"Let's try the next carriage," suggested Stan struggling with Fiona's holdall.

Stan walked down the next carriage. That was equally as busy. However, there was a lady sat next to the gangway, but she had her bag placed on the seat next to the window.

"Excuse me," said Stan politely. "Can my daughter sit there please?"

The lady did not react and maintained her forward stare.

Stan coughed loudly.

"Excuse me," repeated Stan with a louder voice. "Is that seat taken?"

"I am saving it for my friend," replied the lady. "She's getting on this train at Andover."

"You can't do that," remonstrated Stan. "Just let my daughter sit down, please."

The lady did not respond.

"Wait here, I'll sort this," said Stan to Fiona.

A few moments later, Stan returned with a railway guard.

"What's all this then?" asked the guard.

"This lady won't let my daughter take this spare seat," argued Stan.

The guard looked directly at the lady.

"Is this seat taken madam?" asked the guard.

"I'm saving the seat for my friend," responded the irritated passenger. "She will be getting on this train at Andover."

"Sorry, madam," added the guard. "You can't reserve seats like that. Let this passenger sit down please."

"Well, I'm not sitting by the window," insisted the lady.

Stan courteously helped the lady out of her seat and placed the bag that was on the window seat in the overhead storage space. Fiona then struggled across to the window seat and sat down. The lady passenger then took her seat.

"Thank you," said Stan to the lady. "And thank you for your help," he said to the railway guard. "Have a great journey, Fiona," he added as he turned to make his way off the train.

However, to Stan's total horror, as he looked out of the window, he noticed that the train had begun to pull out of the station. Frantically pushing through the standing passengers, Stan battled his way to the train door, only to find it firmly closed, as the train picked up speed.

"You are kidding me," said Stan out loud.

Stan battled his way back through the standing passengers. He could see the guard starting to check tickets at the front of the carriage.

At last, Stan finally reached the guard.

"Can you stop the train please," demanded Stan.

"No can do," replied the guard promptly. "It's a two hundred and fifty pound fine if you pull the stop chord with no good reason. And I suspect your reason is not good."

"I have to get off this train," demanded Stan. "How long until the next stop?"

"Twelve minutes," responded the knowledgeable guard. "First stop for this train is Grateley."

"That will have to do," said Stan in a panic.

Stan walked back through the standing passengers to where Fiona was seated. As Stan arrived, Fiona looking up very smug and smiling broadly.

"I thought you were going to Christchurch," japed Fiona.

"It's unbelievable," replied a frustrated Stan. "You do someone a favour, and this happens."

Fiona burst out into raucous laughter.

"Don't you start," said Stan. "What do I tell your mother? She will have a field day with this one."

Stan looked and smiled at the lady sitting next to Fiona who smiled back ironically.

"What do you think you are looking at?" asked the lady aggressively.

"I'm sorry," responded Stan. "I didn't mean to disturb you. I was just trying to be courteous and polite."

"Don't even think about it," stated the lady.

"Think about what?" asked Stan.

"About sitting here, next to your daughter," responded the lady with a dead pan look on her face.

"I don't want to sit down," replied Stan. "I need to get off at the next station. I shouldn't really be on this train."

"Good," responded the lady. "Because I'm not budging an inch."

"I don't want you to," replied Stan, trying to get himself out of this awkward exchange.

Stan could sense that the train was starting to slow down. He leaned across to bid his farewell to Fiona and made his way through the crowd to the doors. He didn't want to prolong this dire situation any further.

As the train came to a halt, Stan leapt out of the train and onto the platform, eagerly looking for passage to the other side of the tracks. Fortunately, a few yards behind him, Stan spotted a footbridge spanning across the tracks.

Scurrying over the bridge, Stan looked for a ticket office, as he needed to buy a ticket back to Salisbury. However, there didn't appear to be any facilities at this station in the middle of nowhere.

Stan walked up to a lone passenger waiting on the platform.

"Excuse me," said Stan calmly. "Do you know when the next train to Salisbury will be arriving?"

"In fifteen minutes," replied the stranger. "Apparently, it's been delayed."

"Many thanks," replied Stan. "Also, do you know where the ticket office is?"

"You will have to buy one on the train," responded the stranger. "There isn't a ticket office here. Apparently, we aren't important enough at Grateley to merit a ticket office."

"Thank you," replied Stan. "I'm sure this station is worthy of a shiny new ticket office."

"You are welcome," responded the stranger.

Stan paced up and down nervously on the platform waiting for the train. He kept looking at the clock to count down the fifteen minutes, but the clock hands didn't appear to be moving.

Stan's thoughts were suddenly overcome with the vision of a traffic warden. The one that he left waiting by the car in Salisbury station. Surely, he would have gone by now?

The fifteen minutes turned into nineteen minutes, then Stan spotted the welcome sight of a diesel engine approaching in the distance.

A few minutes later, the train pulled up at the platform. One of the doors close to Stan flew open, as a disembarking passenger leapt on the platform. A relieved Stan climbed aboard. This train was far less busy than Fiona's train, and there was plenty of available seats to occupy.

As the train pulled out of the station, the carriage door in front of Stan parted. A tall ticket collector walked through the door into Stan's carriage.

"Tickets please," called out the inspector.

As the inspector approached Stan, Stan patted his pockets to find his wallet. Stan gulped as he realised his wallet was in the glove compartment of the Zodiac. Stan was cashless!

"Ticket please," said the inspector, offering his ticket clipper to Stan.

"I don't have one," said Stan sheepishly.

"Where are you going?" asked the inspector.

"Salisbury," responded Stan confidently.

"That will be thirty pence please," demanded the inspector.

Stan patted down all of his pockets again, desperately trying to find some money.

"This is the thing," uttered Stan with his head bowed. "I was putting my daughter on the train to Worcester just now, and I got stuck on the train by mistake. I wasn't planning on getting stuck on the train, so I haven't got any money on me right now. My wallet is in the car, which is parked up at Salisbury station. I can rush and get the money when we get to Salisbury and pay you the thirty pence. Is that okay?"

The ticket inspector looked back at Stan in disbelief. Was this tall story actually true? Or was this chancer trying to get a free ride to Salisbury on the train? The ticket inspector decided to see if Stan was telling the truth.

"You will have a minute to get the money when we get to Salisbury Station," demanded the inspector. "Not a second more. If you are spinning me a tale then I will throw the book at you."

"Oh, thank you," said a relieved Stan.

"Take off your jumper," ordered the ticket inspector.

"What?" replied Stan. "Why?"

"So that you don't run off without paying," responded the ticket inspector. "I'll keep your jumper until you return with the money. If you don't return, I'm sure I'll get more than thirty pence for this jumper."

Stan reluctantly removed his favourite sweater.

Eight minutes later the train started to slow down. A few minutes thereafter, the train came to a halt in Salisbury Station.

"I'll be back within a minute," said Stan frantically.

Stan waited for the train door to open then ran towards the exit. He headed right to his parked car and caravan, where he could see that the traffic warden was stood chatting with Barry.

"Where on earth have you been?" demanded the traffic warden. "You've been gone nearly an hour. What did you do? Get lost on the way to the platform?"

“I don’t have time to explain,” panted Stan. “Let me go back and pay for my train ticket and I will come back and explain everything. Christine, give me thirty pence, quickly.”

“Thirty pence?” replied a confused Christine. “What do you need thirty pence for?”

“I don’t have time to explain,” responded a desperate Stan. “The ticket inspector is waiting for me. He’s holding my favourite sweater hostage.”

“Hostage?” replied an astonished Christine. “What has British Rail come to? Holding clothes as a hostage.”

“Just don’t worry about that,” yelled an even more distressed Stan. “Has anybody got thirty pence they can give me?”

Everyone checked their pockets, wallets, and purses, even the traffic warden.

After a thorough search the traffic warden came up with the goods.

“There you go,” said the helpful traffic warden. “Twenty pence and two five pence pieces. That’s thirty pence.”

“Thank you,” shouted Stan as he raced back into the station.

As Stan reached the platform his worst fears became a reality. The train he had dashed back to intercept was pulling out of the station, as a plume of smoke belched out of the roof mounted exhaust of the mighty diesel.

Stan bent over in despair and placed his hands on his knees. Gone forever. His favourite sweater. Stan had enjoyed most of his favourite walks in his best woolly mate. But that was that.

Feeling destitute, Stan trudged wearily out of the station to explain his situation to the waiting traffic warden.

"Right then," said the traffic warden calmly. "What has been going on? Do you care to explain please?"

Stan told his story to the attentive traffic warden. How the obstructive lady had delayed Stan's exit from the train. How he had not got his wallet on his person. How the ticket inspector had taken his favourite sweater as a hostage. But was the traffic warden going to buy Stan's sob story?

"It's just not your lucky day, is it," announced the traffic warden, as he started to fill out a parking violation ticket with Stan's name on it.

"Please show me some mercy," begged Stan. "You know I didn't go to Grateley intentionally. It was just a build-up of unfortunate events. If that miserable lady would have given up her seat, instead of fighting like she did, I wouldn't have got trapped."

"I'll make you a nice cup of tea as compensation," suggested a hopeful Christine.

"Stay out of this, Christine," snapped Stan. "Can I appeal to your kind nature, and request that you tear up that parking ticket."

"So, you want me to tear up this official document?" asked the traffic warden. "You want me to put my job at risk just to help you out of a situation of your own making?"

"I'm just asking for you to show me some compassion," pleaded Stan.

"Then there is the attempted bribery," added the traffic warden.

"Bribery?" asked a confused Stan. "I haven't tried to bribe you."

"You asked to make me rip up this ticket," continued the traffic warden, "in return for a measly cup of caravan tea."

"My tea isn't measly," said an irate Christine.

"Christine, keep out of this," demanded Stan. "You've got me on a bribery charge as well now by the looks of it."

"I was only suggesting," added Christine.

"Then stop suggesting," snapped Stan.

The traffic warden spent another few minutes completing the parking ticket paperwork. Once concluded, he ripped the parking ticket from his pad and handed it over to Stan.

"Thanks for nothing," said Stan, whose day was going from bad to worse.

"Can you move your vehicle immediately from the taxi rank," insisted the traffic warden. "If you are still here in five minutes, I'll give you another ticket."

Not wanting to leak any more money, Stan commanded his party to get into the Zodiac for the off.

Stan jumped into Betsy and turned the ignition key. Betsy just coughed and spluttered but didn't fire up into life. Stan's heart dropped two inches in his chest. Not now! Don't break down here in front of this heartless traffic warden. Stan tried again. Betsy was not playing ball as she continued to cough and splutter.

For a third time Stan turned the ignition key. To Stan's absolute delight, the Zodiac roared into life, belching a plume of grey smoke behind her.

"We'll be off now," said Stan to the traffic warden. "Thanks for nothing."

The traffic warden, angered by Stan's attitude, mimicked writing out another parking ticket at Stan as the black Zodiac eventually freed up the Salisbury railway station taxi rank.

"What an obnoxious man," commented Christine as they pulled out of the railway station.

"That's why he's a traffic warden," responded Barry. "The skin as thick as a rhinoceros and the mental strength of a chess master. Deadly combo."

"What do you know about it?" asked Jenifer. "Do you actually know any traffic wardens? He was only doing his job. He expected Dad to be on the platform for five minutes, not an hour. None of this would have happened if princess Fiona hadn't insisted on going back to Worcester."

"You leave Fiona out of this," argued Christine.

Jenifer threw herself back in the back seat in frustration. It seemed that Fiona could do no wrong in the eyes of her mother.

"Right, Christine," said Stan assertively. "I need you to get us on the A338 towards Downton. Do you think you can manage that without resorting to bribery?"

"Enough," snapped Christine, in full knowledge of Stan's attempted cheap shot. "I was only trying to help. I thought he might have sat down in the caravan with us, enjoyed a nice cup of tea with a fig roll, then come to his senses."

"Not possible," interrupted a confident Barry. "We are out of fig rolls. I had the last one yesterday with my bedtime cuppa."

That was it. Stan hit rock bottom. A parking ticket, the loss of his all-time favourite jumper, losing one of the holidaymakers, and now this. Having to face his next brew without a fig roll to dip.

Chapter Eight

Still mourning the loss of his precious sweater, Stan drove in silence as he guided Betsy down the A338 towards Downton. It was now noon, and they were still far from the caravan site entrance in Christchurch.

"I think today is the day," stated Christine, trying to cheer up her husband, as she had noted his sourpuss mood.

"We'll see," responded a dejected Stan. "To be honest, I can't create an arrival picture in my head. I just can't see Betsy driving through the welcoming gates of Home Farm."

Not wanting to jeopardise progress getting Stan out of his gloomy mood, Christine allowed Stan a cheeky mention of Betsy without punishment. This totally surprised Stan as he was in a state of readiness to receive an onslaught.

All was good with Betsy. She had plenty of fuel, oil pressure was normal, engine temperature was normal, and the remaining gauge displayed needles resting in the normal position.

Approximately half a mile outside a small village called Breamore, the holiday's party was about to change yet again. Wondering why the cars in front of him were moving to their right, Stan's reactions were not on top form. The drivers were swerving around a very large pothole in the road. Stan managed to pull Betsy out of the pothole path. However, the twin nearside tyres of the caravan dropped into the abyss, causing an almighty crashing sound as they did so.

After this unexpected trauma to the caravan, Stan tried to get his thoughts together quickly. Aware that he had previously vexed the local constabulary by blocking off a tank crossing, Stan desperately searched the road ahead for a suitable layby or turning, so he could get off the main road and inspect the damage.

"There may be somewhere to stop in this village," said Jenifer from the back seat.

Stan drove gingerly into the village. The caravan just didn't feel right. The handling was vague, and the caravan seemed to be pulling against the towing hook.

Due to Stan's slow and cautious progress, a small tailback of around ten cars had formed behind them. As Stan was in the heart of the village, he spotted a right turn in the road ahead, signposted to Woodgreen. Stan activated his right hand indicator and prepared to turn right.

As the carriageway in front of him cleared, Stan manoeuvred into the turning as the unthinkable happened. Betsy was clear of the main road, but as the caravan progressed over the junction's white painted lines on the road, the front end of the caravan collapsed to the tarmac with a crash.

Stan tried to pull Betsy forward, but the caravan sub-frame had dug itself into the road surface and refused to budge an inch. Stan turned off the engine and started to bash his head gently on the top of the steering wheel.

“What was that bang?” asked a worried Christine. “Go and have a look, quickly.”

Stan didn’t want to get out of the car as he feared the worse. Not only was it yet another possible setback to their journey, but assessing the crashing sounds made by the caravan as it took a dive to the floor, it meant that in all probability that Stan would be opening his wallet again.

Stan jumped out of his unreliable Zodiac and flounced to the back of the car. Looking down at the front end of the caravan, their plight became instantly understandable. The caravan sub-frame had snapped right across one of the iron beams, and it looked terminal.

With two thirds of the caravan stuck on the A338, traffic on this busy road had quickly collected in a growing queue. Drivers at the front of the queue had got out of their vehicles to see what was causing the delays, and to see if they could assist.

Stan stood in silence, scratching his head as he stared down at the buckled steel in front of him. Why him? What had he done so wrong to deserve this continued run of absolutely foul luck?

One of the queuing drivers sidled up to Stan.

"Doesn't look good," said the stranger. "You need to move this before the school run, mate. This road gets so busy around three o'clock.

Stan looked at his watch; it was quarter to one.

"We should be able to get this moved inside two hours," replied Stan. "Maybe we can get a few of these people in the queueing cars to help lift the caravan up? Haven't the schools broken up for the summer down here?"

"You'll be lucky," responded the stranger. "I bet that weighs over a ton. Unless you have made the Incredible Hulk angry because you've trapped his in a traffic jam, then it's highly unlikely. The schools break up this Friday, by the way."

"What am I going to do then?" said a desperate Stan.

A second driver had joined the debate.

"There is a service station in Fordingbridge, just down the road," suggested the gentleman. "They might be able to help. I'll run to the phone box and see if I can raise anybody."

"How far down the road?" requested Stan.

"The garage or the phone box?" asked the gentleman.

"The garage," replied Stan firmly.

"Keep your hair on," responded the gentleman. "I'm just trying to help. No need to get all lairy."

"I'm sorry," replied Stan. "I'm just a bit stressed right now."

"That's okay," responded the gentleman. "The phone box is just around the corner, and the garage is just over a mile away."

"That's great," said Stan.

With the queue of traffic building every minute, Stan decided to try and unhitch Betsy, so at least he could move the car out of harm's way. However, even with the assistance of six bystanders, the weight being applied to the tow hook made the unhitching process humanly impossible.

More and more drivers were getting out of their cars and joining the small crowd that was now gathered. All desperate to be on their way, all wanting an accurate summary of what was going on, and eager to offer advice.

With fifteen minutes now elapsed since the incident, the inevitable happened. Thinking that there had been another accident at the junction, a local resident had dialled 999 and alerted the police, fire service, and the ambulance people.

The police arrived first. Two police officers jumped briskly out of a patrol car, leaving the flashing beacon on in an attempt to warn motorists of the incident. As the police officers reached Stan, the fragrance of inevitability filled the air. It just had to be.

"Good afternoon, Stan," said Sergeant Corthine sarcastically. "So, we meet again. Didn't I politely request you to leave Wiltshire yesterday?"

"I've been trying my hardest to obey your instructions," replied a hapless Stan. "But, as you can see, I've run in to a bit of bother."

Sergeant Corthine and his colleague leant over the front of the caravan to assess the situation.

As they were taking a look at the pile of twisted metal, the Fire Brigade arrived on scene. A fireman, with his bright yellow helmet perched on his head, wandered over to join the debate.

"Any fires or spillages?" asked the fireman.

"No," responded Sergeant Corthine. "I think you can stand down. We've got it from here."

"I think you are going to need some help though," added the fireman. "We could barely get here. The backlog of traffic goes back miles. You might want to get some officers on traffic control duties."

"Let me be the judge of that," replied Sergeant Corthine forcefully.

"That's a good idea," said Sergeant Corthine's colleague. "I'll get on the radio and muster some assistance."

The supporting police officer then ran to his patrol car, seeking assistance.

"We've tried unhitching the car from the caravan," said Stan, "but it's too heavy to lift off without some sort of equipment."

"Have you got a half decent jack in your boot?" asked Sergeant Corthine as he looked across to Stan.

"I do," responded Stan, "but it's buried at the bottom of the boot."

Stan walked over to Betsy, unlocked the boot, and showed Sergeant Corthine the sight of a Zodiac boot packed to the gunnels.

"We've got jacks on the appliance," suggested the fireman. "What have you got in mind?"

"I think, that if we jack up the caravan sub-frame," continued Sergeant Corthine. "Then we could take the weight off the tow hook and unhitch the car. That will take some of the pressure off this junction."

The fireman disappeared to fetch his equipment from the fire engine. As he did so, an ambulance arrived on scene. An ambulance lady waltzed up to Sergeant Corthine.

"Any casualties?" asked the ambulance lady, clutching a first aid bag.

"No, thank goodness," replied Sergeant Corthine. "Just an unfortunate breakdown. I think you can carry on your way. Nothing to concern yourself with here."

"Right you are," responded the ambulance lady, returning briskly to her ambulance. "Good luck!"

"I think we are going to need it," said a frustrated Stan.

The fireman and two colleagues retuned from the fire appliance, all carrying heavy duty jacking equipment. They lay the jacks on the floor next to the crumpled sub-frame to see where they could lift up the front of the caravan. However, as the metal had twisted, there appeared to no suitable places in which to position the jacks.

"What now?" asked Stan.

As they were just about to give up, behind them, a farmer appeared in his dirty, yellow digger. The farmer pulled up to the side of Betsy and turned off his engine.

"Can I be of any assistance?" asked the farmer.

Sergeant Corthine and the fireman looked at the digger and back to the damaged caravan.

"Are you thinking what I'm thinking?" announced the second fireman. "If we fit a sling to the teeth on the bucket of that digger, we might be able to lift up the front end of the caravan."

"Great idea," interrupted Sergeant Corthine. "Do you carry slings on your fire engine?"

"Oh yes," responded a smiling lead fireman.

Fifteen minutes later, the farmer had repositioned his digger, close to the front of the caravan. The fireman had fed a sling around the subframe of the caravan. With the sling now fitted to the bucket of the digger, Officer Corthine gave the order for the farmer to gently raise the bucket.

The farmer cautiously lifted the bucket. As he did so, the twisted sub-frame gradually began to free itself from the tarmac. As the gap between the caravan and the road surface grew, the firemen readied themselves to place support struts under the sub-frame.

As the tow hook on the car started to lift, Sergeant Corthine gave the order for the farmer to stop lifting.

"Try unhitching the caravan now," demanded Sergeant Corthine.

Two firemen stepped forward and attempted to unhitch the car.

"Just another inch and I think we're there," said the fireman.

Sergeant Corthine signalled to the farmer, indicating a fraction higher.

"Stop!" yelled the lead fireman.

The two firemen tried for a second time to unhitch Betsy. At last! Success! Betsy was free!

Stan jumped into the black Zodiac and pulled away from the caravan, parking up out of the way on the side of the road.

With the caravan still being held mainly by the sling and digger, the fireman added a couple more struts under the caravan to make it safe.

As the crowd of gathered onlookers clapped at the completion of the first phase of the recovery, the gentlemen who had tried to call the garage came up to Sergeant Corthine, out of breath.

Bernard will be here in half an hour with a recovery truck," panted the gentlemen.

"Excellent," responded a smiling Sergeant Corthine. "We might have this cleared up in no time. I think you guys can go now."

Sergeant Corthine hinted that it was time for the firemen to clear the scene and go and put out some fires somewhere else.

"We're going nowhere until we get our equipment back," replied the assertive lead fireman.

Not wanting to start an inter-emergency services battle, Sergeant Corthine didn't offer a response. Instead, he returned to his patrol car to get an update from the officers on traffic duty.

"Isn't this exciting," said Christine. "All these people here for us."

"Because of us," snapped Stan. "There is a huge difference."

"Don't be so petty, Stanley," replied Christine. "I bet these firemen are glad to be on a job that doesn't cover them in smoke."

Stan rolled his eyes and returned to the caravan, to await the arrival of the recovery truck.

Nearly forty-five minutes later, the recovery truck arrived with two amber beacons rotating on the cab roof. The driver parked up alongside the caravan and leapt out of his cab.

The recovery truck driver marched up to Sergeant Corthine and shook his hand firmly.

"Afternoon, Bernard," said a relieved Sergeant Corthine.

"Afternoon, Mark," replied Bernard. "Looks like a bit of a mess here."

"Tell me about it," responded a totally aggravated Sergeant Corthine. "I've had these pests in my hair for days now. They are a complete disaster, just one thing after another."

"Bloody tourists," replied Bernard.

Bernard walked over to the caravan to inspect the damage and work out his recovery strategy. The farmer joined him.

"Looks rotten to me," said Bernard as he tapped on the metal subframe.

"Rotten as a pear," added the farmer in a broad Wiltshire accent. "Shouldn't even be on the road."

"These people," continued Bernard. "They think a coat of red oxide and a coat of anti-rust black paint will do the job. They don't realise that these things can rot from the inside out.

"I had no idea that it was in this state," said Stan, joining in the debate.

"See what I mean," laughed Bernard.

"I'll have you know," continued Stan in self-defence, "my brother gave this caravan a thorough once over only two weeks ago. He gave it a clean bill of health."

"Does he wear spectacles?" asked the farmer.

"No," responded Stan firmly.

"Well, he clearly should," replied the farmer in a fit of laughter.

"This mickey taking is getting us nowhere," interrupted Sergeant Corthine. "We need to get this caravan out of here, and pronto. Our traffic queues have now made the news on the local radio station. How are you going to move this hunk of junk, Bernard? And how long will it take you?"

Bernard took a pipe out of his overall pocket, pressed down the tobacco in his pipe with his thumb, lit the pipe, and started puffing on it, sending balls of smoke into the afternoon air.

"Tricky one," announced Bernard. "I reckon, if we move this beauty off those supports, she will just crumble again. I reckon we need the heavy duty recovery truck, the one with the crane, and lift the van onto the truck."

Bernard walked to his recovery truck and fetched a hammer from his toolkit. He then walked around the caravan, hitting each of the caravan's lifting shackles firmly one by one.

"They seem to be okay," declared Bernard after his lifting shackle assessment. "I think we can do this."

"Where is your heavy duty recovery truck?" asked a hopeful Sergeant Corthine.

"Let me think," replied Bernard as he re-lit his pipe. "I reckon she's in Southampton."

"Southampton!" shrieked a shocked Sergeant Corthine. "How long until you can get the truck here?"

"I need to call them," replied Bernard. "I'll go back to the garage and give them a call. If the truck is available, it shouldn't take more than an hour to get here, depending on traffic."

Sergeant Corthine looked down at his wristwatch, then averted his gaze to the giant line of queueing, stationary traffic.

"See what you can do to get them here sooner," responded a worried Sergeant Corthine. "These roads are now at bursting point."

Bernard leapt in his truck and screamed away, back to his garage to rally the cavalry.

Christine, Barry, Jenifer and Rob were sitting in Betsy. Stan had instructed them to stay out of the way in the car, worried that Barry's attempted humour might enflame an already tense scene.

"I wonder if I should go in the caravan and make all these nice people a nice pot of tea?" suggested Christine.

"Don't be daft," replied Jenifer from the back seat. "We're out of milk."

"Well go and take a walk into the village," indicated Christine. "See if there is a shop selling milk."

"No chance," responded a resolute Jenifer. "I'm not moving from here unless there is an earthquake. And what we've had to put up with this week, I wouldn't be surprised if we witness one!"

"Go on," continued Christine, "you can take Penny for her walkies."

"Hang on, where is Penny?" enquired Jenifer.

Christine looked in the footwell, there was no sign of her pampered pooch.

"Isn't she in the back with you?" quizzed Christine.

"No," replied a worried Jenifer. "I thought she was in the front with you."

In a blind panic, Christine, Barry, Jenifer and Rob leapt hurriedly out of the Zodiac. Stan spotted the commotion as he reluctantly tore himself away from a digger appreciation debate with the farmer.

"It's Penny," gasped Christine. "We've lost the dog!"

"You are joking me!" exclaimed Stan. "Whatever next? When did you see her last?"

"I don't remember," replied Christine. "Maybe it was when the ambulance turned up?"

"Think, woman!" shouted Stan.

"Don't be like that!" cried Christine. "She is my dog."

"And you've lost her!" declared Stan.

Christine turned to her family.

"Right, spread out and look for Penny," ordered Christine. "Leave no stone unturned."

Barry rushed to the right and started to search the hedgerow along the line of queueing traffic. Jenifer ran to the left, also checking the hedgerows. Rob jogged up the Woodgreen Road in search of the missing pup.

Christine didn't know what to do with herself. She couldn't imagine life without her beloved pet.

Barry, Jenifer and Rob looked intently for the missing dog. Some of the queueing drivers helped in the search once the word of the missing dog filtered out.

Half an hour later there was still no sign of the missing dog.

However, Sergeant Corthine's colleague appeared from the patrol car.

"Sarge," called the police officer. "I've just had a weird call on the radio. They've come across a dog, loose in the back of an ambulance."

"What type of dog?" asked Sergeant Corthine.

"Hang on, I'll find out," responded the police officer returning to the patrol car.

"Sheltie, they think. Black, gold and grey," replied the police officer.

"That sounds like Penny," announced a jubilant Christine.

"Can they bring the dog here?" asked Sergeant Corthine.

"They are on a call at the moment," responded the police officer. "But they will once they are free."

Stan and Christine breathed a sigh of relief, as Stan gave Christine a big hug.

"I wonder where this recovery truck is?" said Sergeant Corthine. "I need this road unblocked."

Another fifteen minutes passed by. Then, on the wrong side of the road, two recovery trucks came into view, both displaying brightly flashing amber lamps on their roofs.

Bernard jumped out of his truck and guided the heavy duty recovery truck into place. Then, two men from the second recovery truck fitted four hooked slings to the caravan lifting shackles. Bernard jumped onto the roof of the caravan, where he was handed the slings.

The heavy duty recovery truck driver then positioned the jib of his small crane accurately over Bernard's head. Bernard hooked the straps to the crane hook and the crane operator took the slack out of the slings.

"Let me jump off first," shouted Bernard as he scrambled off the roof of the caravan.

With Bernard safely on terra firma, slowly and surely, the caravan was lifted from its resting place and swung into place over the waiting heavy duty recovery truck. Slowly, the caravan came to rest on the bed of the recovery truck.

At last, Sergeant Corthine was almost in a position to open the road and get things moving again.

As the heavy duty recovery truck pulled away, Sergeant Corthine let out a huge sigh of relief.

"Right," said Sergeant Corthine. "Do you know where this garage is, where they are taking your caravan?"

"Yes," replied Stan.

"Get on your way then," ordered Sergeant Corthine.

"I can't", responded Stan.

"Why not?" begged Sergeant Corthine.

"I have to wait for the ambulance people to return the dog," replied Stan.

"Oh yes," responded Sergeant Corthine. "I forgot we were in the middle of a double disaster."

Stan was displeased with where the conversation was heading, so walked away.

With bigger fish to fry, Sergeant Corthine ignored Stan's ignorant departure, focussing on his colleague, who was trying to get the jammed traffic moving at last.

Sergeant Corthine and his colleague stood in the road waving at cars as Stan and his carful of holidaymakers waited patiently inside Betsy for the return of their family pet.

"We need to devise a system," said Stan. "This damn dog is the bane of my life. It's always going missing and getting into mischief."

"She's a good girl," replied Christine defensively. "She doesn't do it on purpose. She's just inquisitive."

"Nosey!" called out Barry from the back seat, preparing himself for the Jenifer punch, which was soon delivered with precision.

"I wonder how much longer we will have to wait," said Jenifer. "It's been ages."

"Just be patient," replied Christine. "I'd rather have her back safe and sound."

"So, what system are you going to put in place?" asked Stan, sticking to his agenda despite appearing to being ignored.

"System?" responded Christine. "This is our family pet, not a machine. I'll make sure she is on the lead at all times from now on. Even if she is sat on my lap in the car."

"At least that's a start," replied Stan, starting to think he was making progress. "We have enough on our plate. So, the additional distractions caused by an adventurous dog need to cease."

"Who said you were in charge?" quizzed Christine, with an ironic smile on her face.

As the debate continued, and with the traffic flow looking much better behind them, finally, the ambulance turned into Woodgreen Road and pulled up in front of the Zodiac.

The ambulance lady got out of the ambulance clutching Penny. The lady walked to the passenger's side door. Christine lowered the window as Penny was handed over. As the handover process was in mid-flow, a male ambulance driver jumped out of the ambulance and walked up to Stan's side of the car. Stan lowered the window.

"We found your dog in the back of the ambulance," declared the ambulance man. "She must have sneaked in when I went to fetch my first aid bag. She must have jumped in when I left the door open."

"Bless her," said Christine.

"Absolutely not," said the irate ambulance man. "She has violated our sanitised ambulance. It's not set up to have dogs roaming about in the back. We have to send this ambulance for a deep clean now, and I have been told that you must pay the bill."

Stan freaked out and slumped back into the heart of the driver's seat. More expense!

"Surely that can't be right?" asked Stan. "I'm sure you have the budget to wash out the back of your ambulance."

"Wash out!" snapped the ambulance man. "We have to deep clean the mess. Who knows what diseases this mutt has let loose in the back of our ambulance?"

"She's not diseased," argued Christine. "She has a bath every other month. And she cleans herself all the time."

"Outrageous," said the angered ambulance man. "You think that's acceptable?"

"Yes," declared Christine.

"In any case," continued the ambulance man, "I'm going to need your full name and address. So I know where to send the bill for the deep clean."

"I'm not going to tell you," responded Stan, folding his arms defensively across his stomach.

"Is that right," declared the ambulance man. "Then I will just have to take this up with Sergeant Corthine."

The ambulance man started to walk off in the direction of Sergeant Corthine, who was busy directing traffic.

"Wait!" exclaimed Stan. "I'll tell you."

The ambulance man stopped in his tracks and returned to the Zodiac.

"I should think so too," said a relieved ambulance man taking a notebook and pencil out of his pocket.

"My name is David," stated Stan, as he gave the ambulance man his brother's name and address, in an attempt to avoid even more unnecessary expense.

The clueless ambulance man wrote down the details given by Stan.

"Thank you very much for bringing her back," yelled Jenifer from the back seat.

"You are welcome," replied the ambulance lady. "Your pup has had quite an adventure today."

The Zodiac passengers watched on as the ambulance U-turned in the road in front of them, driving off to their left towards Salisbury.

"You little monkey," said Christine as she fluffed up the fur on Penny's head.

"More like manky," called out Barry from the back seat. "She's totally ruined the back of that ambulance with her diseases."

Jenifer slapped Barry firmly on the shoulder.

"Leave her alone," said Jenifer, reaching over to stroke Penny.

"We'd better get to this garage now," suggested Stan. "See what's going to happen with the caravan. Even more expense!"

"You and your money," said Jenifer from the back seat. "You are tighter than an arm wrestler's grip."

Barry looked across at Rob in the back seat and shrugged his shoulders. It's not every day that arm wrestlers grips get a shout out in conversation.

As the family bantered in the car, Stan got out of the Zodiac and approached Sergeant Corthine.

"I'd just like to thank you for all of your help and understanding," said Stan in a genuine manner.

"Just doing my job," replied Sergeant Corthine. "Although, you are taking up most of my time this week. Next year, make sure you go on holiday to Scotland."

Stan laughed and gracefully shook Sergeant Corthine's hand.

Stan returned to Betsy, jumped in, and turned the ignition key. Betsy just coughed and spluttered, but the engine refused to start. Stan tried again, nothing. After five attempts, Stan started to hit his head on the top of the steering wheel again.

"Out and push, everyone, except the dog," said a completely exasperated Stan.

Everyone piled out of the Zodiac except Stan and the dog, positioning themselves at the back of the car. Seeing their plight, Sergeant Corthine joined the team.

Just as the push gathered enough speed, Stan tried to bump start Betsy. Her engine roared into life as a small cloud of grey smoke popped out of the exhaust.

"Everyone in, quickly," requested Stan in a panic.

With the car fully laden with passengers, Stan indicated right and manoeuvred onto the A338, waving farewell to Sergeant Corthine and his colleague.

Stan had barely travelled a mile when he arrived at the garage. The garage was set back from the forecourt of a petrol station and café. Stan instantly spotted his caravan positioned in front of the workshop doors. Stan parked up in the petrol station car park and strolled over to the caravan, where Bernard was waiting for him.

After a firm handshake, Stan prepared himself for Bernard's feedback.

"I've had a look at your caravan sub-frame," said Bernard puffing on his pipe. "It's rotten through at the front. I'll have to replace it all. I can get the box section and reinforcement plates from our Southampton depot. I've already checked with them, and they have confirmed that they have the steel in stock. If I leave in the next half hour, I will be back by five. However, we shut at five, so I won't be able to start the repairs until tomorrow morning."

"What!" exclaimed Stan. "Can you not start the work tonight, considering that this is an emergency?"

"Emergency?" asked Bernard looking across at the assembled Zodiac passengers. "Can you define 'emergency' please."

"We were supposed to be in Christchurch last Friday," responded Stan. "It's now late Wednesday afternoon and we have made it to Fordingbridge so far. That's a travel emergency in my opinion."

Bernard relit his pipe, to give him an opportunity to ponder the situation.

"If I start tonight," declared Bernard. "Then it will cost you extra."

"Extra?" responded a deeply concerned Stan. "Why extra?"

"Overtime," replied Bernard assertively.

"Tell me, what's the estimated bill without overtime?" quizzed Stan, trying to establish the extent of the impending damage to his finances.

Bernard had another time out, puffing on his pipe frantically.

"Eighty pounds for parts," announced Bernard. "Seventy pounds labour, without overtime."

"And when would the job be completed?" requested Stan.

Bernard again puffed on his pipe, looking pressurised by Stan.

"Around two o'clock tomorrow afternoon," replied Bernard. "That's if everything goes to plan."

"And how much with overtime?" added Stan. "And when would you be finished by?"

Bernard looked again at the caravan in front of him, trying to justify his estimating attempt.

"One hundred and ten pounds labour," replied Bernard nervously. "I reckon I would be all finished by around eleven o'clock in the morning."

"What time do you start in the morning?" asked Stan, trying to apply more pressure on Bernard.

"Nine," responded Bernard smartly. "We always start at nine and close at five. Just like every other garage around here."

"Can you start earlier in the morning?" requested Stan, trying his luck."

Stan relit his pipe, he needed inspiration.

"Let me check with Jeff," added Bernard. "He'll be working on the job with me."

Bernard opened the smaller door within the larger, main garage doors and walked into the workshop. Stan followed him in.

After a lengthy and animated conversation with Jeff, Bernard was once again ready to engage with the testy Stan.

"Jeff can start at eight," declared Bernard. "So that will take another hour off the end time. So that'll mean you will be on your way at ten in the morning. Take it or leave it."

"And what is the final cost?" asked Stan nervously.

"Two hundred and twenty pounds, all in," responded Bernard adamantly.

"Two hundred pounds and we have a deal," said Stan, trying his luck.

"You are not really in a place to bargain and negotiate, are you," replied Bernard. "Like I said, two hundred and twenty ponds. As a goodwill gesture, I won't charge you for recovery."

Seeing a cost saving in there somewhere, Stan thrust his hand forward at Bernard to shake on the deal. The pair shook hands.

"Are we okay to sleep in the caravan in the workshop tonight?" asked Stan nervously.

Bernard and Jeff looked at each other nervously. Seeing no negative reaction from Jeff, Bernard was happy to allow the family to sleep in the caravan.

"We'll make sure the caravan won't collapse on itself," said Bernard reassuringly. "Just don't touch anything in the workshop."

"Thank you," said Stan, shaking Bernard's hand again. "We will be model guests."

Chapter Nine

Stan was restless, he had a lot on his mind to compute. Still not completely over the loss of his revered knitwear, he also had the guilt of the parking ticket to consider. Pacing up and down the petrol station car park like an expectant father, Stan's thoughts turned to the bill that was going to be handed to him in the morning. Fuming that he found himself unable to reason with Bernard over the cost of the repairs, Stan was also peeved to be paying extra for labour. It was no use. Stan needed a distraction to take his mind off his woes.

Stan opened the driver's side door of the Zodiac and grabbed the map that was located in the door pocket. Spreading the map out on the bonnet, Stan looked at it for a possible ride out.

Salisbury looked the best bet. It was only twelve miles away, plus Stan already knew a number of pull in spots should Betsy continue to let them down. It was decided. Stan walked over to the petrol station café, where Christine, Barry and Rob were sitting behind mugs of tea. To the left of the café, Stan spotted Jenifer sitting on a wall with Penny sat on her feet. It appeared that the café was a non-dog zone. Stan waved at Jenifer and wandered into the café.

"Bernard is going to be in Southampton for a while," stated Stan. "He's gone to fetch some steel to repair the caravan."

"We know," responded a tetchy Christine.

"What I thought, was," continued Stan, "to pass the time, how about if we had a ride to Salisbury to take a look at the cathedral? I've heard it's quite impressive."

"Sounds okay," replied Christine. "But I want to finish my mug of tea first. I'll go and fetch you one. Sit down, chop-chop."

Stan had no choice. Christine sprang from her seat to fetch Stan a hot brew. Christine was quite pleased to part with Stan's hard earned cash. Even if it was only forty pence for a mug of tea. It all mounts up.

Being sat down and having time on his hands, Stan took out the parking ticket from his back pocket, unfolding it under the table. To his deep joy, Stan noticed in the small print, that if he paid in person at the police station within fourteen days, he would get forty percent knocked off the fine.

Stan needed a street map so he could locate the police station. This was too good a cost saving opportunity to miss. Stan remembered that Jenifer was the last person to use the street map, when she went to fetch a replacement rod for the engine.

Stan jumped off his stool and rushed out of the café, just as Christine arrived with his mug of hot tea.

“Where’s he off to?” asked Christine.

Rob and Barry looked back at Christine with vacant looks on their faces, shrugging their shoulders.

Outside, Stan was sitting with Jenifer and Penny.

“Have you still got that street map of Salisbury?” asked Stan.

“Let me think,” responded Jenifer. “Last time I recall having it was in the caravan. It’s in the side pocket of my holdall, I definitely remember placing it there for safe keeping.”

“Great,” responded Stan. “Is your holdall in the small bedroom?”

“Yes, it is,” said Jenifer.

Stan wandered over to the workshop doors and tried to open the smaller access door. It was padlocked. Stan then rattled the larger access doors, to see if he could open them, but they were bolted shut.

Stan walked to the office and peered inside. Sadly, there was no visible signs of life.

“Bother,” said Stan out loud. “They both must have gone to Southampton.”

Unperturbed, Stan returned to the café, waving once more to Jenifer.

“Where have you been?” asked Christine as Stan sat down for his fresh brew.

“I wanted the street map of Salisbury,” responded Stan. “I need to find the police station.”

"Why do you want to find the police station?" requested Christine. "Haven't you had enough of Sergeant Corthine already?"

Stan smiled at Christine.

"If I go in person to the police station," continued Stan, "and pay my fine in person, I will have a forty percent discount."

"Oh, I see," replied Christine. "That's the real reason for the trip to Salisbury. Not for the pleasure of a trip out with you wife and family. You just want to save money on a parking ticket."

"Not at all," pleaded Stan. "I had already decided to take you to Salisbury, before I found out about the parking ticket rebate."

"Likely tale," grunted an unimpressed Christine.

"I'm going out for a cigarette," announced Rob.

"You will have to go well away from the petrol station," advised Barry, smugly.

"I want to use the phone box as well," added Rob. "Is that far enough away?"

Rob looked over to Barry for his reaction.

"Probably," responded Barry.

"I'll go and tell Jenifer about our trip to Salisbury on my way to the phone box," continued Rob.

"I'll do that," snapped Barry. "She's my girlfriend, I'll tell her."

Barry immediately dropped off his stool and barged past Rob. Rob was pleased to see Barry react in a jealous manner. Job done.

Rob disappeared out of the café.

"I wonder who he's phoning?" pried Christine. "I bet he's going to tell his mother and father about this disastrous week."

"That's up to him," replied Stan. "It's a free country."

Stan and Christine finished their mugs of tea. They walked out of the café and beckoned Barry, Jenifer and Penny to join them in the Zodiac. Christine was quite excited about the visit to Salisbury, at last it started to feel like she was on holiday.

Everyone except Rob was waiting in the Zodiac, anxious to make the most of the remaining daylight. Ten minutes passed by and the mood inside Betsy was starting to grow tense.

"Shall I go and fetch him?" suggested Barry. "How long does it take to smoke a cigarette these days?"

"Leave it," responded Jenifer abruptly. "He'll be here in a minute."

"Look at you," said Barry, not happy with Jenifer defending Rob. "Why don't you go and find him, then you can have a snuggle."

Jenifer smacked Barry on his upper arm.

"Grow up," snarled Jenifer. "It's you that goes off flirting, not me. I bet you are still in contact with that Natasha!"

Barry backed off. Realising that Jenifer had the upper hand, Barry decided that silence was his best defence right now.

"Pack it in you two," said Christine, turning around to face the back seat. "We've got enough going on without you pair keep rowing. Just settle down."

"It's him," responded Jenifer.

A denim jacket clad Rob appeared around the corner of the hedgerow that bordered the petrol station. At last, the journey to Salisbury could get under way.

Unbelievably, Betsy made the entire twelve miles to Salisbury without a hitch. Everyone commented and laughed when they passed the Woodgreen Road junction, the location of their earlier breakdown incident.

"We broke down in a pretty dangerous spot," said Stan as they were parallel to the Woodgreen Junction. "We were lucky not to have had a nasty accident there."

"Could anyone actually understand what the digger driver was saying?" asked Rob from the back seat. "He sounded like he'd be at home on the stage with The Wurzels."

"They have a really nice accent around here," responded Jenifer. "I could listen to it all day."

Barry folded his arms in anger, not happy at seeing Jenifer siding with Rob.

"Stanley," said Christine, "try and find somewhere to park in Salisbury where you won't get a parking ticket."

"At least I'm not towing the van this time," replied Stan. "I can head for a normal car parking space."

The banter continued in the Zodiac until they were parked up in the centre of Salisbury. Everyone got out of the car and looked around. To their left, they spotted the unmistakable spire of Salisbury Cathedral in the near distance. The sun was out, the sky was blue, the weather was warm. Time to start the holidaymaking.

"I fancy a Cornish pasty," stated Christine. "Let's find a pasty shop, and go and sit in the grounds of the cathedral."

"Good idea," agreed Jenifer. "I haven't had a pasty in ages."

The group wandered off towards Salisbury on the hunt for a pasty shop. Within fifteen minutes they had located their target. Christine and Stan were stood in a queue of five people waiting to be served. It was a nice shop. They sold pasties and an endless variety of stunning looking cream cakes.

"Five Cornish pasties please," said Christine as they reached the front of the queue.

The shopkeeper packed five pasties into a large white paper bag.

"Anything else, my dear?" asked the shopkeeper.

"No, that's it," responded Christine.

"That will be four pounds, please," requested the shopkeeper.

Stan opened his wallet close by his side and covertly removed a twenty pound note. Stan handed the note to Christine. Christine offered the note to the shopkeeper. The shopkeeper handed the change to Christine and they left the bakery.

"This way," said Barry pointing towards the spire in the near distance.

Finding two empty benches in the grounds of Salisbury Cathedral, Christine handed out the pasties.

"Have you still got my change Christine?" asked Stan nervously, feeling aggrieved that he was still missing some of his precious cash.

Christine fumbled around in her pocket and handed Stan his change.

Stan looked down at his change.

"There's only six pounds here," fumed Stan. "Where's the other tenner? I gave you a twenty!"

"No, you didn't," snapped Christine, digging around in her pocket again, to check if she had any more notes in her pocket. Christine's pocket was empty.

"I definitely gave you a twenty," continued Stan. "On Penny's life."

"Don't you use my dog's life as a means of validation," growled Christine. "Look, you gave me a ten pound note, let that be an end to it."

Stan was adamant. He didn't flash twenty pound notes willy-nilly. He knew he was in the right.

"I'm going back to the pasty shop to get my tenner," said a vexed Stan.

"Don't be ridiculous," replied Christine. "Just sit down and enjoy your pasty."

By the time that Christine had uttered the 'pas' of 'pasty', Stan was already up and off to reclaim his precious ten pound note.

A few minutes later, Stan stormed into the bakery. There were two people waiting in the queue. The shopkeeper smiled across to Stan, recognising him from their recent encounter.

Stan bided his time in the queue impatiently, tapping his foot on the floor as he waited. At last, he was at the front of the queue.

"Afternoon," said Stan sheepishly. "I was in here just earlier."

"I know," replied the shopkeeper, smiling. "I recognise you."

"Look," pleaded Stan. "There appears to have been a mistake. My wife, Christine, paid for our pasties with a twenty pound note. But you only gave her change for a ten pound note."

"That can't be so," replied the shopkeeper confidently. "I've been working here for fifteen years, and I don't make mistakes."

"On this occasion," responded Stan nervously, "I think you may have made your first mistake in fifteen years."

The shopkeeper brought her hands down to the counter in an aggressive manner.

"Like I said," responded the shopkeeper with the sternest of looks on her face. "I don't make mistakes. Are you calling me a liar?"

Stan now found himself on really thin ice. He needed to engage brain before opening mouth. But his instincts overpowered his reasoning.

"I definitely recall taking a twenty pound note out of my wallet," counterargued Stan. "I don't take twenty pound notes out of my wallet without due care and attention."

"How old are you?" asked the shopkeeper.

"None of your business," snapped Stan. "What's that got to do with it?"

"Come on, humour me," continued the shopkeeper. "How old are you? Forty-two?"

"That's not a bad guess," replied Stan. "I'm actually forty-three. What's that got to do with anything?"

"Looking at you," replied the shopkeeper, "I reckon you had your first wallet when you were twelve years old. So, in my estimation, that's the first time you have made a mistake with twenty pound note in over thirty years."

Stan was speechless, he had been duped by a pasty shop worker.

"I'm not leaving here until you give me my ten pounds you owe me," announced Stan, folding his arms across his chest defiantly.

"Well," responded the shopkeeper. "There's only one way to sort this out."

The shopkeeper walked into the back room, closing the door behind her. The shopkeeper reappeared a couple of minutes later.

"What's going on?" asked Stan anxiously.

"You'll see," replied the shopkeeper. "Now stand aside whilst I serve this customer."

Stan shuffled sidewards to let the customer past him.

For the next fifteen minutes, Stan tried to extract his fate from the shopkeeper, but she stood firm with tight lips. Suddenly, Stan became aware of his fate as a patrol car pulled up outside the pasty shop. It just had to be. It was Stan's old nemesis Sergeant Corthine.

Sergeant Corthine walked into the pasty shop confidently. Sergeant Corthine scanned the shop and spotted Stan.

"No!" growled Sergeant Corthine. "Surely, not you again. Didn't I order you out of Wiltshire?"

"You did, sir," replied an embarrassed Stan. "But I am still waiting for the caravan sub-frame to be repaired."

"Of course, I forgot, the dreaded caravan," responded Sergeant Corthine in disbelief. "Look, I'm done with you. I'm going to get my colleague, Officer Walton, he's in the car. He can deal with this."

Sergeant Corthine stormed out of the pasty shop to fetch his colleague.

Officer Walton entered the shop. After listening to both sides, and with Stan unable to provide the serial number of his prized twenty pound note, Officer Walton suggested that Stan was at fault and asked Stan to leave the shop.

"I'm not going anywhere without what's mine," said a determined Stan.

"This is your last warning," replied Officer Walton. "If you don't leave now, I will arrest you for obstruction."

Stan dropped into deep thought mode. He'd only recently committed his first offence with the Salisbury Station parking ticket. Did he really want to double up his record with an arrest? Absolutely not.

"Okay, you win this time," admitted Stan. "I will go, but, for the record, I'm not happy."

"Good choice," said Officer Walton. "You don't want to be spoiling your holiday with a stay in jail."

"By the way," added Stan. "I need to go to the police station to pay a parking fine. Can you give me a lift? As I don't know where it is."

"You are kidding me?" said an astonished Officer Walton.

"No, I'm for real," replied Stan.

"I'll have to talk this over with Sarge," responded Officer Walton. "This one is above my pay grade."

Officer Walton and Stan wandered out to the patrol car, to put Stan's request to Sergeant Corthine.

To Stan's absolute astonishment, Sergeant Corthine agreed to Stan's proposal and opened the rear door of the patrol car to welcome Stan in.

Stan was taken a mile or so to the police station, where he not only paid off his parking ticket, but enjoyed a tour of the police station at the hands of Officer Walton. The pair enjoyed a mug of tea in the rest area, where Stan shared his week's adventures and mishaps with Officer Walton. Once the full story was told, Officer Walton returned Stan to the pasty shop.

"Thank you so much," said Stan through the open front door of the patrol car. "Not only informative, but I saved myself a few bob."

"For a normal looking bloke," replied Officer Walton, "you appear to be a serial offender."

"Not at all," responded Stan. "I've just been blighted by incredible bad luck this week."

"On your way now," responded Officer Walton. "And like Sergeant Corthine said, don't darken our doors again."

Stan closed the patrol car door and made haste to Salisbury Cathedral. When Stan entered the grounds he spotted his gang, still sitting on the same benches.

Stan sat next to Christine and picked up the white paper bag from the bench. Stan then took a bite of his pasty.

"This is cold!" complained Stan.

"I should think so," replied Christine angrily. "It's been sat there for hours. Where have you been all this time?"

"To the police station," stated a proud Stan.

"You haven't gone and got yourself arrested? Have you?" asked Christine nervously.

"Don't be daft," added Stan. "The kind police officers took me to the police station to pay my parking fine. That's all done and dusted now. Plus, I saved forty percent."

"And what about your change?" asked Jenifer from the adjacent bench.

"I don't want to talk about it," grunted Stan. "You win some, you lose some."

"And we are losing most of them this week," said Barry.

Jenifer administered the traditional slap to Barry's upper arm.

The holidaymakers spent another half an hour browsing around the centre of Salisbury. However, Stan was getting restless again. He needed to know if Bernard had returned from Southampton with the steel. Time was ticking and it was gone four o'clock. He wanted to be at the petrol station, to check that Bernard was good to his word. So, at any given opportunity, Stan suggested that they returned to the petrol station. The others wanted none of this. They knew the agenda behind Stan's suggestions, plus, there was no entertainment back at the petrol station, so boredom was inevitable.

Eventually, Stan persuaded his gang to return to Fordingbridge, to put Stan out of his misery. For a change, Betsy started first crank which indicated to Stan that his run of bad luck could be coming to an end.

After an event-free twelve miles back to Fordingbridge, Stan pulled up outside the workshop. Noticing that Bernard's truck was parked up next to the workshop, Stan assumed all was well.

Stan jumped out of the Zodiac and sprinted through the open workshop access door.

"Everything okay?" asked Stan as he approached the overall clad Bernard and Jeff.

"I think so," replied Bernard, much to Stan's relief. "We have all the steel we need, so I think we are good to go. Make sure you keep your people out of here when we are working. Welding and grinding are dangerous work. The last thing I want is to injure an onlooker."

"Leave that with me," replied Stan.

Stan wandered back out of the workshop to brief the troop about the workshop etiquette.

As the familiar sound of a cutting tool on steel filled the air, Stan rushed back into the workshop to monitor progress. Christine, Jenifer and Barry had been ordered to sit out of the way in the café, with Rob detailed to Penny watch outside.

Stan looked on as Jeff set about cutting away the damaged parts of the caravan sub-frame. In between the flying sparks and debris, Stan moved his head in to inspect Jerry's work.

"This has to stop right now," ordered Jeff, looking at Stan.

"What?" responded Stan innocently.

"You," added Jeff, "checking my every move, it's putting me off."

"Look, Stan," interrupted Bernard. "You are just going to have to trust us. We know what we are doing. We've been doing this for years. I've got certificates in the office for welding."

"I don't doubt your abilities," responded Stan. "I'm just eager to get the job done and to see how you are progressing."

"You are slowing us down," said a frustrated Jeff. "If you keep nosing about, it will take a week to get this job done."

This was a wakeup call for Stan. He needed the job doing quickly, with absolutely no more labour costs added to the already pricey job.

"Okay, I get it," replied Stan. "I'll back off. Can I sit over there on that chair in the corner, and watch from there?"

"We'd rather you not watch at all," said Bernard assertively. "Just go and join your family in the café. We will call you in when there is something worth seeing."

Begrudgingly, Stan agreed to Bernard's suggestion, and made his way to the café to join Christine.

Good to his word, Stan sat in the café. He dared not take his eyes off the workshop doors, just in case Bernard would appear with news of progress.

“Just try and relax,” said Christine, attempting to calm Stan down. “You are acting like a cow on heat.”

“It’s imperative that we get this job done quickly,” replied Stan. “Tomorrow is Thursday. Time is fast running out. Even if we get to Christchurch tomorrow, we will only have three nights at the caravan park, instead of the planned nine. It’s just like I’ve failed you all.”

“No, you haven’t failed us all,” said a comforting Christine. “All these horrid things that have happened to us are not your fault. You didn’t puncture the caravan tyre. You didn’t break the exhaust pipe. You didn’t break that stick thingy that you fitted in Devizes. You didn’t break the front of the caravan. So don’t beat yourself up.”

“I did lose my favourite jumper!” responded Stan. “And I lost a tenner in the pasty shop.”

“Like I said, don’t beat yourself up,” added Christine. “I’ll buy you a lovely new sweater. And what’s ten pounds these days?”

“In my book,” responded Stan, “a tenner is a tenner. I don’t like spending money, as you well know. But to get robbed is another matter.”

“You didn’t get robbed,” replied Christine calmly. “You must have made a mistake.”

“I know what I did,” scowled Stan. “Enough of this, I’m going to have a tinker under Betsy’s bonnet. Just to make sure everything is in order.”

"You and that car!" said Christine. "You think more of that car than your entire family."

Stan refused to get involved in such a judgemental debate. So, he jumped off his stool and headed out to work on his beloved Zodiac.

Time rolled on. It was now seven o'clock in the evening. Stan was sitting alone in the front seat of his vehicle. Tinkering was over for the evening. Stan was actually delighted that Bernard and Jeff appeared to be still at work on the caravan.

Bernard appeared from the small access door to the workshop. As Bernard looked around to try and locate his customer, Stan read the signs and decided to leap out of the Zodiac. Bernard waved at Stan after spotting him in the car park.

When inside the workshop, Stan looked nervously down at the caravan. Bernard and Jeff had completely stripped away what appeared to be all of the front sub-frame. This made Stan feel extremely nervous.

"What do you think?" asked Bernard. "Tidy or what. We've got rid of all the rusty metal. This sub-frame will last longer than the entire caravan once we've finished with it."

"So, it's taken you all evening to just chop it all off?" asked a concerned Stan.

"No," responded Bernard confidently. "Take a look at this."

Bernard led Stan and Jeff over to a workbench to the side of the caravan. On the workbench was the shape of the caravan sub-frame laid out. It hadn't been welded up yet, but Bernard and Jeff had cut all the metal to size, ready for a welding session in the morning.

"Looks impressive," said Stan as he looked over their work. "When are you going to weld it together?"

"First thing," replied Bernard. "It's gone seven o'clock now, I need to get home. I have things planned for tonight."

"Can't they wait?" suggested Stan, trying his luck.

"Look, matey boy," said an angered Bernard. "We are doing you a favour staying until seven. I had to convince my wife that this job was an emergency. I'm not staying any later."

"Maybe I could weld it up tonight?" appealed Stan. "I'm pretty handy with a welding torch."

"If you so much think about touching our welding equipment," said an angry Bernard, "you will find yourself having to deal with the long arm of the law. Believe me, I will have no hesitation."

Stan, convinced that Bernard's threat was real, immediately backed out of the conversation.

"In any case," added Bernard "just as a precaution, I'm going to take the fuses out of the fuse box and take them home with me."

"There is no need to go to those lengths," insisted Stan.

"I don't care," continued Bernard assertively. "I've seen enough. The look in your eye tells me that you would be more than willing to give it a go. Therefore,

I'm going to completely remove the temptation from you."

"I understand," admitted a beaten Stan.

"Furthermore," added Bernard. "Once Jeff and I leave the premises, we are going to lock you inside the workshop. If you want to stay in your caravan tonight, then those are the conditions. I can't afford a break in. So, take it or leave it."

"I need to talk to my family first," responded Stan.

"Do what you have to," replied Bernard. "There are no other choices. Once we have locked you in, any equipment inside of my workshop is out of bounds. If I find one thing out of place in the morning, I will hold you personally responsible, Stan."

"And if my wife refuses to be locked in, can we move the caravan outside before you leave?"

"How?" howled Bernard. "There is no sub-frame in place. How on earth do you propose we move the caravan off the ramp? Heavy duty magic carpet?"

"I see," admitted Stan, realising the nonsensical comment he had just made.

"I'm serious about this, Stan," continued Bernard. "There is some pretty dangerous stuff in here. I don't want anyone coming to harm. You have to promise me that once you are locked in, you all stay in the caravan."

"As I said," responded Stan, "let me have a quick chat with the family."

Stan returned to the petrol station café to discuss the rules with his family. At first, Christine and Jenifer were totally opposed to being imprisoned in the caravan for the night. But after Stan explained the dangers in the workshop, and the risk of break in if the workshop remained unlocked overnight, both came round and agreed to the demands.

Barry was not bothered either way, as long as he had a soft pillow to rest his head.

Stan finally walked outside the café to inform Rob, who was sitting on a wall on Penny watch.

Stan explained Bernard's demands to Rob. Almost immediately Rob refused to co-operate. He didn't want to be stuck in the caravan for the night with a snoring Barry. Stan's plan contained the sub-plot that Rob and Barry would sleep in the dining area, on the pull out beds. This would position Rob just a few feet from the midnight orchestra.

"Can I sleep in the car?" pleaded Rob.

"No," said an adamant Stan. "I don't want the wear and tear on the seats. It's only for one night. Just do as we ask, please."

Already shattered due to lack of a decent night's sleep since Friday, Rob stuck to his guns.

"Just think," said Rob, pleading his case, "if I sleep in the Zodiac tonight, I will be like a guard dog. What would you feel like if your beloved Betsy was stolen in the night? With me in there sleeping, the chances of that reduce dramatically."

Stan hadn't considered that angle. Stan had no idea how safe this location was, so Rob's suggestion seemed more than feasible.

"Okay, you can sleep in the Zodiac tonight," confirmed Stan after due consideration. "Just make sure you take your training shoes off. And watch that sleeping bag zip on the leather seats."

"I will treat her with the utmost of respect," confirmed Rob.

Now Stan had a full buy in to Bernard's rules, he revisited the workshop to tell Bernard that they all had agreed to the ground rules.

Stan chaperoned his gang into the workshop as Bernard and Jeff prepared to leave.

"I'm not going to give you any keys," said Bernard. "If anything happens in the night, and you need to get out fast, just put one of the office chairs through the window. I can replace a pain of glass really easily."

"Got you," replied Stan, winking at Bernard.

Rob waved his farewell and took up his residence inside Betsy in the car park.

Bernard swung the main doors to the workshop shut, then double checked the padlock on the smaller access door.

"I'm really not comfortable with this," said Bernard to Jeff.

"I know," replied Jeff. "But that bloke is just too tight to put his family up in a hotel room tonight. Beggar's belief."

"It's going to be so boring in there tonight," added Bernard. "Especially for the younger ones. They will be going out of their minds in no time at all."

"At the end of the day, it's their own decision," responded Jeff. "Just remember that. So don't feel responsible for their position."

"They will be okay, you'll see," said Bernard, getting into his truck.

"You certainly know how to treat a lady," said Christine as Stan closed the caravan door behind him.

"We've still got our home comforts," responded Stan. "It could be worse."

"How?" growled Jenifer. "I didn't even want to come on this pesky holiday. I wanted to go to Blackpool with Amanda."

"There's gratitude for you," mumbled Stan.

After dealing with the initial complaints, Stan had everyone settled down within the hour. Christine rustled up a nice pan full of hotpot for dinner.

"I've just thought," said Christine. "How are we going to get the hotpot to Rob? We are locked in."

"He'll be okay," replied a smug Barry. "There is a café out there, if he can afford to smoke, then he must have money to buy some food from the café."

"You've never liked Rob, have you," said Jenifer.

Chapter Ten

It was a weird evening for the caravaners in the workshop. Bernard was kind enough to leave the fuses for the lights, so nobody broke their bones travelling to and from the toilet. Stan mused around the workshop as expected. He didn't touch any of the equipment, but it all interested him.

Christine's hot pot went down a storm, so, with everyone fed and watered, they tried to decide on how to fill the remainder of their time for the evening.

Barry's Monopoly suggestion was unanimously binned immediately. That game was poison in the household. The game was taken too seriously by all competitors which inevitably led to confrontation and fall out.

"How about a game of whist?" suggested Jenifer.

"Boring!" chanted Barry immediately.

"Old Maid?" said Christine, a fan of old school games.

"Even more boring!" recited a disruptive Barry.

"Well, you suggest something," responded an irate Jenifer.

"Poker," announced Barry. "Texas Hold 'Em". Stan can win back his change from the pasty shop."

"Not even funny," replied Stan with a scowl on his face.

"Come on," added Barry. "It's more of a mind game than a card game. You have to get into the heads of the other players."

"They won't find much in yours!" declared Stan, trying to get one back over Barry.

"We might as well play Monopoly," said Jenifer. "It sounds like poker is just as competitive. In any case, I think it's only you that knows how to play, Barry."

"I can teach you if you like," suggested Barry. "If we play for just pennies, we won't win or lose a great amount."

"You are not playing for the dog!" interrupted Christine.

"Pennies, pence, not Penny the dog," explained a bemused Barry.

"I'm not playing for money," declared Christine. "Carry on without me."

"Me neither," added Stan, worried that there was a good chance he would be parting with more cash.

"There is no point playing with just the two of us," said Barry. "Just forget it."

"Worried I might beat you?" declared Jenifer.

Barry ignored Jenifer's taunts, got up and walked over to the fridge to get a can of pop.

"It's only early evening, what are we going to do?" said a bored and frustrated Jenifer.

"We could clean the caravan," suggested Christine. "It needs a good going over. You can hoover, Jenifer, and I will dust."

"You've brought a hoover?" asked Stan. "No wonder the caravan sub-frame has broken, it's the weight of all the appliances you have smuggled on board."

"It's only a small one, and it's light as a feather," explained Christine.

"I haven't come on holiday to be a cleaner," replied Jenifer. "Count me out. I'm going to read a book."

"Great," responded Barry. "What am I going to do?"

"Beat yourself at poker!" sniped Jenifer.

The pattern of events for the evening pretty much followed the same tracks. Suggestions for possible activities to kill the time were debated at length then binned. At one stage, the badminton rackets actually made their way out of the storage bin, instantly replaced when Jenifer and Barry noticed how cluttered the low ceilinged workshop was.

Eventually, they all retired to their respective sleeping bags and turned in for the night.

Thursday morning dawn had broken; beams of bright sunlight started to filter through the workshop windows, lighting up the caravan.

Stan was first up. With nobody about, he returned to closely inspecting the interesting equipment in the workshop, picking up tools and shadow pretending to use them.

Stan's tour was rudely interrupted by the jangle of keys outside the workshop doors. It was Bernard and Jeff arriving early to make a start on the sub-frame. Stan watched on as Bernard arrogantly walked over to the main fuse box, returning the fuses to their respective positions. Bernard looked over at Stan with a smirk on his face after he had replaced the final fuse.

This grated with Stan who looked away in disgust.

"Can your missus knock up a brew?" asked Bernard. "That will save us time, so Jeff and I can make a start on the welding. The sooner we start, the sooner we can finish. Milk and one sugar in both, please."

Desperate to save time, Stan rushed into the caravan to wake Christine from her slumber.

Stan made his way to the main bedroom in the caravan, where he found Christine still asleep, with her back facing him.

Stan patted Christine's shoulder, but this did not rouse her. So he began shaking her lightly as he called out her name.

"Christine, Christine," said Stan just, louder than a whisper. "The workers are here. They need a cup of tea."

Christine began to stir and rolled over on her back.

"What do you want now?" asked a half asleep Christine.

"Bernard and Jeff are here," responded Stan in hope. "They have asked you specifically to make them a cup of tea, to save time."

"You make it!" declared Christine. "I'm going to have another half an hour in bed."

Christine rolled onto her side again, displaying her back to Stan in disdain.

Stan opened the second bedroom door gently, to see if Jenifer was awake and available to rectify the tea making situation that faced him. Unfortunately, Jenifer was still snuggled up in bed asleep. Knowing how Jenifer could react if she was inadvertently woken up, Stan chose not to disturb her.

Not trusting Barry even to hold a hot kettle, Stan resigned himself to doing the job and set about making the brews.

Fifteen minutes later, with Bernard and Jeff already hard at work welding, Stan presented the two cups of tea proudly to his customers. Jeff walked over to Stan to collect the refreshments. He took a look at the offerings.

"These look as weak as dishwater," said a disappointed Jeff. "How long did you leave the teabag in for? Five seconds?"

"Tea making is not really one of my strengths," admitted Stan. "I did want my wife to make them, as she is a dab hand, but she's still asleep."

"Then I recommend that you get her out of bed," suggested Jeff, giving the two mugs of tea back to Stan.

"I'll make them," announced Rob arriving in the workshop from outside. "I could murder a cuppa."

Rob took the mugs from Jeff and made his way to the caravan kitchen.

After they were presented with an acceptable cup of tea, Bernard was getting fed up with the gathering group watching on as they tried to work.

"Right, everyone out!" commanded Bernard. "We are going to start welding again in a minute, so I don't want anyone getting arc-eye."

"What's arc-eye?" asked Christine, standing there in her hair rollers.

"It's nasty," replied Stan. "If you look at the flame without a welding mask when they are welding, the intensity of the flame burns your eye covering. A few hours later, it feels like your eyes are full of sand."

"Oh dear," responded a worried Christine. "We don't want that. Come on, everybody out."

Christine took the lead and made sure everyone who should be was removed from the workshop, leaving Bernard and Jeff in peace to carry on working.

Stan had asked the group to assemble in the café, to make sure they were out of the way and to again gauge team morale and willingness to continue on their way to Christchurch. Barry was missing from the group, as it was his turn on pup watch.

"By my reckoning," said Stan "we are less than twenty miles from our destination."

"Oh, we are doing so well," interrupted Jenifer sarcastically.

"Looking at what Bernard and Jeff have to do this morning," added Stan. "I reckon we could be on the road at about ten o'clock. Maybe earlier. So, are you all still up for cracking on to Christchurch?"

"Why wouldn't we be?" asked a bemused Rob. "We are so close now, why would we ever want to turn around and head back home?"

The others grouped around the table nodded in approval.

"Well, that's it then," continued Stan. "We'll crack on."

"And that's it?" quizzed a disappointed Christine. "You called a big meeting just for that?"

"I wasn't sure how people were feeling," pleaded Stan. "I just wanted to make sure it was not just me who wants to carry on."

"Very nice," replied Christine patting the top of Stan's head. "Now go and make yourself useful and polish your precious car."

Not wanting to be in the crosshairs for more mickey taking, Stan retreated from the café to spend more precious time with his beloved Zodiac.

Ten o'clock came and went. Stan was getting nervous as Bernard had broken through his predicted finish time. Wanting to pop his head in the workshop to see what was going on, Stan resisted and continue to apply wax to Betsy's bonnet.

At twenty to eleven Bernard appeared from the workshop. Stan's eyes were filled with delight as Bernard started to open the main workshop access doors. Was the job done?

Bernard casually swaggered over to Stan.

"You can reverse your car into the workshop," announced Bernard. "Job done."

Stan was ecstatic.

"Can I take a look first?" asked Stan.

"Sure, why not," responded Bernard.

Stan dashed into the workshop to take a look at the repairs. He was thrilled at what he discovered. The caravan was fitted with the most splendid of new sub-frames. The welding was precise and neat. Plus, Jeff had applied a perfect coat of black paint. The caravan looked better than new.

Stan ran out of the workshop, sparked Betsy into life, and reversed her up to the caravan. Jeff guided Stan, just in case his reversing skills weren't up to scratch.

With the repaired caravan hitched up Stan proudly drove out of the workshop, into the sunshine of the petrol station forecourt.

Christine had spotted the unfolding events and had gathered the troops on the forecourt. There were smiles a plenty.

Bernard escorted Stan into the office to settle the bill, whilst Christine herded the holidaymakers into Betsy.

Ten minutes later, an elated Stan indicated left and pulled out onto the A338, with an enormous smile across his face.

"Where are we heading?" asked Christine with a map partially unfolded on her lap.

"Ringwood," replied Stan confidently.

Christine frantically looked at the map to find Ringwood. However, it wasn't glaringly obvious.

Barry leaned over from the back seat and snatched the map from Christine's lap.

"Hey, what are you doing?" growled Christine as Barry had accidently bumped Penny in the nose as she sat on Jenifer's lap.

"Just trying to help," responded Barry.

Barry soon discovered that Christine was looking at the wrong part of the map. Christine was looking at the map covering the Worcester area by mistake. Barry started to refold the map so that the correct area was displayed. However, Barry and maps don't get on well, as he struggled to fold the map neatly and correctly.

"Stop it!" requested Stan who was now distracted by the melee in the back seat. "You are completely distracting me with your antics."

With Stan's attention focussed on Barry's feeble map folding, he had not noticed the debris on the carriageway ahead. In a second, Stan had inadvertently driven the Zodiac over the debris. The car shook as did the caravan as they passed over the debris.

"Look what you've made me do," complained Stan.

"What was that?" asked a concerned Jenifer from the back seat.

"I've no idea," responded Stan. "I was too busy being distracted by your boyfriend."

Stan proceeded with caution as Betsy was handling poorly. Stan spotted a farm entrance on the other side of the road, big enough to park up with the caravan. After letting two cars pass by, Stan pulled up in the entrance.

After spending a few seconds headbutting the steering wheel gently, Stan got out of the car to inspect the damage. Barry also climbed out to be nosey, with Rob jumping out for a nerve calming smoke.

Stan walked around to the nearside of the car and looked down. As suspected, the front tyre was flat as a pancake. In addition, Stan quickly looked at the rear tyre. That was also deflated.

Stan looked to the heavens and screamed in frustration.

To complete the inspection exercise, Stan timidly walked to the caravan wheels expecting the worst. However, much to his surprise, both tyres were fully inflated. It appeared that Betsy had taken the full force of the contact.

Christine and Jenifer joined the group of onlookers.

"What now?" asked a subdued Christine.

"I only have one spare, so we are going to need some help here," replied Stan.

"It's not so bad," declared Barry. "The tyres are only flat at the bottom."

Everybody looked at Barry with disgust. This was not the time or place for a poor attempt at humour. Jenifer couldn't even bring herself to administer her expected right cross punch.

Stan walked to the car and returned to the group holding an invoice.

"I have Bernard's phone number on this invoice," said Stan. "We need to find a phone box. Then hope Bernard can come out and help us."

Stan sent Barry southbound and Rob northbound along the A338 to search for a telephone box. Both had Bernard's number written down on a piece of paper. Stan, Christine, Jenifer and Penny returned to the caravan. Christine had offered to make a brew whilst they waited for news.

They had been sitting in the caravan for twenty minutes, when the group heard a vehicle pull up on the gravel surface next to the caravan. Christine pulled the net curtain to one side and looked out of the window.

"Oh no," declared Christine. "Not again."

It was a police car.

Moments later, a police officer poked his head through the caravan door; it was Officer Walton.

"I'm sorry, people," said Officer Walton. "You can't stop here and have a picnic."

Stan stepped forward.

"Good morning, Officer," said Stan politely. "We are not having a picnic. We have broken down as two of our tyres have been punctured. We have sent out two lads to look for a phone box, so we can phone a garage for assistance."

"Hang on a minute," said a bemused Officer Walton. "Don't I know you?"

"Yes, I think so," responded Stan, looking at the floor in embarrassment.

"The pasty shop!" added Officer Walton. "You were trying to make ten pounds out of those innocent shop keepers."

"That's rubbish," replied Stan angrily. "They made the mistake, not me."

"That's all history," interrupted Christine, putting her arm across Stan, trying to get him to back off. "Can you help us, Officer?"

Officer Walton considered his position and ill feelings towards Stan. But at the end of the day, he was there to help and serve the public.

"Who were you trying to get in contact with?" asked Officer Walton.

"Bernard, at the service station," replied Stan.

"I know that place," replied Officer Walton. "That's not too far up the road, isn't it?"

"Yes," responded Stan in complete embarrassment.

"Come on, jump in with me," offered Officer Walton. "I will take you up the road."

"Thank you very much," responded a surprised but delighted Stan.

Stan quickly jumped in the patrol car with Officer Walton. The gravel flew everywhere as the police vehicle sped off from the farm entrance.

Half a mile up the road, Stan spotted Rob camouflaged in a plume of cigarette smoke trotting down the pathway. As Rob was deep in concentration, he failed to spot Stan in the patrol car. Stan ducked down as they passed Rob. Stan didn't want to confuse the situation any further.

Just over five minutes later, Officer Walton pulled onto the petrol station forecourt. Stan spotted Bernard in the office, munching on a sandwich.

Stan opened the office door and walked in.

"You again!" declared Bernard. "What do you want now? Has that caravan sub-frame broken already?"

When Officer Walton came into view in the office, Bernard took on a different attitude. He cowered back into his chair.

"What is the law doing here?" asked Bernard nervously.

"He rescued me," said Stan. "I hit some debris a mile or so up the road, and it punctured two of the car tyres. Can you help us?"

Bernard dropped his sandwich and looked across at Officer Walton apprehensively.

"I guess so," responded Bernard. "It just depends on what tyres you need? I don't carry much stock. What tyres are you looking for?"

"Six forty by thirteen's" replied Stan confidently.

"Okay, I'll go and see what I have in stock," replied Bernard.

Stan and Officer Walton followed Bernard out of the office.

"You stay here in the office," demanded Bernard, not wanting the long arm of the law looking around his workshop. "I'll take a look myself."

Officer Walton reluctantly returned to the office with Stan. Why didn't Bernard want company in the workshop? What could he be trying to hide?

With Bernard out in the workshop, the telephone sitting on Bernard's untidy desk started to ring. Officer Walton and Stan looked at each other.

"Should we answer that?" asked Stan.

"Maybe," replied Officer Walton. "It's not our business though."

"Might be important?" added Stan "I'll answer it."

Stan picked up the phone.

"Hello," said Stan nervously. "Can I help you?"

"I hope so," came the voice from the other end of the phone. "We've broken down, two of our tyres are flat. We need you to come out and assist us."

"Is that you, Barry?" asked Stan, recognising the dulcet tones.

"Yes, it is," responded a confused Barry. "Who is that?"

"It's Stan, Jenifer's father," replied Stan.

"Stan?" said an even more confused Barry. "What are you doing at the garage? I thought you were with Christine and Jenifer, at the farm entrance."

"We have been rescued by the police again," confirmed Stan. "The officer kindly brought me to the garage. Isn't that kind of him."

"So you just abandoned me," replied an angry Barry. "I could have been all day looking for a phone box."

As Barry complained, the pips went on the phone, so Stan returned the phone in the office to its receiver.

"Who was that?" asked Officer Walton.

"My potential future son-in-law," replied Stan.

"How did he know you were at this garage?" inquired a disturbed Officer Walton.

"He didn't," responded Stan. "I sent him out to look for a phone box, armed with the phone number of this garage. I also sent out Rob to look for a phone box in the opposite direction."

"To cover your bases?" suggested Officer Walton.

"Exactly," replied Stan. "Would I make a good police officer?"

"I'm not sure?" said Officer Walton. "Sending people out to look for a phone box won't catch too many criminals."

As Officer Walton was finishing his sentence, Bernard returned to the office.

"Criminals?" asked Bernard timidly. "What criminals?"

The awkward state of Bernard had placed Officer Walton's suspicions on high alert. What was in the workshop?

"Have you got the tyres in stock?" asked Stan, trying to break the growing tense ambience.

"No," replied Bernard. "I'm going to have to check with our Southampton branch."

Stan couldn't believe his luck.

Bernard reached out to the telephone on his desk to contact the Southampton branch. As he reached out, mysteriously, it began to ring. Bernard picked up the receiver.

"Hello," said Bernard.

"Hello," replied the caller.

"Can I help you?" asked Bernard.

"I hope so," added the caller. "We are towing a caravan down the road, and the car has got two punctures. Can you come out and help us?"

Bernard held the receiver to his chest, to block the earpiece and mouthpiece with his overalls.

"Would you believe it," said Bernard to Officer Walton and Stan. "Someone else who has got two punctured tyres. What are the chances?"

"Ask the caller if his name is Rob," suggested Stan.

With a look of total confusion on his face, Bernard did as he was instructed.

"Is your name Rob?" asked Bernard down the phone.

"Yes," replied Rob. "How did you know?"

"I think I have your dad or father-in-law in my office, with a policeman."

What?" reacted Rob. "Father-in-law? I don't have a father-in-law?"

Bernard dropped the phone to his chest again.

"What is your name again?" asked Bernard pointing at Stan.

"It's Stan," said Stan.

"This bloke in the office with me is called Stan," stated Bernard. "Do you know him?"

"Yep," responded a disappointed Rob. What was Stan doing there already, thought Rob. "Can you put him on the phone, please?"

Bernard handed the phone receiver to Stan.

"Hello, Rob," said Stan.

"What's going on?" asked a confused Rob. "How come you are at the garage and what are the police doing there?"

"Well," said Stan.

As Stan started his response, the pips once again came to Stan's rescue, as he slammed down the receiver to get himself out of a difficult explanation.

At the other end of the line, Rob shouted a couple of unanswered 'hellos' before returning the telephone receiver firmly. With no more change in his pocket, Rob was unable to prolong the discussion, and was now faced with the trek back to the caravan.

In the office, Bernard took the phone from Stan, pressed down on the phone receiver tags, and listened for a dialling tone. Turning his back on Officer Walton and Stan, Bernard dialled the Southampton number using the phone dial.

Officer Walton and Stan watched on as Bernard inquired about the availability of the required tyres. After a brief conversation, Bernard replaced the phone receiver.

"I've got good news and bad news and more bad news," announced Bernard. "The good news is that they have two tyres in stock. The bad news is that I have to fetch them. The very bad news is that I am due to appear in court today, so I can't drive over to Southampton."

Officer Walton was most intrigued with Bernard's news.

"What are you in court for?" asked Officer Walton.

"Never you mind," replied Bernard abruptly.

"Come on, spill the beans," continued Officer Walton.

"Can you take Stan to Southampton?" suggested Bernard. "To collect the tyres. Jeff can fit them for you."

"Why can't Jeff drive to Southampton?" asked Officer Walton.

"Because he's working on an important job for me," responded an uncomfortable Bernard.

"Let me see," considered Officer Walton.

"You don't have time," replied Bernard, trying to wriggle off the hook of suspicion. "You need to get Stan over to Southampton."

"It's not official police business," added Officer Walton. "I'll be in for it if I get found out for taking civilians on a joyride."

"It's not a joyride!" interrupted Stan, trying to keep his needs alive. "It will be an act of public service. You can't leave me abandoned, blocking a farm entrance on a busy road."

Officer Walton considered his options.

"Come on then," said Officer Walton. "What is the address in Southampton?"

Bernard scribbled the address on a blank envelope that happened to be lying on his desk and handed the envelope to Officer Walton.

"Can we have the blue lights and siren on?" asked an excited Stan.

"No," replied Officer Walton firmly.

Officer Walton and Stan rushed out of the office and set off on their quest to Southampton. Bernard went immediately to the workshop to find Jeff.

"I'm sure that copper will be mooching about in here when he gets back from Southampton," said a concerned Bernard. "Make sure all of that dodgy knock off welding equipment is dumped. Take it to my house and put it in my garage, out of harm's way."

"Got it, boss," replied the loyal Jeff.

Officer Walton and Stan made good time to Southampton. Without managing to get lost, they found the Southampton branch. When they pulled into the depot, they were greeted by an animated gentleman.

"Good day!" said the exuberant host. "My name is Darren. Have you driven from Fordingbridge to collect two tyres?"

"That's right," replied a relieved Stan. "Where are they?"

"In the office," responded Darren. "Wait here and I will fetch them."

Darren swaggered over to the portacabin located a few yards away, soon wheeling two brand new tyres on his return swagger.

"There you go," said Darren. "That will be one hundred and fifty pounds please."

"One hundred and fifty pounds?" exclaimed Stan. "What are they? Gold plated?"

"Do you want them or not?" asked Darren.

"Yes!" replied Stan in a state of shock. "But you are charging me double the usual asking price."

"These tyres are rarebines," added Darren. "Seventy-five pounds each is the going rate."

"That is daylight robbery," responded Stan. "I pay fifty pounds for a new tyre back home."

"You are not at home now," replied an arrogant Darren. "Now, do you want them or not?"

Stan again found himself in a position of vulnerability. Again, he was not in a position to demand the terms. Reluctantly reaching for his wallet, Stan was resigned to being ripped off by a chancer.

As Stan patted each pocket in turn, Stan's mood reached a new low as he realised that his wallet was in the caravan, back in Fordingbridge.

"I don't appear to have my wallet on me," admitted Stan.

"How convenient," replied Darren.

Stan looked over to Officer Walton.

"Have you got any money on you, that I could borrow?" pleaded Stan.

Officer Walton reached inside his uniform and produced his wallet. After briefly looking inside, Officer Walton looked back at Stan.

"I've got fifteen quid on me," said Officer Walton. "I don't usually carry too much cash on me."

"So, I guess I can take these tyres back to the warehouse," said a disappointed Darren, looking like he was going to miss out on a steal.

"Look, my wallet is in Fordingbridge," added Stan. "I can pay Bernard and he can give the money to you."

As this was too good a profit to miss out on, eventually, Darren agreed to Stan's terms and rolled the two tyres over to Stan.

"I'm going to phone Bernard right now," stated Darren. "I'm going to order him not to start work on the tyres until you hand over the one hundred and fifty pounds. End of conversation."

Stan reluctantly agreed and loaded the tyres into the back of the patrol car.

"Pleasure doing business with you," said Darren as Stan and Officer Walton jumped back into the patrol car.

Stan complained at Officer Walton for the entire trip back to Fordingbridge. Officer Walton must have said, "It is what it is," approximately twenty times during the journey.

When they arrived back at the petrol station in Fordingbridge, the patrol car was greeted by a smiling Bernard. Fortunately, Jeff had sufficient time to clear the workshop of stolen goods, so Bernard felt far more at ease.

After a brief discussion, Officer Walton bid his farewells and drove off down the A338 towards Salisbury.

"Darren told me you need to pay me before I start work," said Bernard.

"My wallet is with the caravan," replied Stan. "I will pay you when we get to the caravan."

After a firm handshake, Stan jumped in the recovery truck with Bernard to fetch the punctured tyre from the stricken Zodiac.

When they arrived at the caravan, there appeared to be an ongoing argument. Christine, Jenifer and Rob were facing off to an angry farmer, arguing with them as they were blocking his access. Barry was standing around twenty yards away from the group with Penny.

He was under strict orders to keep Penny away from the confrontation.

Bernard knew the farmer well, as he had been servicing the farmer's vehicles for years. In no time, Bernard had explained Stan's plight to diffuse the situation.

Stan begrudgingly walked over to the caravan, took out his wallet and handed over the required cash to Bernard.

"Expensive tyres!" exclaimed Bernard.

"Tell me about it," replied Stan in a sulk.

Fortunately, Bernard had a number of jacks on his recovery truck. After informing the caravaners not to enter the Zodiac until the jacks were removed, Bernard went about his business, removing the two damaged wheels from the Zodiac.

Once the offending wheels had been removed, Bernard climbed aboard his recovery truck and sped off to complete the puncture repairs.

"I paid a hundred and fifty pounds for those pesky tyres," said Stan glaring angrily at Barry.

"How much?" replied a shocked Christine.

"Exactly," added Stan. "If that kid hadn't interfered with your map, none of this would have happened."

"Don't be ridiculous," responded Christine. "You leave him alone. You were holding the steering wheel at the time. How can it be Barry's fault?"

"I need a cup of tea," suggested Stan. "It's been a tough day already, especially for my wallet."

“I’ll make you one, dear,” replied Christine. “Go and sit down in the caravan.”

“Any fig rolls?” requested an expectant Stan.

“We need to get some,” replied Christine, much to Stan’s disappointment.

A distraught Stan jumped into the caravan to wait for his hot mug of tea. Pondering on the week’s events, a wry smile came across Stan’s face.

“What are you smiling about?” asked Jenifer, who was reading her book in the corner seat.

“I’m just baffled,” replied Stan. “I don’t think I’ve ever been on a holiday like this. I can’t get my head around the series of events that have unfolded.”

“Yeah, but,” responded Jenifer, “you’ve managed to get us through whatever has been thrown at us.”

“Indeed,” replied Stan. “But the money is running out. If my wallet takes another major hit, my brother David will have to take us back to Worcester, on his way back from Cornwall.”

“It won’t come to that,” said Jenifer confidently. “The only way is up from here.”

Christine placed a nice, hot mug of tea under Stan’s nose, as he waited for Bernard to return with the repaired tyres.

Chapter Eleven

Time seemed to be standing still as the luckless band of holidaymakers waited for the recovery truck to appear on the A338. Despite the advice, Christine was sitting in the front seat of the Zodiac, reading a newspaper she had purchased from the petrol station shop. Rob was leaning up against a telegraph pole smoking, with Barry and Jenifer deep in conversation by the caravan. Stan was pacing up and down the farm entrance with Penny on her lead. Stan found it difficult at such times to stand still, he needed to fidget.

At last, after another half an hour waiting, the group's spirits lifted as Bernard and his recovery truck came into view. It was just like watching the cavalry again.

In no time, Bernard had the two repaired wheels fitted. Betsy was as good as new again. After handshakes all round, Bernard jumped back into his recovery truck, leaving Stan and his guests ready for the off. Stan looked at his wristwatch; it was fast approaching three in the afternoon. Christine fussed around and instructed everyone to get in the Zodiac. Christine was desperate to get on their way.

“Unbelievably, we are now close to our destination,” announced a resolute Stan. “Everyone keep the faith. I am confident that Betsy is in good working order. I’ve checked all of the tyres to make sure they are all okay. Unless the road parts in front of us, I see no reason why we can’t get there this time.”

“You are wasting time with all of these noble speeches, Stan,” said an angry Christine. “Just get going, you’re squandering valuable time.”

Without further ado, Stan sparked Betsy into life and at last pulled away from the farm entrance.

The traffic was relatively light, so Stan made good progress, trying to drive as sympathetically as he could. He knew Betsy was a temperamental princess.

Once they reached the A31 junction, Stan became nervous.

“Keep a look out for the A338,” declared Stan. “It’s imperative that we get back on the A338, so we can find our camp site easily from that road.”

“Leave it to me,” replied a confident Christine. “I’m a good navigator!”

Stan looked across with anguish at Christine. If Christine thought she was a good navigator, then she was very much mistaken. Christine alone had probably got them lost over thirty times in the past, for one reason or another. Distraction being the main reason.

Now on a dual carriageway, at last Stan felt he could really make good progress. The weather was warm again today which had brought the midges out in force. To try and reduce the crust of insects on the windscreen, Stan activated Betsy's washer jets and windscreen wipers. The jet wasn't exactly reminiscent of an Icelandic geyser as the pitiful limp jet of water barely reached six inches up the screen. The first meeting of the wipers with the water was disastrous. The wipers smeared the crust of dead insects across both the driver's and passenger's field of view. Forward visibility was extremely vague to say the least.

Not happy with the state of the windscreen, Stan attempted repeat blasts of washer jet water. Slowly but surely, the windscreen field of vision began to clear.

"You should have cleared off those insects before we left the farm entrance," advised Christine, with her arms folded across her chest.

"Now you tell me," responded Stan rolling his eyes. "Just keep your eyes peeled for the A338 junction."

As the vehicle entered St Leonards, Christine was convinced that there was something wrong. Studying the map on her lap, she noticed that the A338 turning was way before St Leonards. They may have missed the turning during the windscreen clearing debacle.

"Stan, my dear," said Christine.

Stan braced himself for bad news. Christine was rarely this pleasant when opening a conversation.

"What's wrong?" asked Stan suspiciously.

"I think we've gone too far," continued Christine. "We should have turned off on the A338 before St Leonards according to my map."

"I thought I saw the junction back there," added Barry from the back seat.

"Why didn't you say something?" snapped Stan.

"Nobody usually listens to me," responded Barry.

"I will listen to you if you have anything useful to say," continued Stan, "instead of all that nonsense talk about football."

"That's exactly why I kept quiet," sulked Barry. "You never seem to take anything I say seriously."

"Look," interrupted Christine. "There, a sign with the A338 on it."

Stan reacted quickly and turned left. At first, Stan thought he had been directed down a leafy lane. Both sides of the roads were heavily populated with tall trees, looking like they were standing to attention as Stan passed them.

As they progressed along the minor road, the trees started to overhang the carriageway, forming a gracious arch above the road. However, the arch became lower and lower, as the top of the caravan started to clatter into the lower hanging branches.

"Steady on, you mad fool," nagged Christine.

"There's nothing I can do," responded Stan in a panic. "We'll just have to take it steady."

The low hanging branches continued to rattle against the roof of the caravan, reverberating as loud as a John Bonham drum solo at times.

Fortunately, within half a mile the tree arches gave way to a more open panorama. The scenery became far more appealing. The holidaymakers were sure that they were in the depths of the New Forest. The road cut through clearings, then transformed into deep, thick forest, lush with undergrowth.

Sadly, another quarter of a mile down the road, the tree arches returned, drumming on the caravan roof. Stan slowed down at this point. The last thing he wanted to do was to replace the caravan roof, or remove an errant tree trunk from the main bedroom.

The midge problem again reared its ugly head down this particular road. It must have been due to their location in the forest. Betsy's windscreen became thickly coated in insect debris, so Stan administered the washer jets. This time his luck was out. As the wiper arms swung into motion, the washer bottle must have been empty, as there was no water to be spread across the target area.

"Blast!" shouted an angry Stan. "We need to stop as soon as we can. I can barely see out of the windscreen."

Stan was literally in a blind panic. Not knowing the road, he was desperate to find a safe haven and get the windscreen cleaned.

Within two hundred yards, Rob who had thrust his head out of the open side window to assist with forward vision, spotted a turning to the right dead ahead.

"Stan, there's a turning ahead on the right," said Rob.

"How far?" asked Stan desperately.

“Couple of hundred yards,” responded Rob.

Stan pressed down his indicator stalk and signalled to turn right, desperate to get off the minor road. Crawling forward at a dangerously low speed, Betsy reached the turning.

When the Zodiac pulled into the turning, within thirty yards of the front of the car was a set of steel gates, adorned with a roll of nasty looking barbed wire. On the gates was a warning sign, white characters on a red background:

“PRIVATE PROPERTY — STRICTLY NO ADMITTANCE.”

“I wonder what’s behind those gates?” asked Stan.

“We aren’t here to spy,” replied a frustrated Christine. “Go and sort those wipers out.”

Stan couldn’t contain himself and walked up to the gates, trying to establish what was behind them.

“Stanley!” barked Christine. “Get back here, now, and sort out this windscreen.”

Stan immediately and sheepishly returned to the car. Reaching inside the driver’s door, Stan popped the bonnet, then propped it up using the bonnet stay.

Stan knew he had an abundance of water in the caravan, so briskly trotted to the caravan. Armed with water, a couple of cloths and some cleaning agent, Stan gave a cloth to Rob as he passed the back window of the car.

“Start cleaning the screen, mate,” requested Stan, “whilst I fill the screen wash bottle.”

Rob jumped at the chance of freedom from the Zodiac; if nothing else, it was a ciggie opportunity.

Stan and Rob beavered away at their tasks. With the windscreen clear and the washer bottle full, Stan and Rob returned to the car. Begrudgingly, Stan swung the car and caravan round the turn in, and back onto the minor road. He was still anxious to investigate what secrets lay behind the barbed wire.

Two miles down the minor road, Stan reached a T junction.

"Which way now?" asked Stan, desperate for Christine to give him instructions.

"What?" asked a surprised Christine, lifting her head out of the newspaper she was engulfed in.

"Which way do we turn?" requested Stan desperately.

"I don't know," replied Christine in a state of fluster. "How should I know?"

"Because you are the one with the map!" shouted Stan.

Christine guiltily lifted the map from the door pocket.

"Oh!" responded Christine. "You mean this one."

Stan snatched the map from Christine's grip. After a brief glance at the map, Stan decided to turn left.

As they progressed, once more, the tree canopy arched over the roadway. The drumming branches returned, performing their percussion acts on the tin roof of the caravan. Jenifer was so irritated by the clatters, she covered her ears with her palms.

As the thick tree population cleared to their left, ironically, Stan spotted the A338 within touching distance. So near yet so far. Stan had to press on, there was no opportunity to get on the A338 from their current location.

A mile down the road, the carriageway started to get very narrow, barely wide enough for one vehicle to pass safely, let alone two.

"I hope we don't meet anything coming the other way," said Barry breaking the tense silence of the car.

"Don't jinx it," replied Jenifer as she smacked Barry on the lower arm.

"I'm just saying," responded Barry, trying to defend himself.

But, as luck would have it, once again it wasn't their day. Ahead of them, coming in the opposite direction was a tractor pulling some farming equipment. There was no way that the two vehicles could pass each other at this point.

As the tractor pulled up in front of Stan, it appeared to fill the entire road. The tractor driver jumped out of the cab and approached the Zodiac.

"Morning," said the farmer. "Nice day for it."

"For what?" asked an irritated Stan.

"For you to back up and let me pass," replied the farmer assertively.

"I can't back up," responded Stan. "I'm towing a caravan and I don't know the road."

"Well," continued the farmer. "I'm towing a seed planter, and my rig is bigger than yours."

Stan and the farmer exchanged childish banter for a further minute or so. Eventually, Christine reached her limit with the exchange.

"I'll make you a nice cup of tea if you back up," suggested Christine to the farmer.

Being a sucker for a nice mug of tea, the farmer soon crumbled.

"Deal," said the farmer. "In any case, I only have to back up thirty yards. The entrance to my top field is only back there. You would have to have backed up nearly five hundred yards."

Stan was astonished at the stance the farmer had taken, now knowing that he had been holding the trump card.

The farmer jumped back in his cab and reversed the thirty yards to his field entrance. Stan crept forward, keeping just a few feet between Betsy and the tractor. As the farmer reversed into the wide gateway, Stan pressed the accelerator hard and sped off.

"Where's my cup of tea?" berated the farmer, waving his clenched fist angrily above his head.

"At last, a win!" said a jubilant Stan as he sped down the minor road.

"You're just a selfish beast at times, Stanley," replied an unimpressed Christine. "I promised that nice man a cup of tea."

"Nice man!" snapped Stan. "He was just playing with me. He knew exactly who had to back up the shortest distance. He was just making sure he humiliated me. Anyway, enough of that. Just get your head in that map and get us on the A338."

Stan steered the Zodiac for a few more miles down the minor road. They didn't seem to be making headway, as the road meandered in and out of heavily forested areas, narrowing to a slither at times.

Gradually, it appeared that civilisation wasn't too far away. Grand, expensive mansions and houses in ample grounds popped up on both sides of the road. It looked like they had stumbled upon the local millionaire's row.

A further half a mile down the road, Stan spotted a roundabout in the near distance.

"Look for the A338 to Ringwood," said Stan desperate to get back on track.

As they approached the roundabout, Christine spotted the signpost that Stan was desperate to find.

"There you go," shouted a jubilant Christine. "The A338 to Ringwood."

Stan followed the sign. It took them back on the A31, exactly in the same place as they found themselves nearly an hour ago. They had just driven in one big circle.

Within two minutes, Jenifer leapt forward in the back seat.

"Look, A338 to Christchurch," screamed a proud Jenifer.

At last, back on track. Stan peeled off left with a huge smile on his face. They were nearly there, could it be that they would overcome all the odds and actually find the caravan park.

Twenty minutes later, with no more obstacles, breakdowns, or emergencies to tackle, Stan pulled up at their final destination. Nearly taking out the overhead sign with the caravan, Stan pulled up in the marked bay close to the site office.

A huge cheer rang out from Betsy.

"I'll go and check us in," said a totally relieved Stan. "Just wait here, I don't want people wandering off."

"I'm just going to have a quick smoke," said Rob, jumping out the back seat.

"I need the loo," added Barry, also leaping out of the back seat.

"Me to," said Jenifer, closely following Barry.

"Christine looked at Penny who was sitting alone on the back seat, wagging her tail gently.

"Just me and you girl," said Christine, patting Penny's head gently.

Stan approached the reception area within the office for new arrivals. A smartly dressed lady got up from her desk to attend to Stan.

"Good evening," said the lady. "I'm Anna, welcome to Christchurch Caravan Park, formerly known as Home Farm. How can I help you?"

"Good evening," replied Stan politely, looking at his wristwatch to confirm it was evening. "Stan Spencer here, I have a booking."

Anna ran her finger down the list of names in the booking ledger. Finding the booking, she looked up with a look of surprise.

"You were booked in for last Friday," stated Anna. "That's nearly a week ago. I think we have given your pitch away to passing trade. I need to check."

"Anna walked over to the site map behind her. It was populated with different coloured cards, with the name on the booking and length of stay displayed on the cards. Anna scoured the map for some time, making sure she reconfirmed her suspicions.

"As I thought," said Anna returning to the counter. "We assumed you weren't honouring your booking, so we've given your pitch to the Campbell's. They arrived on Tuesday without a booking."

"You can't do that!" exclaimed Stan. "My wife, Christine, has been on the phone to you many times. Telling you that we will be arriving late. You can't just give out pitch away.!"

"Let me check," said Anna. "I'll have a chat with the other girls."

Anna turned away and headed for a group of ladies, sitting at desks at the back of the office. After a few minutes' consultation, Anna returned holding a bunch of handwritten notes.

"I have your case notes here," declared Anna showing Stan the handwritten notes.

"Case notes?" asked Stan firmly. "We are here for a holiday, not to have my tonsils out!"

Anna smiled and ignored Stan's attempted humorous response.

"The last we heard from you was Tuesday," added Anna. "As we didn't hear from you again, we assumed you had given up and gone home."

"Outrageous!" said an angry Stan. "I demand you give us our pitch, immediately."

"Please don't lose your temper, Mr Spencer," replied Anna assertively. "I will ask you to leave if you carry on in this way."

Stan calmed himself down. Clearly, he had to be in control of himself right now.

"I apologise," said Stan. "It's been a trying week, to say the least. Is there any way you can accommodate us?"

Anna returned to the site map to investigate. A few minutes later Anna returned.

"We have one pitch for tonight I can let you have," replied Anna. "But the Gandy family have it booked for a week from tomorrow."

"That's a start," responded a relieved Stan. "Where is the pitch? Do you have a site map I can have?"

"Certainly," replied the helpful Anna.

Anna fetched a site map for Stan, drawing the route to follow on the site map with a red biro.

"Just follow that line," continued Anna. "You are to set up on pitch number thirteen. It's down by the river."

"That's great," responded Stan. "Thank you so much for all of your help and understanding."

"That's fine," replied Anna. "By the way. Do you have a Mr Rob Williams in your party?"

"I'm not sure?" said Stan. "We have someone called Rob with us, but I don't know his surname. Let me check."

Stan wandered out to the car and peered inside the driver's window.

"What's Rob's surname?" asked Stan.

"What?" replied Christine. "All this time and you don't know his name?"

"What is it?" asked Stan again impatiently.

"It's Williams," responded Christine.

Stan saluted at Christine and rushed back into the office, where Anna was still waiting.

"Yes," panted Stan. "We have a Mr Rob Williams in our group. Why do you need to know?"

"We have an urgent message for him," responded Anna handing Stan a piece of paper with a handwritten message on it.

Stan looked at the piece of paper, it read:

'Urgent, Mr Rob Williams to contact his father at home as soon as possible.'

Stan was intrigued. What was going on at home? Had someone been taken ill, or worse. Had a family pet passed away? Why would Rob's family take the trouble of getting in touch with the caravan site?

"I'll make sure he gets it," said a reassuring Stan leaving the office.

"Have a great time!" yelled Anna as Stan just went out of earshot. "We will discuss further plans tomorrow about where you set up your caravan."

Stan walked over to Betsy and jumped in. Stan handed the note to Christine.

"What do you think of that?" asked Stan.

Christine unfolded the paper and digested the contents.

"Interesting," said Christine. "I wonder what's going on? Maybe someone has be taken ill? Or worse?"

"Exactly what I thought," replied Stan, pleased to be on the same page as Christine.

Christine smacked Stan gently on the arm.

"You are morbid," yelled Christine.

"You thought the same as me!" exclaimed Stan.

"That's different," snapped Christine. "You always think the worst of a situation, Stanley."

Stan rolled his eyes in disbelief.

"Have you given the note to Rob yet?" quizzed Christine.

"I haven't had chance," replied Stan in frustration. "You've literally just watched me come out of the office with the message. I'm not a psychic. I can't transmit the message to Rob using just my mind."

Christine smacked Stan again.

"Don't be ridiculous," responded an agitated Christine. "Stop messing about and give the note to Rob. I'm dying to know what his business at home is about."

Spotting Rob walking out of the phone box next to the office in his side mirror, Stan jumped out of the Zodiac to deliver the note to Rob.

"You need to go back in," said Stan, handing the note across to Rob.

"Go back in where?" asked Rob taking the paper from Stan.

Rob unfolded the note and read the contents.

"You need to phone home, urgently," stated Stan. "Have you got enough change?"

Rob checked his jeans pockets. He had two ten pence pieces. Stan also checked his pockets and handed Rob another two ten pence pieces.

"Thank you," said Rob, surprised that Stan had given up twenty pence without a fight. "I'll go and phone right away."

Rob turned around and jogged the short distance back to the phone box. Once inside, he urgently dialled his home phone number. His father picked up the phone.

"Hello," said Graham.

"It's me," replied Rob. "I got a message to contact home urgently. What's wrong?"

"Ah, number one son," responded Graham. "Are you having a nice time?"

"Not really," snapped Rob. "Why do you want me to ring home urgently? What's going on?"

"Why aren't you having a nice time?" asked Graham. "The weather has been gorgeous. You aren't at school, so why aren't you having the time of your life?"

"Because," responded Rob, getting more and more frustrated as he couldn't get to the heart of the matter.

"Because what?" quizzed Graham.

"Because we keep breaking down," replied an agitated Rob.

"Keep breaking down?" asked Graham.

"Look!" snapped Rob. "If you keep repeating me, we aren't going to discuss what the real issue is here, are we."

"I told you that Zodiac was an unreliable rust bucket," added Graham. "What did I tell you? I said that car would never make it all the way to Christchurch. Didn't I."

"Yes, you did," admitted Rob "Now why did you want me to call urgently?"

Before Graham could answer, the pips went on the line. So, Rob shovelled in a ten pence piece to keep the phone call alive.

"Are you still there?" asked Rob.

"Yes," replied Graham. "Are you?"

Rob rolled his eyes in exasperation.

“So, what did you want?” quizzed Rob.

“Hang on,” responded Graham. “Before we go in to all that, where did you break down?”

“I haven’t got much money,” responded an irritated Rob. “Why did you want me to phone you?”

“You’ve run out of money?” asked Graham. “Is that why you are in a mood with me? Do you want me to send you some?

“No, I haven’t run out of money,” responded Rob. “I just don’t have much change for the phone box. Now, what do you have to tell me?”

“Right,” said Graham.

Again, before Graham could spill the beans, the pips on the line went off again. Rob quickly inserted another coin.

“These ten pence pieces don’t last long,” said Graham. “It must be because you are calling from Dorset.”

“Enough of all that!” snarled an angry Rob. “What is going on at home that is so important!”

“Right,” added Graham. “Your sports master from school has been up to the house.”

“Up to the house?” asked Rob. “Why would he come up to the house? Term is over. What did he want?”

“It is the first eleven versus the old boys cricket match,” continued Graham. “The day after tomorrow. It’s the yearly event, I remember you played in the fixture last year, and took a couple of wickets.”

"What has that got to do with me?" quizzed Rob. "I told the teachers that I was away on holiday and can't play."

"It appears that circumstances have changed," continued Graham. "Apparently, both of the first choice opening bowlers have got themselves injured and can't play. With one of the second choice bowlers on holiday in Spain, the school are adamant that you return from Dorset and play in the fixture. Without you they have no bowling attack."

"You are kidding me?" scowled Rob. "There has to be someone else?"

"Apparently not," responded Graham. "And there is more."

As Graham delivered his commentary, the pips went off on the line again. Rob desperately fed another coin into the slot.

"What more?" asked Rob.

"Your sports master said," continued Graham, "that if you don't come back and play, they will suspend you from school for a month at the start of the autumn term. Plus, you will be banned from playing football and rugby for three months at school."

"They can't do that to me!" exclaimed Rob down the phone.

"Apparently, they can," responded Graham. "That's why I have agreed to come and pick you up tomorrow night. I'll be there at about eight in the evening. Just make sure you are ready."

“This is a nightmare,” said a distraught Rob. “Why me? I’m not really that good a bowler.”

“They seem to think so,” replied Graham. “Make sure you are ready to leave straight away. I don’t want to be hanging around. See you tomorrow.”

After a click on the line, all Rob could hear was the dull buzz of a dialling tone in the phone receiver. His father had hung up.

Rob threw open the phone box door and instantly lit a cigarette. He couldn’t believe his luck. It had taken the best part of six days to arrive. Now this.

After smoking his cigarette, Rob threw his fag butt to the floor and screwed his foot over the top of it. Looking up to try and find the Zodiac, all Rob could see was an empty parking space where the Zodiac had been parked up when he went to the phone box.

“Great,” said Rob to himself.

Rob walked into the reception area of the office to try and find out the whereabouts of Betsy. After the helpful Anna had explained, Rob walked the two hundred yards to pitch thirteen.

Jenifer spotted Rob and ran up to him with a concerned look on her face.

“Is everything okay at home?” asked a concerned Jenifer.

“Yes, no problem,” replied Rob. “It’s nothing really.”

“Nothing?” exclaimed Jenifer. “Then why did you have to call home urgently if it was nothing?”

"School," responded Rob bluntly.

"School?" responded a disbelieving Jenifer. "School has finished for the term, why on earth would you have to phone home urgently because of school? Are you fibbing to me?"

"No, I'm not," replied Rob. "There is a traditional end of term cricket match every year. The cricket first eleven take on a team of Grammar School old boys. They rotate who plays at home each year. Allegedly, two of the main bowlers are injured so can't play. Another possible replacement is on holiday in Spain, so he can't play. Apparently, I am a last resort."

"You and your cricket," replied Jenifer. "You know it's the main reason Fiona wanted to break up with you?"

"Her choice," responded Rob abruptly. "She knew what she was taking on. I was sports mad long before I met Fiona."

"In any case," continued Jenifer, "just don't turn up. If you stay here with us, it's not like they can do much about it."

"There's more," added Rob. "If I don't play, they have threatened to suspend me at the start of next term. Plus, they will ban me from playing sports for three months."

"They can't do that," responded a surprised Jenifer, "can they?"

"It's a grammar school," replied a resigned Rob. "I guess they can do what they want."

"You can't play, in any case," said Jenifer.

"Why not?" quizzed Rob.

"Because you are here, and the match is in Worcester," responded Jenifer.

"My dad is coming to pick me up," continued Rob. "He will be here around eight o'clock tomorrow evening."

"Really?" asked Jenifer, hardly believing what Rob was saying.

"Really," responded a dejected Rob.

"I had better tell my mum," said Jenifer. "She will be devastated. First Fiona, then you. Her dreams of you and Fiona getting back together are crumbling fast."

"It was never going to happen," admitted Rob.

"I know," replied Jenifer as she coyly winked at Rob. "But we all know we have to play along with her games."

Barry arrived on scene just as Jenifer had coyly winked at Rob, getting entirely the wrong impression regarding the subject matter of the conversation.

"What's going on?" asked a jealous Barry as he took a position between Jenifer and Rob, facing his back to Rob.

Rob took a couple of steps back and lit a cigarette.

"Not a lot," said Jenifer. "Just discussing why he has to go home tomorrow with Rob."

Barry's face lit up.

"Oh no, you have to go home tomorrow?" added Barry sarcastically. "That's a shame. Why have you got to go home? Are you missing your mummy too much?"

"I have to play cricket for the school on Sunday," stated Rob.

"Cricket?" responded Barry. "That's not a real man's game. All that padding. I don't even wear shin pads when I play football. That's a proper man's game."

Not wanting to get involved in some petty jealous banter, Rob walked off. Rob wanted to make one more phone call today, so set off back to the site phone box.

News quickly filtered through to Stan and Christine about Rob's pending departure. Christine was not thrilled. With all the commotion of the journey down to Christchurch, she had barely had a chance to get her talons into Rob. In Christine's opinion, Fiona and Rob as an item was still a possibility.

"Enough of all this news," stated Stan. "Let's get that awning up and the comfy chairs out. It's time to start the holiday."

Stan unhitched the Zodiac from the caravan and started to empty the contents of the boot. It was time to justify bringing all of the equipment with him.

It was a pretty good pitch. The river Stour flowed gently behind the caravan, meandering its way towards the sea, littered with wildfowl and the odd swan.

Christine was in charge of sorting the caravan interior. She could almost be heard barking her orders at Jenifer from the site office, such was the ferocity of the commands. Everything had to be just so.

Jenifer poked her head out of the caravan door, about to shake the dust from a bedsheet. Scanning around, Jenifer suddenly came over quite nervous.

"Who's got Penny?" asked Jenifer. "I haven't seen her in a while."

Stan dropped the holdall he was carrying from Betsy on the floor.

"I haven't seen her in a while," added Stan. "Go and check with your mother."

Jenifer scurried into the caravan.

Chapter Twelve

Thank goodness! Penny had not taken herself away on a solo adventure, she was curled up on Jenifer's bed in the small bedroom in the caravan. The hustle and bustle evident during the arrival process was proving to be too much for the sensitive pet.

"We only have this pitch for one night," announced Stan. "They had cancelled our booking as we were so late. This isn't actually the pitch we booked, but Anna in the office kindly let us stay here for the night."

"So, what are we going to do tomorrow night?" asked a concerned Christine.

"I will go and speak with Anna," replied Stan. "As a first night treat, I'm going to treat everyone to a chippy tea, so on my way to the chippy, I will drop in on Anna and negotiate."

"Don't you go losing your temper with her, Stanley!" warned a concerned Christine. "Your objective is to keep us on site for at least two nights."

"Why only two nights?" enquired Barry.

"Stan has to go to work on Monday," responded Christine. "He needs to keep a week's holiday back for summer camp."

"Well, it's summer now," added a confused Barry.

"Not this trip," said Christine. "We go away for a week with the youth club."

"Oh, I see," responded Barry. "So, we all have to go back on Sunday?"

"You can stay if you want to," replied Stan. "But you will need to find somewhere to stay and a means to get yourself home. Betsy, the caravan and I are going home on Sunday."

"All this effort and hardship for two nights?" added Barry. "Was it really worth it."

"Your call," replied Stan. "Anyway, I'm off to see Anna now, then fetch the chippy tea. I'll just get five potions of fish and chips."

Stan jumped inside Betsy and crawled his way up the sloping gravel road, towards the office.

In the office, without losing his temper, Stan managed to persuade Anna to leave them on pitch 13. Anna had contacted the Gandy family, explaining the battles that Stan had gone through. So, the Gandy's, being reasonable and friendly folk, agreed to park their caravan on pitch number seventeen. Stan was delighted. At last, the gods seemed to be with him.

Christine and Jenifer prepared the dining table for the arrival of the chippy tea. Salt, pepper, malt vinegar, tomato ketchup and half a loaf of buttered bread. It was going to be a feast. Everyone on the trip was totally taken by surprise when Stan offered to buy a chippy tea. Maybe he was carrying guilt, down to the failings of

Betsy and the caravan sub-frame. But at least they were here now, and the sun was still shing brightly.

Stan drew up to the side of the caravan nearly an hour later. Huffing and puffing about the enormous queue in the chip shop, Stan finally delivered the large brown paper bag full of chippy teas to Christine.

In fairness, the quality of the food was excellent. In mid-feast, Stan tried to engage the party with an activity conversation.

"As it's Rob's last day with us tomorrow," said Stan, "where do you fancy going?"

"Beach!" exclaimed Jenifer. "Bournemouth beach."

"Same," added Barry.

"Not bothered," said Christine.

"Me neither," said Rob.

"Bournemouth beach it is then," announced Stan. "We need to leave reasonably early, as Rob needs to be back here at eight, for his lift home."

"Can't he make his own way here?" asked Barry. "I think we should stay in Bournemouth until late tomorrow."

"Don't be so selfish," said Jenifer, slapping Barry on his left arm.

Barry cowered back and rubbed his arm, not best pleased to see Jenifer coming to Rob's defence again.

"What is it with you and Rob?" sniped Barry. "Have you two got something going on in secret? It's not like Rob has a girlfriend."

Jenifer smacked Barry's arm again, increasing the power a notch.

"How dare you!" shouted Jenifer. "We are just good friends. If you can't handle that, then I'm not sure we have a future together."

Jenifer clambered over the soft furnishings that surrounded the dining table, grabbed Penny and her lead, then stormed out of the caravan.

"Wait!" yelled a distressed Barry, clambering after Jenifer. Barry still managed to glance over to Rob as he clambered, cutting him the meanest look he could muster.

"I don't know," said Christine. "Those two love birds, what are they like."

"Annoying," responded Stan. "Always at each other's throats. It more like a roller coaster of emotions, rather than a platonic relationship. Rob sticking his oar in now and then doesn't help matters."

"What?" said an angry Rob. "I haven't done a thing. It's Barry, he gets jealous at the drop of a hat. He needs to realise that he has a great girlfriend who he can trust implicitly. If he didn't get so jealous, the relationship would run a lot smoother."

"I agree," added Christine. "He does drop the 'J' bomb all the time."

"'J' bomb?" quizzed a confused Stan. "What on earth is a 'J' bomb?"

"J is for jealous," snapped Christine. "Oh, do keep up Stan."

"What is the bomb part of it then?" requested Stan.

"It's just a figure of speech," replied a frustrated Christine. "Nobody is dropping bombs as such. It's what the kids say these days."

Stan, not impressed with the dropping of any type of bombs, cut out of the conversation and returned his devout attentions to the delicious chippy tea.

"So, Rob, why haven't you got a girlfriend?" asked Christine seeing an opportunity to matchmake. "Are you still holding out for Fiona?"

"No, I'm not holding out for Fiona," replied Rob firmly. "That ship has sailed for both of us. We had a 'clear the air' chat in Cheltenham, both agreeing that we would continue the holiday as just mates. Fiona has a new boyfriend now, plus, I have been working on someone."

"Who?" asked an intrigued Christine.

"Time will tell," responded Rob, tapping his index finger on the side of his nose.

"Anyone I know?" quizzed Christine, now in full interrogation mode.

"Maybe," replied Rob, not trying to give too much away.

"Come on, who is it?" asked Christine, increasing the volume a couple of notches.

"You'll see, soon," replied Rob.

"Leave him be," interrupted Stan. "Can't you see he doesn't want to talk about it."

"Well, I do," snapped Christine.

"I've finished my chippy tea," declared Rob. "I'm off for a smoke and to make a phone call."

"To your girlfriend?" asked Christine, grinning from ear to ear.

Rob turned his head and winked at Christine as he walked out of the caravan door.

As the sun began to dip beyond the distant range of hills, Christine cleared up the chippy tea debris, Stan retired outside to his comfy recliner to watch the world go by, and Rob was listening to music on his Walkman, having returned from making his secretive phone call. Still no sign of Barry and Jenifer. Everyone assumed they were either in the middle of a heart-to-heart conversation, belting two bells out of each other, or just taking Penny for a long walk.

When Christine had finished her tidying up, she joined Stan in the comfy recliner zone.

Forty minutes of peaceful bliss was broken, as Barry and Jenifer returned to the pitch holding hands. This was a good sign. Barry walked across to Rob who was lying on the grass, listening to Led Zeppelin though headphones. Barry tapped Rob on the shoulder, who jumped in surprise following the disturbance. Rob removed his headphones.

"I'm sorry, mate," said Barry, offering his hand for a ceasefire handshake. "I'm just being a bit daft. I get a bit jealous. I don't know why. Please accept my apology."

Rob shook Barry's outstretched hand.

"No worries," replied Rob. "No need to worry about me. Jenifer and I are just good mates. I'm almost considered part of her family."

"No, you are not," butted in Stan.

"No hard feelings?" added Barry.

"None, apology accepted," replied Rob.

Christine sat back in her comfy recliner with a smile on her face and a warm feeling inside.

With everything patched up, everyone started to consider retiring for the night. It had been another long and eventful day. The constant crisis navigation was really starting to take its toll on the hapless holidaymakers. But at least they had some interesting stories to share when they returned home.

After Stan had pinned an 'out of bounds' notice on Betsy, Rob was resigned to another night in the awning, listening to another one of Barry's solo symphonies. At least it was for just one more night. Rob decided to sleep with his Walkman playing in an attempt to drown out the droning.

Friday morning, yet another sunny summer's day, as the sun rose in a clear azure blue sky. Stan had been up a while, checking Betsy's washer bottle and radiator levels, not wanting to be caught out again.

Christine had made toast for breakfast and was part way through making up a loaf of sandwiches for the beach. Jenifer was still in her bedroom fast asleep, Barry was still snoring in the awning, whilst Rob was nowhere to be seen. He was at the phone box again, trying to contact his mystery lady.

Stan walked into the caravan to see what the state of play was.

"Where is everyone?" asked a disappointed Stan. "We need to get going soon. That beach will fill up in no time, we need to get going, otherwise we will be parking miles from the sea."

Stan walked into the awning and kicked Barry's camp bed. Barry woke with a jolt.

"Oh, I'm terribly sorry," said Stan. "I didn't wake you up, did I?"

A half asleep Barry rubbed his eyes and sat up in his sleeping bag.

After successfully waking Barry, Stan wandered back into the caravan, banging on the small bedroom door to get Jenifer out of her pit.

"Come on, wakey-wakey," shouted Stan. "We're off soon. Get out of bed."

An unimpressed Jenifer rolled over, pulling the continental quilt up over her head, to block out the light.

Stan returned to the kitchen area.

"Where's Rob?" asked Stan.

"Phone box," replied Christine with her mouth half full of toast. "Talking to his girlfriend I suspect."

"He's never around when you need him," complained Stan. "We need to get ready, and pronto."

Stan stormed out of the caravan and started to pack the car ready for the beach.

A full hour later, Stan had managed to get the group assembled in Betsy. Stan adjusted his rear-view mirror. He was amazed at the sight that greeted him.

In the back seat, Barry, Jenifer and Rob were sitting with an inflatable green alligator, a pink and cream rubber ring, a blue and white rubber ring, and an inflatable swan. The scene through Stan's rear view mirror resembled a blow up safari park, giving him no rear view visibility whatsoever.

"Why on earth have you inflated those toys now?" asked a bemused Stan. "Why not wait until we get to the beach?"

"It's my idea," responded Barry confidently. "It will save us time. Plus, we won't get sand in our mouths when we blow them up."

"So, how am I supposed to see what's behind me through my rear-view mirror?" asked Stan.

"Use the mirrors on the doors," responded Jenifer. "At least you haven't got the caravan behind you."

"Just take the air out of them." ordered Stan. "I need to use my rear-view mirror."

The three rebels on the back seat remained unmoved in silence, none wanting to deflate the inflatables.

"I can sit here all day if you want me to!" said an irate Stan. "There'll be no beach from anyone."

There was still no reaction or movement from the back seat.

Stan turned Betsy's engine off, folded his arms across his chest and sat back in the driver's seat.

"Come on, Stan!" said Christine sternly. "We haven't got all day. Remember, it's Rob's last day, let's get going."

Stan sat motionless for a few more minutes before he cracked. Casting an angry look into his rear-view mirror, Stan started Betsy's engine.

Christine unfolded a local map on her lap as Stan reversed onto the grave track.

It was only a four mile journey to Bournemouth from where they were caravanning. The route would take them along the Boscombe Road, which ran alongside the sea. Noting that there were not many free parking spaces when they arrived at Boscombe Beach, Stan made the call to pull over and park up.

"What are you doing, Dad?" screamed Jenifer from the back seat. "We are nowhere near Bournemouth yet."

"Look how busy it is!" replied Stan. "You can bet your bottom dollar there will be no parking near Bournemouth beach. It's a beautiful sunny day and it's the first week of the Midlands holidays."

Reluctantly, the group started to pile out of the car. Extraction from the back seat was extremely difficult. The multitude of inflatable toys filled the space making the slightest of moves difficult. Eventually, the holidaymakers accessed the beach via the wooden steps located a few yards in front of Betsy. Once at the top of the dunes the beach and sea came into full view. There was a light breeze coming of the flat calm sea.

"Beautiful!" declared Christine. "All those mishaps on the way were worth it."

"Really?" responded Barry. "I would have preferred to come straight here."

"You know what I mean," snapped Christine.

The group made their way down the crowded beach, trying to find a suitable spot close to the sea, but not too far from the amenities.

Barry and Jenifer grabbed an inflatable each and ran towards the sea. Rob lit a cigarette and sat himself down on his towel. It was still a bit early in the day for Rob to go in the sea. The water would still be a bit too cold.

The holidaymakers enjoyed a fabulous morning on the beach. Barry and Jenifer spent most of their time in the water. Christine joined them for an occasional paddle. Stan confined himself under his trusty parasol. Stan was not a great fan of the sun. His skin type was not suited to sunbathing. Stan went as red as a cherry if he exposed himself to the sun for more than fifteen minutes. So, wearing his favourite floppy hat, Stan buried his head in car magazines for the majority of the morning.

Christine announced that it was lunch time and started to lay out the picnic on their light and dark blue chequered blanket. It was a mighty feast. Sandwiches, sausage rolls, pork pies, salad, the variety of food on offer was endless.

As the group set about demolishing the beach banquet, Jenifer was keeping a beady eye on Barry. True to form, every time a bikini clad beauty walked past, Barry's adoring eyes followed, time after time. When the twentieth lady walked past the picnic, Jenifer flipped.

"That's it, I've had enough!" declared a distraught Jenifer looking towards Barry. "You just can't keep your eyes to yourself, can you!"

Jenifer grabbed her towel and flip flops, wrapped the towel around herself and stormed off.

Barry jumped up immediately to try and remedy the situation.

"Don't bother following me!" scowled Jenifer as she increased her pace to a trot.

Barry still maintained the pursuit, kicking sand up behind him as he desperately tried to get traction in the sand to make up ground.

"Do they ever stop arguing?" asked Stan.

"I'll go after her," said Christine, struggling to get up off the sand with any form of dignity.

"Fabulous last day?" said Stan. "I bet you are really glad you came."

"It's been a trip with a difference," replied a smiling Rob. "At least I know how to fit a rod between the oil pump and distributor of a Zodiac."

"I'll have you in a Zodiac if it's the last thing I do," added Stan.

"Absolutely no chance," responded Rob. "I'd rather ride a push bike. Plus, it's a lot faster than a Zodiac."

Stan smiled, enjoying the banter with Rob.

Two and a half car magazines and nine cigarettes later, Christine, Barry and Jenifer appeared, walking down from the sand dune path. Christine was holding two cups of coffee.

When Christine reached the pitch on the beach, she handed the coffee's to Stan and Rob.

"Thanks," said Stan and Rob in unison.

"Where have you been?" asked Stan as he looked at Christine. "You've been gone ages."

"It's you daughter," replied Christine. "She's a feisty one. We were pretty much at Bournemouth pier when we persuaded her to stop and turn around. I'm pooped. It's hard work walking on that sand."

"What's wrong with her now?" quizzed Stan.

"It's Barry's wandering eye I think," replied Christine. "I think our Jenifer has had enough of it now."

"Looking never hurt anyone," responded Stan. "What's the harm in window shopping?"

"Every waking hour?" replied Christine. "Once in a while maybe, but not all the time."

Stan shrugged his shoulders and returned to his car magazines.

“Stanley!” said an animated Christine.

Stan lifted his head in surprise.

“There was plenty of parking near Bournemouth pier,” continued Christine. “So, why have you pitched us miles away from the pier, in the middle of nowhere?”

“How was I to know?” replied Stan.

“You just can’t be bothered to check,” continued Christine. “Next time, we go all the way to Bournemouth, got it!”

The remainder of the day on the beach went without further incident. Barry barely lifted his chin up off his chest, determined to avoid the wrath of his girlfriend. Rob managed to get through a packet and a half of cigarettes, with Stan managing to read all of his car magazines. After a final paddle, Christine hinted to Stan that she was ready for the off.

“It’s gone six,” said Christine. “Less than two hours until Rob’s father arrives to collect him. We probably need to get going.”

Stan was up in a shot. He bolted out of his deckchair as if a starting pistol had gone off. The beach was not Stan’s favourite place. The sun, the pesky sand that gets everywhere, the cold water. Give Stan a motor museum any day of the week.

“Make sure you deflate all of those toys,” requested Stan, trying to guarantee vision through his rear-view mirror. “There’s no time to be saved deflating them back at the caravan.”

Barry and Jenifer took the deflating responsibilities, jumping on the animals and rubber rings to speed up the process. With all hands to the deck, their space on the beach was soon clear as they all made their way back to the Zodiac.

"Don't get any sand in the car!" commanded Stan as he opened the car boot. "I've spent hours getting Betsy in pristine condition. That sand gets everywhere and it's a beggar to hoover out."

Everyone made doubly sure they bashed as much sand off their person as possible. Locking horns with Stan over sand in the car was not the best of ideas. Stan had extra gears when it came to protecting his pride and joy.

With everyone sat in their respective seats, Stan turned the ignition key to start Betsy. She cranked over but didn't spark into life. There was a slight odour of petrol in the air. Stan tried again without success, and the stench of petrol grew stronger.

"You've flooded her I reckon," suggested Barry from the back seat.

Stan tried again, nothing.

"Can you smell that fuel?" asked Barry from the back seat. "You've definitely flooded her."

Stan turned and looked at Barry. Stan was furious and Barry wasn't helping the situation. After a single headbutt of the steering wheel, Stan popped the bonnet and went to investigate. Barry opened the nearside rear door.

“You stay inside!” commanded Stan. “I’ll sort this myself.”

Barry sheepishly jumped back in the car, smartish.

Stan took a cloth and an aerosol can to the front of the car. His activity was blocked by the raised bonnet, so the onlooking expectant ‘experts’ were unable to comment on proceedings.

After ten minutes of tinkering and the bonnet still open, Stan returned to try and start the engine. Two attempted turns of the ignition key proved fruitless, so Stan returned to the front end of the car.

With a couple of magic, well directed squirts from the aerosol can, Stan attempted to start the engine again.

Success! Betsy boomed into life as her engine roar filled the air. It was smiles all round. Stan closed the bonnet and returned to the driver’s seat.

“If you don’t sell this car when we get back to Worcester,” said an angry Christine, “Then you will be finding another wife. And I’m not joking.”

“She’s just a bit temperamental at times,” responded Stan. “Just like your daughters. You don’t threaten to leave me when they start playing up.”

“We don’t rely on them to get us from A to B, do we,” replied Christine.

Taking little notice of Christine’s latest barrage of complaints, Stan pulled out and headed back to the caravan park.

The beachgoers arrived back at the caravan park at ten minutes to seven. Rob ran up to office to check if his father had arrived yet, but the office hadn't seen him as such.

Christine decided to cook hot dogs for tea, so that Rob's father could join them for a snack before the drive home. She figured Rob's dad was more likely to stop and eat if she provided finger food, hence the hot dog decision.

Rob had already packed his bag. Travelling light, it took just over five minutes to stuff his crumpled clothes into his Adidas holdall.

"I bet you can't wait to get away from this madhouse?" asked Jenifer, sitting down next to Rob. "I don't blame you if you are in a rush to get off. I would be."

"I'm torn," replied Rob. "You guys are nice people and always make me feel welcome. Well, most do."

Rob looked across at Barry who was staring across at Rob and Jenifer's chat with jealous eyes.

Just as Barry was on high alert to spring forward to split up the cosy chat, Rob's father came slowly down the gravel track towards pitch thirteen.

Rob got up to greet his father. To his great surprise, there was a passenger sat in the front seat next to Rob's dad. It was Ruth. The girl that Rob had been phoning constantly, trying to get her to go out with him.

Graham and Ruth stepped out of the car. Ruth was wearing a fashionable blue denim jacket and a short blue denim mini skirt. Rob looked across at Ruth with approving eyes.

"You're a sight for sore eyes," said Rob to Ruth, placing a gentle kiss on her left cheek. "What are you doing here?"

"You convinced me to come down and pick you up," replied Ruth. "Just to keep your dad company. Don't read too much into it."

Rob laughed and gave Ruth a small hug.

"I've cooked hot dogs!" announced Christine. "Come and join us. Have something to eat before you set off back to Worcester."

Ruth and Graham smiled and walked into the caravan awning, not wanting to decline Christine's polite invitation. Christine had set up a table and some chairs in the awning, throwing Barry's bed and belongings unceremoniously behind the caravan to create more room.

"How was the journey down?" asked Christine.

"No problem at all," replied Graham looking at his wristwatch. "Took us about two and a half hours. We had a bit of a delay at Downton."

"It took us over six days," responded Barry in a very sarcastic tone. "You must have broken the sound barrier on your way down."

Graham smiled.

"What happened?" asked Graham. "Why did it take so long to get here?"

"I'll explain on the way back," added Rob. "I think we've all had enough of the tales of woe for now."

As the conversation developed, Christine couldn't take her eyes off Ruth. Christine knew Ruth from the youth club she helped out at in Worcester, she was one of the girls who use to attend the Friday Youth Club.

"So, what brings you to sunny Christchurch?" asked Christine, unable to contain her emotions any longer.

"I've come to meet Rob," replied Ruth calmly.

"How did you know Rob was here?" quizzed Christine.

"He's been phoning me all week," responded Ruth. "Bless him, he must have spent a small fortune on phone calls."

"Has he?" replied Christine as she glared across at Rob.

This was not what Christine had planned. Her main task for the week was to work on Rob and get him back together with Fiona. The arrival of this more than real threat to her plans just wasn't good enough.

"So, are you two an item?" asked Jenifer, sensing her mother needed back-up.

"Maybe," replied Rob. "It just depends on Ruth."

Ruth bowed her head with embarrassment. Being forced into the spotlight was making her feel uneasy.

"You won't see him much at weekends," continued Jenifer, on the offensive. "He'll be playing football in the winter, and cricket in the summer. You will be a sports widow in no time."

"I quite like cricket," replied Ruth. "And I've heard Rob is pretty good. So, I look forward to watching him in the sun. I can top up my tan."

"This is England," said Stan. "It rains in the summer."

Christine was happy that Stan had decided to join in with his pincer attack.

"If it rains," added Ruth, "at least I will spend more time with Rob."

"But what about the football?" said Barry, joining the unpleasantries in search of brownie points. "It's frosty and cold in winter."

"Then I'll see Rob when he's finished, we can meet up somewhere warm," replied Ruth.

"Can't see it lasting," added Christine inappropriately. "You don't share common interests."

"Don't we?" responded Ruth, taking off her denim jacket to reveal the Led Zeppelin T-shirt she was wearing proudly.

This put Christine on the back foot. She knew of Rob's obsession with anything related to Led Zeppelin. Ruth had played a master stroke.

"What do you know about Led Zeppelin?" asked Barry, guessing that Christine and company were losing the battle.

"Plenty," replied Ruth confidently. "For starters, the band members are Robert Plant, Jimmy Page, John Paul Jones and John Bonham."

"Who plays the drums then?" asked Jenifer, trying to catch poor old Ruth out.

"Bonzo, of course," responded Ruth.

"Ah, you are wrong," interrupted Barry. "It's John Bonham. So, you know less than you think."

"Bonzo is John Bonham's nickname," said Rob, putting his arm affectionately around Ruth.

"He lives just outside Droitwich," continued Ruth. "He drinks at The Chequers pub and drives kit cars."

Stan, Christine, Barry and Jenifer were overwhelmed by Ruth's genuine knowledge and interest in Led Zeppelin. It appeared to be more than an act. Feeling ashamed by their inappropriate and unfounded attack, Christine tried to make amends.

"Anyway, I hope it works out for you," said Christine, offering Ruth a hot dog in peace.

Ruth took the hot dog with a smile.

"What's that you are driving?" asked Stan trying to change the subject.

"Mark Three Ford Cortina," replied Graham. "Nice tan interior."

"I don't like the shape of these modern vehicles," replied Stan. "They don't have the lines of the classics."

"It's got an engine that makes it from Worcester to Christchurch on the same day!" quipped Barry, trying to add some humour.

"Then feel free to take a ride home in it," replied an offended Stan.

Barry waved his arm to Stan attempting to apologise. His humour seemed to have landed him in warmer water than he intended.

"I'm not too bothered," continued Graham. "I just need a car to get me from A to B. It's a tin box on wheels. I've never really been into cars."

This comment infuriated the classic car obsessed Stan.

"Classic cars are incredible," said Stan, laying his cards on the table. "I get hours of joy tinkering with the Zodiac. She has great character, charm and makes a beautiful sound when she's running right."

"She's also a massive drain on your wallet," chipped in the long suffering Christine.

"She's worth every penny," replied Stan defensively. "I wouldn't be without her."

"You will be when we get back to Worcester," snapped Christine. "And I'm not joking!"

Sensing the atmosphere turning negative, Rob got up from his chair.

"We'd better be off. It will be dark in an hour," said Rob. "The further we can get in the light, the better."

"Totally agree," added Graham, getting up from his comfy recliner. "Thank you very much for the snack. Thank you for having Rob this week and entertaining him with such variety. Nice to see you."

Stan and Christine both got to their feet to bid their farewells. Barry and Jenifer remained seated.

After Stan had shaken Graham's hand firmly, he walked immediately back into the caravan. He didn't feel comfortable with Rob abandoning the trip, not convinced that the cricket excuse was for real, so wanted no part of the farewell ceremony.

Christine gave Rob and Ruth a small hug and shook Graham's hand.

Graham led the way to the Cortina, with Rob and Ruth directly behind him in his wake.

Assuming Ruth wanted to sit in the front, Rob jumped in the back seat. However, Ruth followed Rob into the back of the car, much to the absolute disgust of Christine. This was the final and most brutal of insults.

Rob and Ruth waved farewell as the bottle green Mark Three Ford Cortina pulled away on the gravel driveway.

"I told you, didn't I!" said Rob to Ruth as they passed the caravan park office.

"Told me what?" asked Ruth.

"Swat up on Led Zeppelin, just in case the mafia closed in!" added Rob. "And they did!"

"You were spot on," replied a smiling Ruth.

"As was your revision," continued Rob. "And where did 'Bonzo' come from?"

"New Musical Express," replied Ruth proudly. "I had even more in my locker. Album names, descriptions of album covers, single releases, lyrics, I had it all."

Rob grabbed Ruth's hand and gave it a gentle squeeze of approval.

"Do you actually like Led Zeppelin?" asked Rob.

"Of course, I do," responded Ruth. "Genuinely, I think they are brilliant, but they don't play my favourite song."

"What would that be then?" quizzed Rob.

"*I Don't Believe in Miracles* by Argent," responded Ruth proudly.

"Good call!" exclaimed Rob. "That's definitely in my top three all-time favourite songs."

"You'd better make it your favourite if you want me to stick around," replied Ruth, squeezing Rob's hand playfully.

Chapter Thirteen

With Rob gone, the dynamic of the group changed immediately. For some reason, the reduction in numbers seemed to bring the four remaining holidaymakers closer together. Siege mentality?

Christine collared Stan and ordered him to take her to the supermarket. Supplies were getting low in Christine's kitchen.

With Stan and Christine on the supermarket run, Barry and Jenifer decided to kill the time by taking Penny for a romantic walk along the riverbank. It was an idyllic spot. The River Stour was flanked by thick rushes, brightly coloured wildflowers and reedbeds. Trees in full leaf stood to attention in the wind-free late summer's evening. As the sun lowered towards the horizon, the ambient light cast a romantic mood across the babbling water.

By the time Stan and Christine had returned from the supermarket, darkness had fallen across the caravan park. Barry and Jenifer helped Stan and Christine unload the shopping. Further signs that a tighter knit community was forming and developing.

Jenifer peeped into bags as they were removed, passing positive and negative comments based on the products in question. This was one of Jenifer's traits that irritated Stan immensely. Jenifer adopted this behaviour at home as well, making Stan feel the most of inadequate shoppers, as the majority of Jenifer's comments were negative and aimed at Stan.

Christine prepared a light snack consisting of cheese and biscuits for quickness. After devouring the late supper, the four weary holidaymakers retired for the night. They needed to charge their batteries to make full use of the following day ahead, as it was to be their last before starting the journey home.

In the middle of the night everyone's sleep was disturbed by the unwanted. The caravan roof sounded like small pebbles were being evenly dropped on it, causing the most irritating tinny drone. Barry was also awoken in the awning as the accompanying wind was blowing the awning around violently.

Fearing that the awning could actually blow away, Barry collected together his sleeping bag and bedding, heading into the sanctuary of the caravan for the remainder of the night.

The storm didn't abate. At sunrise, the rain was still biblical but the wind had eased. Stan pulled back the net curtain in the bedroom, watching the endless stream of raindrops battle their way to the bottom of the caravan windowpane.

"Is it still raining, Stan?" asked Christine.

"Just listen," responded Stan rolling his eyes.

Christine listened. The heavy rain falling on the caravan roof was very much still audible. It was if a calypso steel band was in residence.

"I'll take that as a yes then," stated Christine, rolling over in the bed, showing no interest in rising from her warm sanctuary.

Stan got up to put the kettle on. As the kettle was warming up, Stan strolled to the bay window at the front of the caravan and opened the curtains.

"Oh no!" exclaimed Stan.

"What's wrong?" asked Barry, startling Stan, as Stan assumed Barry was still in the awning.

"Someone left the car boot open," added a distraught Stan. "And it's been raining for most of the night."

Stan instantly fetched his bright yellow waterproof jacket and set off to close the boot. Battling through the stinging rain drops, Stan looked into the boot. Thankfully, the water level in the boot was minimal, mainly due to the holes that Stan knew existed in the bodywork in that area. Another job Stan was yet to get round to sorting.

Stan slammed the boot shut and sped back to the dry caravan.

The excitement of the open boot was sufficient to trigger the three remaining holidaymakers to rise from their slumber. Over a piping hot mug of tea at the dining table, the assembled caravaners were trying to discuss what to do on their last rain soaked day of the holiday.

A visit to Corfe Castle, a walk around the shops in Bournemouth, a trip to Poole Harbour were all discussed and rejected on a variety of grounds. As a mooch around Christchurch harbour was being discussed, Barry broke the thread of conversation.

"Was the river that close before?" asked a concerned Barry. "I am sure it was a lot lower when we walked Penny along the riverbank."

All four immediately moved to get a good vantage point to look at the rising river level.

"Blimey!" exclaimed Jenifer. "You are right, it was a lot lower. It won't flood the caravan site, will it?"

Stan took a close look at the river, then looked up the gentle slope to the left of pitch thirteen, that led up to the site office.

"You know, I'm going to check right now," stated an apprehensive Stan.

Once again, donning his trusty yellow waterproof, Stan scrambled out of the caravan, up the gravel roadway towards the site office. The rain was still incredibly heavy. Stan tried to look in the distance, in the direction of the inclement weather source, but there appeared to be no break in the low, heavily laden, slow moving grey clouds.

Stan returned to the caravan thirty minutes later. An increase in the ferocity of the rain forced Stan to wait for a suitable break in the downpours. Stan opened the caravan door, panting, as he had attempted to jog the majority of the way from the office in cumbersome wellington boots.

After removing his soaked outer garment, Stan started to dry his drenched hair with a fluffy towel handed to him by Christine.

"Anna said we are to be on alert for an immediate evacuation," said a still out of breath Stan. "The river floods the lower site once in a blue moon. Today it looks like it's a blue moon day."

"How deep does it get?" asked a concerned Barry. "Should we not just move to higher ground, just in case?"

"It depends," responded Stan. "If the rain continues at this rate, then I agree. We need to move. However, it would have to be either home, or to another site. They have no more pitches available on higher ground."

"Can't we just set up on the central grassy area by the site office?" suggested Jenifer.

"I asked them exactly that," continued Stan. "But there are two main reasons why they can't. Firstly, the local council only agreed to planning permission if only commissioned pitches are used by touring caravans. Secondly, the ground is soft, and we would make a muddy mess in the grass. The caravan park manager has forbidden any caravans on that grass, period."

"Fair enough," replied Jenifer. "It was just a suggestion."

"I think we just hold tight for now," added Stan. "The forecast is mixed and contradictory. Some say the storm will pass by ten this morning. Others say it will clear at four this afternoon."

"Why don't we just pack up and go," suggested Christine, waiting for her moment. "If we stay, there is a risk that we could get flooded out. Also, it's no fun trying to have a day out in rain this heavy. I say we go home."

"What do you think Jenifer and Barry?" asked Stan.

"I say we go home," replied Jenifer.

"Me to," added Barry. "Not much to keep us here now. Plus, Betsy seems to be behaving herself. Maybe we can take advantage of that good run of form. Plus it looks like the wind is getting up again."

"Okay, that seems to be unanimous, we go home," announced Stan. "I will clear up the awning and the outside stuff. I'm already soaked. I'll bring Betsy up to the caravan when I've packed the awning, to reduce the time you will have to spend in the rain."

Everyone set about packing the holiday gear. After packing their bags and holdalls, Christine made the beds, Jenifer did the washing up, and Barry collected the bags, holdalls and equipment in the dining area.

It took Stan a while to win his battle with the awning. The now fresh, gusting wind made it a difficult one man task. Stan was unable to keep hold of the parts of the removed awning, as they blew around trying to squirm their way out of Stan's grip.

Eventually, seeing the trouble Stan was having, Barry threw on his parka and joined Stan's battle. With Barry sitting on the bulky sections of the removed awning, Stan was able to reach up and slowly release the remaining sections.

Fifteen minutes later, the awning was down and rolled up in a tight cylinder shaped package.

"I'll just move the car now," said Stan to Barry.

Stan jumped into Betsy and turned the ignition key. There was a brief clicking sound, then silence. Stan wondered what was going on. It was most unlike Betsy to behave in this way. At worse, she normally tried to cough and splutter into life, but on this occasion, she was completely lifeless.

Stan started gently headbutting the top of the steering wheel.

Barry strolled over to the Zodiac to investigate the lack of running engine.

"What's up?" quizzed Barry. "Won't she start again?"

"Look," replied a distraught Stan pointing at the main headlamp switch.

"What am I looking at?" responded an ignorant Barry.

"The headlamp switch is in the 'on' position," replied a weeping Stan. "I must have left the headlamps on and the boot open last night, when we returned from the supermarket. I was distracted by Jenifer's item by item analysis of the shopping."

"Disaster!" exclaimed Barry. "We need to get this sorted, and quick. What if the river bursts it's banks?"

"Exactly!" responded a concerned Stan. "I'll run up to the office and see if they can help."

"I'll go, I'm faster than you," replied Barry eagerly.

"You stay here," said Stan sternly. "You know nothing about cars. What are you going to ask them to help with?"

"You can brief me," replied Barry. "Just tell me what to say."

"I'll go," responded Stan assertively.

Stan shot out of Betsy to speak to the site office, whilst Barry ran into the caravan to spread the bad tidings.

"The car won't start again," announced Barry.

"What's wrong with it this time?" yelled a completely frustrated Christine. "I've had it with that car. I say we leave it in the river if it floods, and let the water wash it down into the sea."

"Here, here!" added Jenifer. "We need a reliable, proper family car. Not an antique serial breakdown unit. I'm sick and tired of being stranded in remote places."

The holidaymakers continued with their packing duties, waiting for Stan to bring news from the office.

Thirty minutes later, Stan entered the caravan puffing and panting.

"They can help us," spluttered Stan. "In an emergency such as this, they use a local farmer to help them. He is a brilliant mechanic, apparently, plus he has a big, meaty tractor. So, if the worst comes to the worst, he can at least tow us out of harm's way. He's going to try and get the Zodiac started first."

"Just leave the car, Stan!" suggested a fed up Christine. "Let the river do its worst."

"Don't be ridiculous," replied a surprised Stan. "I'm not letting any river flood my precious classic car."

The debate was interrupted by the sound of the chugging of an approaching tractor. Stan walked out of the caravan to take on the supervisor's role.

"Morning," said the friendly farmer. "I'm Ted. Anna in the office tells me that you are having car trouble. How can I help?"

"Nice to meet you, Ted," replied Stan. "I've got a flat battery. I left the headlamps on last night. She won't start."

"She?" quizzed Ted. "What do you call her then?"

"Betsy," responded a proud Stan.

"Each to his own," replied an unimpressed Ted. "I need to go back to the farm workshop and get some jumper leads. I would have brought them with me if I'd have known you had a flat battery."

"I did tell them that in the office," insisted Stan, trying to clear his name.

"They don't know a jumper cable from a spare wheel in that office," chuckled Ted. "No worries, I'll be back in a jiffy. Just keep an eye on that river level. It won't be long until you need a boat."

Stan and Ted walked up to the low wooden barrier adjacent to the riverbank. Their wellington boots squelched in the waterlogged grass, indicating that they didn't have much time.

"We'd better get a move on," stated Ted. "I'll get off."

Ted climbed the small ladder into his tractor cab, fired up the tractor, and drove away up the gravel roadway.

Stan returned to the caravan to wait for Ted to return with the jumper cables. He was not best pleased with the communication breakdown with the office. Time appeared not to be on their side as the persistent rain continued to beat down.

"We're just about ready now," announced Christine. "Just the car to pack once you get it started. Are we going to head back straight away?"

"I see no good reason to hang around," replied Stan. "The sooner this nightmare of a week is over, the better."

They waited for another forty-five minutes before Ted and his tractor appeared on the gravel roadway.

"Couldn't find these pesky jumper cables," said an embarrassed Ted jumping out of his tractor. "Come on then, let's get to it."

Ted, Stan, and Barry walked over to the Zodiac to prepare for the jump start. Once the cables were attached to Betsy's battery, Ted started up his tractor and manoeuvred it close to Betsy's flank.

Once the cables were attached to the spare car battery that Ted had brought with him, Stan turned the ignition key. Nothing, absolutely nothing. Not even a click.

"Is there any charge in that battery?" asked Stan. "Did you check it?"

"I thought it was okay," replied Ted. "To be honest, I didn't check it."

Stan walked around to the back of Betsy and started to rummage around the boot. He knew he had a small black plastic box containing a voltmeter. Stan didn't go anywhere without his bits and pieces.

Stan returned to the front of Betsy armed with his voltmeter.

"This battery is dead as a dodo," announced Stan in a state of disbelief. "Why would you bring a flat battery to help with a jump start?"

"Just hook the cables up to the tractor battery," suggested Barry.

"No can do," replied Ted smartly. "It's twenty-four volts. If I had two twelve volt batteries, we would have been able to. But that's a twenty-four volt battery."

"It's all just electrics and batteries, isn't it?" argued Barry. "Just hook it up."

Ted and Stan ignored Barry's plea.

"Have you got any other batteries we can jump from?" asked Stan.

"No," responded Ted. "Why don't we see if we can get some help off your fellow caravaners?"

"Great idea," responded Stan.

Ted walked up the gravel roadway to try and get some assistance. All the caravans by the river had packed up and moved off, assuming that it was only a matter of time before the river flooded the area.

Ten minutes later, Ted appeared, followed by a welcome fellow camper, edging his Ford Capri down the sloping gravel road. Suddenly, the Ford Capri stopped and the driver got out.

"I need to test that ground before I go any further," declared the good Samaritan.

The gentleman walked down to Stan's caravan. As soon as the water started to cover his wellington boots, the gentleman turned to Stan and Ted.

"I'm not going to be able to help," said the waterproof jacket clad caravaner. "If I take my motor down there, it will just get stuck. The ground is already waterlogged."

"You will be okay," insisted Stan, not wanting his rescuer to leave the scene.

"No chance, mate," responded the gentleman. "It's just too wet."

The would-be rescuer then got in his Capri and reversed up the bank.

"Can't you just tow us up the bank?" suggested Barry. "At least if the car and caravan are above the flood line, then time is not so crucial."

"Good thinking young man," stated Ted. "Why didn't I think of that?"

"Have you got a tow hook fitted?" asked Stan.

"No," responded Ted. "My tractor is set up ready to hitch the plough. We are going to have to use a tow rope, have you got one?"

"Yes," responded Stan. "In the boot."

Stan walked over to Betsy and took a blue nylon tow rope with a metal hook at one end from the boot.

"Are you sure this is man enough?" asked Ted after Stan presented him with the dubious looking nylon."

"Never let me down yet," responded a proud Stan.

"So, you do this sort of thing all the time?" asked Ted.

"Literally, all the time," jumped in Barry.

"Let's try the caravan first," suggested Ted. "If that floods, it will be a massive clean-up job. If we get the caravan to higher ground, at least you will have somewhere dry for your family to shelter."

"Agreed," replied Stan.

Ted walked to his tractor and manoeuvred it in front of the caravan, whilst Stan took the nylon tow rope to the front of the caravan.

As soon as Ted had reversed up adjacent to the caravan, the immediate problem facing them was instantly apparent.

"There is too much height difference," said a demoralised Stan. "The caravan will just scrape along the ground."

Ted jumped out of his tractor cab, not hearing what Stan had to say above the noise from the tractor engine.

“My hitch point is too high,” declared Ted.

“I just said that!” responded Stan angrily. “What are we going to do?”

“No idea,” replied Ted. “All of my vehicles with tow hooks are out working. I have no way of getting in touch with them.”

Christine decided to brave the heavy rain and joined the gathering. Stan and Ted brought her up to date with recent events.

“Why don’t you try and see if any of the caravaners here will help?” added Christine. “They must be able to tow caravans, otherwise, how did they manage to get their caravan’s here in the first place?”

“Tried that,” snapped Stan. “Nobody wants to take the risk of getting stuck in the soft, wet ground.”

“Why don’t you call for roadside assistance?” suggested Christine. “They might be able to tow the caravan out of here?”

“We might have to,” said Stan. “I guess we are out of options.”

With the rain still heavy, and the river level slowly inching towards pitch number thirteen, Stan walked briskly to the phone box by the site office.

Fifteen minutes later, Stan came scurrying down the gravel roadway.

“They will be here between one and two hours,” announced Stan. “Apparently, they are having a very busy day, due to the weather.”

“That figures,” said Ted. “We’ll just have to wait.”

Ted jumped in his warm tractor cab to wait. Christine, Barry and Jenifer huddled up nervously in the caravan, keeping watch on the river level. Stan decided to try and knock the caravan doors again, to see if he could persuade one of his fellow caravaners to assist him.

Two of the requested caravaners walked to the top of the bank, but as soon as they saw how close the caravan was to the rising river, took a big step back and returned to their respective safe and dry caravans.

Giving up on any assistance from on site, Stan begrudgingly returned to his caravan.

Christine had prepared sandwiches whilst they waited for the recovery truck. Stan took some to Ted in his tractor, along with a mug of piping hot tea.

An hour passed, no sign of the recovery truck. The river was now half a foot from the pathway, which was only a foot from the top of the riverbank. Palms were starting to get sweaty.

After waiting for another forty minutes, finally, the recovery truck appeared at the top of the gravel throughfare.

In no time, Gavin, the recovery truck driver was positioned and hitched up to the front of the caravan. Christine, Barry and Jenifer had been ordered to wait at the top of the grassy bank out of the way. Gavin needed no distractions. Ted and Stan looked on as Gavin inched forward.

As the full weight of the caravan was now under tow, the rear wheels of the recovery truck started to spin on the saturated grass, cutting a rut into the forming mud.

Gavin backed off the power, then applied it again, trying to tug the heavy caravan from its grassy berth. With the rear wheels of the recovery truck still spinning, Ted and Stan rushed to the back of the caravan and started to push with all their might.

Barry, spotting an opportunity to impress, ran down the grassy bank to join the heavers.

Inch by inch, the caravan started to move. As it did so, the rear wheels of the recovery truck started to spin faster and faster, spraying plumes of wet mud higher and higher up the front bay windows of the caravan.

"Those windows are going to take some cleaning," said Christine, watching events unfold from the top of the bank.

The caravan had now moved around three feet in the soft ground, when the recovery truck hit a spot of particularly saturated ground. Progress halted as the rear wheels span in a circular frenzy. Sensing a lack of progress, Gavin eased off on the power and put the recovery truck into neutral.

Gavin jumped out of his cab to assess the situation.

"It's just too soft," declared Gavin. "We need to put something down on the grass so that my tyres can get a bit of traction."

"What about if I hook up my tractor to your truck?" suggested Ted. "Then we can both pull out the caravan together."

"Great idea," responded Gavin. "I'll get a tow rope."

"No need," interrupted Stan. "You have one here."

Stan pulled a sturdy looking tow rope from the open locker of the recovery truck, he had spotted it inside the locker earlier.

As Ted started his tractor and moved it in front of the recovery truck, Stan tied the tow rope to the front of the recovery truck.

Once Stan had secured the tow rope to the tractor, he gave the thumbs up.

Ted applied the gas to the tractor, and Gavin did likewise to the recovery truck. However, after five seconds of manic engine revving, the tractor shot forward, pulling the recovery truck bumper behind it. Ted had just pulled the front bumper clean off the recovery truck.

Gavin leapt out of his truck to inspect the damage.

"What have you done?" gasped Gavin, looking at his bumper less front end. "Why didn't you attach the tow rope to that towing eye?"

Gavin squatted down next to his truck and placed his index finger on the very obvious and visible towing eye.

"Sorry, I didn't see that," replied a guilty looking Stan. "I thought the bumper looked man enough."

Gavin looked across at his buckled front bumper, which was lying in a sad state behind the tractor.

"Really?" said Gavin in a filthy mood. "If you want anything doing, do it yourself."

Gavin walked over and recovered his bent front bumper. Stan bent down and picked up the now free tow rope.

"Oh no you don't," said an irate Gavin, snatching the tow rope from Stan.

Gavin took the tow rope and attached it to the towing eye on the recovery truck, pulling on the rope to ensure it was attached properly. Gavin put his thumb up to Ted and got back into his vehicle.

This time, as both engines revved into life, and with the slack taken out of the tow ropes, the caravan began to move with ease from its muddy lair. Ted steered his tractor gently onto the gravel roadway, closely followed by Gavin and then the caravan. As soon as they were well clear of the sloping ground, Ted stopped and unhitched the tow rope.

There was quite an audience gathered at the top of the bank, despite the torrential rain that was still falling.

"You need to go back for the car," suggested Ted. "I haven't got the right gear on the back of the tractor."

"Right you are," replied Gavin.

Gavin carefully reversed the recovery truck down the gravel road, not wanting to turn round on the saturated ground by Betsy, just in case he got stuck. Stan walked alongside the recovery truck, guiding Gavin as he progressed.

Stan attached his blue nylon tow rope to the front of the Zodiac, and placed the metal hook at the other end of the tow rope on the back of the recovery truck.

Once in position, Stan got into Betsy to steer her away from the threat of the rising river. He put his thumb up to Gavin.

Gavin revved up his engine and started to pull forwards. After only a few feet, once again, the rear wheels of the recovery truck began to spin. The ground had become much wetter, traction was almost impossible. Seeing the dilemma, Ted jumped in his tractor, drove down the bank and positioned himself in front of the recovery truck. It had to be a tractor pull to get everyone out of the saturated quagmire.

Ted attached Gavin's tow rope to the back of the tractor and sparked the tractor engine into life. With Stan waving his thumb at Gavin out of the driver's side window, and Gavin doing the same to Ted, inching forward, the tractor took up the slack from both tow ropes.

Ted and Gavin increased power as the three vehicles started to inch forward, out of the sticky surface. After Betsy had moved about a foot, there was a large twanging sound followed by what sounded like glass cracking.

Stan hadn't fitted the hook securely to the back of the recovery truck. As the tow rope filled with tension from the tow, the metal hook had slipped out of its location and flew backwards at great speed into the top of Betsy's windscreen. Fortunately for Stan, the hook hit the top of the windscreen with more of a glancing blow than a direct hit. But the damage was done, as the windscreen had cracked from top to bottom.

Stan jumped out of the Zodiac in a state of shock, almost as if he was escaping a swarm of bees that had come to rest inside the car. Stan looked at the damage.

Gavin joined Stan to look at the cracked windscreen.

"You were mighty lucky!" said Gavin. "That could have been a lot worse if it would have hit the screen lower down. Are you okay?"

"Just a bit shaken," replied a trembling Stan. "Have you got another tow rope?"

"I have," responded a concerned Gavin. "But don't you want to get yourself together first? You've had a nasty shock."

"We don't have time," replied Stan. "Look at that water level now."

Gavin looked across at the river which was now literally inches from breaking its banks.

Gavin quickly returned to the recovery truck to obtain another tow rope, just in case the fit was the cause of the slippage. Once the different tow rope was fitted and tested, the three drivers returned to their driver's seats.

This time, all tow ropes did their job, as slowly but surely Betsy popped out of her muddy prison, inching her way to the safety of the gravel roadway. As Betsy's back wheels reached the gravel, a ripple of applause broke out from the hilltop onlookers.

Ted piloted the convoy to safe, flat ground before pulling up to a halt. After both of the tow ropes had been removed, Christine walked across to inspect the damage to Betsy. When she realised how close a call it had been for Stan, she walked across to him and gave him a huge hug.

"What was that for?" asked Stan once Christine had pulled away from the affectionate hug.

"Because you are safe and sound, my dear," said Christine. "Anything could have happened if that tow hook had hit the windscreen any lower."

Pleased with the show of affection, Stan afforded himself a broad smile.

"I don't know what you are smiling about now," added Christine. "But I'm sure not cleaning those caravan bay windows. You made the mess, now you can clean it up, Stanley!"

Gavin opened Betsy's bonnet and peered inside. Once he was satisfied, he walked across to Stan.

"I can take you into Bournemouth if you like," said a helpful Gavin. "You can buy a new battery. I know a place where they stock that model you have fitted."

Concerned about having to spend more money, Stan tried his luck.

"Do you have a battery charger on board?" asked Stan cheekily. "Maybe all it needs is a good charge?"

"Look," continued Gavin. "I am offering out of the goodness of my heart to take you to buy a new battery. I don't really have to do that, but I can see the dilemma you are in. I have other calls to make after this one, so I can't wait here for hours whilst you charge a car battery."

"Then leave the charger with me, then come and fetch it later," suggested Stan.

"Take it or leave it," responded an irritated Gavin. "It's either go now to Bournemouth, or I am out of here."

Five minutes later, Stan climbed into the passenger seat of the recovery truck, on his way to buy a new battery.

Christine walked over to Ted to thank him for his kind assistance.

"Thank you, Ted," said Christine, smiling. "We are ever so grateful for your help and assistance. We will be forever in your debt."

"No, you won't be," replied Ted. "I'm off back to the farmhouse now, to create an invoice."

"Invoice?" asked a confused Christine. "For what?"

"My rescue services don't come for free," announced Ted. "I don't do this thing out of the goodness of my heart. I should have been ploughing today. But instead, I've been pulling rusty cars and caravans out of mudholes."

"Our car and caravan aren't rusty!" argued Christine.

"Whatever," replied Ted flippantly. "But you will still be getting a bill from me."

Chapter Fourteen

Stan sorted out the bill with Ted, begrudgingly, despite his arguments and counterarguments, Stan eventually had to hand over far too much folding for his liking. Stan decided to travel home with the cracked windscreen. Although it was damaged, Stan was still able to see clearly past the minimal crack.

Still in victim mode, Stan decided to set a task for Barry and sent him to talk to the office to establish if they had a hose pipe that they could use to clean the front bay windows of the caravan. After the tug of war battles in the quagmire that was pitch thirteen, the caravan now resembled the look of an off road scrambling motorcycle rather than a comfy sanctuary for family holidays. A glacier like flow of dripping mud was cascading down the entire front of the caravan. In addition, Christine had now refused to get in the car until the caravan had been made respectable. She was not willing to be exposed to the public in such a shabby looking caravan.

Barry had been away for over twenty minutes on his hose pipe quest and Jenifer was getting suspicious. Choosing to investigate the reasons for the lengthy search, the reason for the delay became crystal clear to Jenifer immediately, as she spotted her ill-disciplined boyfriend leaning over the counter flirtatiously, deep in conversation with an attractive site office receptionist.

"At it again!" shrilled a vexed Jenifer as she entered the site office. "You just can't resist temptation, can you."

Barry instantly bolted upright, looking over to Jenifer with his best puppy dog eyes.

"Anna here has sent out the maintenance man to fetch a hose pipe from Ted," replied Barry, trying to convince Jenifer that all was above board. "He will be back soon, you see. I was just waiting here innocently with Anna."

"That doesn't give you a licence to flirt with the locals," snapped Jenifer angrily.

"He wasn't flirting," butted in Anna, the receptionist. "But to be honest, I find him a little boring. I don't really like football. It's ice hockey all the way for me. Far more a man's game. Those footballers are just a bunch of pansies."

Barry looked up at Anna with a look of shock and horror.

Jenifer afforded herself a wry smile. At last, Barry had been called out. Not everyone found his wealth of football trivia and anecdotes interesting. Here was the living proof.

“I’ll leave you to it then,” stated Jenifer as she left the office feeling far more comfortable with the situation.

The hose pipe arrived within ten minutes of Jenifer’s controlled exit from the site office. Anna gave directions to a suitable standpipe for Stan to connect the hose pipe to, recommending that he take great care with his car, so as not to make too much of a mess on the neat looking but saturated caravan park grass.

As Stan hosed down the caravan, Barry helped with a broom, trying to dislodge the collection of thick mud that had been liberally sprayed on the caravan. Christine invited Jenifer and Anna to join her in the caravan and made a fresh pot of tea, whilst Stan and Barry toiled outside.

With the caravan spick and span, the pot of tea devoured, and the holidaymakers seated comfortably inside Betsy, it was at last time to set off for Worcester. Anna waved them off with a big smile on her face.

“Have we got time to stop at Stonehenge on the way home?” asked Barry from the back seat. “You did promise on the way down that we could visit Stonehenge.”

Stan was reluctant to answer. The trials and tribulations of the previous week were weighing heavily on Stan’s shoulders. All he wanted to do was cross his fingers, and make sure Betsy got them home in one day.

“Let me think about it,” responded Stan reluctantly.

"You did promise!" added Jenifer, trying to strengthen Barry's case.

"We have the caravan to consider," replied Stan. "It's awkward to park and manoeuvre on those types of car parks. It might be busy as well, so parking will probably be difficult, even without the caravan."

"I have a great idea," added Barry. "We could find a lay by close to Stonehenge, park up the caravan, then go to Stonehenge without having to tow anything. Easy to park and easy to get there and back."

"Good idea," said Jenifer, patting Barry's arm gently in a show of appreciation, rather than the usual attacking slaps.

Stan was not happy. It appeared that the case for the Stonehenge stop off was strengthening.

"That's settled then," announced Christine. "The rain has eased off, and after all, we haven't done much sightseeing this week."

"Just petrol station forecourts, car dealerships, building sites and muddy caravan parks," added Barry.

"That means we have to go back the way we came," replied Stan. "I wanted to go back a different route, to try and change our luck."

"Don't be ridiculous, Stan," responded Christine. "That's just mumbo jumbo. Take a different route from Stonehenge if you want to do something different."

It was no use. Christine, Barry and Jenifer seemed to have an answer to all the obstacles that Stan was putting in front of them. So, much to his disgust, Stan headed down the A338 towards Salisbury and to Stonehenge.

It wasn't long before they passed through Fordingbridge. There was much banter, jollity and chatter regarding the previous events at the fateful caravan breakdown junction. Stan didn't join in with the light-hearted banter. He just kept his eyes on the road and on Betsy's gauges. Stan was very much aware that they considered him a suitable target for the brunt of the cheap shots and general teasing being banded around.

As Stan reached Salisbury, all was looking good with Betsy. Every warning gauge was reading normal, she was responding well to any throttle applications, purring like a contented lioness. Stan thought it must have been the new battery that was giving the Zodiac a new lease of life.

"Take care through Salisbury," said Christine. "We don't want any more meetings with our old friend Sergeant Corthine."

"Why would you say that?" replied a downbeat Stan. "I just need positive energy inside this car. We are doing well, and nothing is going wrong. Just try and be positive for once."

Christine threw her nose in the air in contempt, then folded her arms across her chest defensively, not impressed with her unjust telling off from her husband.

Salisbury was negotiated at a canter. Light traffic and a lucky run of consecutive green traffic lights meant that Betsy eased through the city without issue. Was this the change in luck that Stan was so desperately dreaming of? The holidaymakers continued with their journey, everyone scanning for a suitable lay by or parking spot in which to temporarily abandon the caravan.

As Stan drove through Salisbury Plain, everyone was in awe of the change and sheer openness of the surrounding vista. Huge fields of crops rose gently up to perfectly rounded hills in the near distance, garnished on top with neat looking groves of tall, evenly cultivated trees.

As they drew nearer to Stonehenge, Barry spotted an opportunity.

"What about this pull in ahead?" suggested Barry. "That looks like a great place to leave the caravan."

"It's the entrance to a farmer's field," responded Stan. "We can't block that!"

"We wouldn't block it," insisted Barry. "It's wide, plus there are no 'no parking' signs. Even if a farmer needed access, there is still plenty of room. And it's away from the busy road."

Stan wasn't convinced. They had already been in hot water with a farmer this week, breaking down and blocking his entrance. Stan didn't want a repeat performance.

"Maybe as a last resort," replied Stan. "Let's keep looking for now."

Stan drove on. As they approached the roundabout that accesses Stonehenge, Stan drove Betsy completely around the roundabout and returned to the southbound carriageway of the A338.

"We may have to use your option Barry after all," said Stan reluctantly. "There is nowhere else suitable to leave the caravan. I think we should be okay. I suggest we stay at Stonehenge no more than an hour and a half tops. That should be long enough."

The holiday crew nodded in agreement.

As they approached the field entrance, Stan carefully guided the caravan as far to the left of the entrance as he could. Once happy with the positioning, Stan jumped out and unhitched the caravan. Stan then waited until the busy road was clear to cross the road. Stan wanted a different perspective to make sure this temporary stop was feasible. After careful consideration, Stan convinced himself that the caravan was not obstructing access.

Betsy took the holiday crew down the A338 to Stonehenge. When they arrived at the entrance, Stan was disgusted.

"Look at this car park!" announced Stan. "It's vast, and a good surface. There was no need to ditch the caravan, we could have parked here easily with the caravan. I'm going to fetch it."

"If you want to fetch it, you go alone," said Christine firmly. "We haven't got long here, and I don't want to waste another half an hour fetching the caravan."

Stan was in a quandary. He was keen to take in the wonders of Stonehenge, but he was also concerned for his caravan. After an internal debate, Stan decided to stay and enjoy the attraction.

Once the tickets were purchased, the group proceeded with excitement to this most iconic of tourist attractions. Stan gazed in wonder at the sarsen stones, towering wondrously from the soil, forming a giant circle around him. Goose bumps filled Stan's arms as he tried to picture days gone by, trying to recreate possible ancient ceremonies or rituals in his mind. Christine was equally impressed with the collection of ancient stones. She had managed to collar a local historian, who was telling Christine all about the history and legends that surrounded this marvellous neolithic wonder. Penny just looked at other dogs in the locality, wagging her tail gently.

Barry and Jenifer wandered around the stone circle alone. Barry was still trying to repair the damage caused by his alleged flirtatious behaviours in the caravan site office. They just needed a bit of alone time for now.

With the weather on the horizon starting to look threatening, Stan suggested that they made their way back to the car. They had spent an hour at the stones which was long enough to milk the mystery.

Much to Stan's relief, Betsy started second time. Things were looking up. It appeared that Betsy was finally playing ball.

It took fifteen minutes battling through the stream of vehicles to get out of Stonehenge. It looked like most of the visitors also had a watchful eye on the building gloomy weather.

Twelve minutes down the A338 southbound, Stan approached the farm entrance. Stan's jaw dropped in astonishment. The caravan was not there! It must have been stolen.

"I don't believe it!" said Stan angrily. "Why did I agree to your ridiculous suggestion Barry? It's quite clear now that this was not a safe place at all to leave the caravan."

"You did fit the wheel lock, Stan?" asked Christine.

"It's broken," responded Stan. It was broken when they towed the caravan out of the river. I forgot it was still fitted. The strength of Ted's tractor broke the device."

"That's just asking for trouble," continued Christine. "What are we going to do now?"

Stan jumped out of the Zodiac and scanned the farmer's fields for any sign of the caravan but detected nothing. Stan walked up to the passenger side of the car. Christine wound down the window.

"Anything?" asked a hopeful Christine.

"Nothing," replied a despondent Stan. "I've got no choice but to call the police."

"There was a phone box outside Stonehenge," suggested Barry.

Stan couldn't bring himself to respond to Barry. It was his idea to abandon the caravan in this ill-fated spot.

Stan climbed back into Betsy and set off back to Stonehenge. After a confused discussion on the phone, Stan returned to the car.

"We have to wait here for the police," said Stan. "I didn't know the exact location of the crime scene, so they will meet us here and I will take them to the scene."

"I bet the Wiltshire Constabulary will be pleased to see you!" chortled Barry.

This earned Barry a customary slap and telling off from his girlfriend.

The destitute gathering waited for another fifty minutes in silence until a police car came into view on the distant roundabout. As the police car pulled up, Stan spotted a familiar face behind the steering wheel. The police officer climbed out of his patrol car and ambled over to the Zodiac.

"Well, well, well!" said Sergeant Corthine. "I knew it had to be you when the call came in. How could it be anybody else? How was the holiday? I assume you actually made it to Christchurch in the end?"

"We did and it was fine," replied an embarrassed Stan. "The end of the holiday was as interesting as the start."

"I don't want to know!" responded Sergeant Corthine shielding his face with both hands.

Stan then explained the situation, describing how and where they had parked up the caravan. Sergeant

Corthine insisted that Stan took them to the location where the caravan went missing.

Fifteen minutes later, Betsy and the patrol car were on scene. Sergeant Corthine got out of his police car and started to survey the scene. Stan joined him to take a look around.

"Look, there," said Sergeant Corthine. "Those tractor tracks are fresh, and they look like they disappear up that hill. Jump in my car and we will go and investigate further."

After instructing Christine, Barry and Jenifer to remain in the Zodiac, Sergeant Corthine took Stan up the sloping muddy track that split the green field in front of them. Once they eventually reached the summit of the hill, Sergeant Corthine spotted a farmhouse about half a mile away.

"Let's go and check that farmhouse out," suggested Sergeant Corthine. "A good place to start."

The pair proceeded to the farmhouse. After a quarter of a mile, Sergeant Corthine spotted a gateway to a lane. They took this option to reduce the risk of getting stuck on the muddy track.

Once at the farmhouse, there were no signs of life. Sergeant Corthine instructed Stan to remain in the police car whilst he took a look around. Stan was not best pleased with the instruction. He was desperate to get his beloved caravan back.

Ten minutes later, Sergeant Corthine returned to the police car, accompanied by a farmer.

"This chap has got your caravan," informed Sergeant Corthine. "It's safe and sound in a barn around the corner. The farmer took it in because he feared it might have been stolen."

"Did he tell anyone about taking the caravan?" asked Stan. "It would have saved a lot of worry."

"I am going to Salisbury this evening," responded the farmer. "I was going to report it then. I was going to make a special trip to the police station."

"That's kind of you," replied Sergeant Corthine.

Stan was far less impressed. He wanted to let rip on the farmer for meddling with his caravan and causing great concern in the camp.

"I'll take you back to your car," offered Sergeant Corthine. "You can drive back down the lane and fetch your caravan."

"That's very kind of you," replied Stan.

Stan offered a handshake to the farmer, which was duly accepted.

Stan jumped in the patrol car with Sergeant Corthine. They drove slowly down the narrow, winding farm lane. Once at the Zodiac, Stan brought the family up to date with affairs, sharing the great news that they still had a damage free caravan.

Stan returned to the farm and waited for the farmer to bring round the caravan. To Christine's disgust, when the caravan came into view, mud was plastered down both flanks of the clean caravan.

"It got a little messy," admitted the farmer. "I took a short cut, but the brook was up due to all the rain we've been having. It got a bit sticky down there."

"Have you got a hose pipe?" asked a disgruntled Christine. "You can clean up that mess you have made."

"There's gratitude for you," replied the farmer. "In any case, I haven't got time to mess about with hose pipes. I'm a busy farmer. If you want to wash your caravan, that's up to you."

"Just go, Stanley!" screamed Christine, wanting to get away from this rude, meddling farmer as soon as possible.

Stan shook the farmer's hand, then walked across to Sergeant Corthine to bid his farewell.

"Now, get out of Wiltshire!" said Sergeant Corthine grinning from cheek to cheek.

Stan climbed aboard Betsy and drove off down the narrow farm lane.

With mixed feelings, Stan turned on to the A338 and headed home. It seemed there was a mountain to climb one day after another. If it wasn't the unreliable car, it was the belligerent caravan. Stan just couldn't wait to get home and leave this disastrous week behind him.

The journey back home progressed well. Marlborough came and went event free. Swindon was soon in Stan's rear view mirror and he was feeling far more comfortable with life and Betsy's performance. Her impeccable behaviour resulted in Stan coming off gauge watch. Instead, Stan tried to take in the countryside and the high spirited conversations that were rattling around the Zodiac.

Now on the tree lined A419, as they approached Cricklade, Betsy starting to cough and hesitate.

"Not again!" said Christine. "What's wrong with this wretched car now?"

"I'm not sure," replied a concerned Stan. "She seems to be losing power."

Stan scanned the gauges, all seemed to be displaying normal, except one. With all the distractions, along with a return to good behaviour by Betsy, Stan had come off gauge watch, including the fuel gauge. They were pretty much running out of petrol.

"Oh no!" announced Stan. "I think I know what the issue is, we are low on fuel."

"Low?" quizzed Christine. "It will still go if you have low fuel, surely."

"Not this low," admitted a distraught Stan.

Spotting a side road turning, Stan turned off the busy main road and spluttered to a halt twenty yards up the side road.

The mood in the car once more dropped to the floor.

"Why didn't you check the fuel, Stanley?" nagged Christine. "It's not rocket science!"

"I don't know," responded Stan. "There have been so many distractions, my attentions were turned away from fuel level."

"I hope you have a jerrycan?" asked Christine.

"There is one in the caravan side locker," responded Stan confidently. "I will go and fetch it."

Stan got out of the Zodiac to fetch the jerrycan. On opening the side locker, Stan's nerves became even more frayed. He hadn't used the jerrycan for some time now, so was surprised to see a rotten pile of metal resembling a jerrycan in front of him. As Stan picked it up, liquid dribbled out of the rusty holes in the bottom of the jerrycan.

"That's all I need!" said Stan to himself.

Stan returned to Betsy and sat down in the driver's seat, leaving the door open.

"Where's the jerrycan?" asked Christine desperately.

"Hmmm," replied Stan. "It looks like it's not fit for purpose."

"What do you mean?" continued Christine.

"It's full of holes," responded Stan. "It's as rotten as a pear."

"I don't believe it!" replied Christine, turning up the volume of her voice. "Did you actually think about this holiday at all?"

"I didn't plan on running out of petrol!" snapped Stan.

"So, what now?" begged Christine.

"We need to find a petrol station and hope they have a jerrycan," responded Stan. "Can anyone remember going past a petrol station recently?"

Nobody answered Stan's call for hope.

"I'll go and look for one," suggested Barry. "I can try and flag a motorist down for assistance."

"If you are sure you don't mind," replied Stan. "I'd appreciate you going. My legs are tired after all that walking at Stonehenge."

Stan handed over some money to Barry.

"Try and borrow a jerrycan, rather than buy one," requested Stan, trying to reduce his imminent spending.

Barry trotted off in search for a petrol station.

"Cup of tea anyone?" asked Christine.

"Any fig rolls?" quizzed Stan.

"No!" shouted Christine. "You and your pesky fig rolls."

Stan, Christine and Jenifer managed to get through two pots of tea and still no sign of Barry returning to the caravan. Moments later, a blue Triumph sportscar pulled up in front of Betsy. Barry jumped out of the passenger door and a leggy, slim blonde lady jumped out of the driver's door.

"Typical!" snarled Jenifer. "Trust him!"

Fortunately, Stan spotted Barry holding a shiny bright red jerrycan, excellent news! Barry presented the jerrycan to Stan, who preceded to pour the precious petrol into Betsy.

"This kind lady lent us the jerrycan," said Barry as he walked up to Stan. "But there is a condition."

"Condition?" asked a concerned Stan.

"That you fill up your tank at her petrol station up the road," explained Barry.

“Fill the tank?” quizzed a concerned Stan. “Or just put enough fuel in to get us home?”

“Full tank,” responded Barry. “And Helen wants to do it, just in case you want to try and cheat her.”

Stan was resigned to the fact that he had to splash out even more money for unnecessary fuel.

“I guess so,” said a reluctant Stan.

With gas in the tank, it took Stan a few cranks to spark the Zodiac into life. At the third attempt, Betsy roared into life, jettisoning a plume of grey smoke out of the exhaust.

Stan carefully backed onto the main road with the assistance of Barry. It was well into the evening, so the road was not as busy as earlier. Closely following Helen, they eventually reached the petrol station. For once, Stan managed to arrive at the fuel pumps without taking out any forecourt canopies. Helen took control of the petrol filling process. She wanted her pound of flesh for the loan of the lifesaving jerrycan.

With the fuel tank now full, the intrepid holidaymakers were soon on their way home. Only Barry waved back at Helen as they pulled out of the fuel station, which earned him the customary slap to the arm.

Stan was gentle on Betsy, not wanting to overload the Zodiac engine. He drove with great care past Cirencester. The drop down Birdlip Hill was a nervous affair. Stan didn’t want to go too fast, but equally didn’t want to cook the brakes. It was a heart thumping ten minutes.

As Betsy entered the M5 motorway, Stan let out a sigh of relief. It felt like it was the last leg of the most fretful of journeys. Plus, the M5 was populated with emergency phones at regular intervals, just in case Betsy threw a last gasp wobbler.

As they were passing the Tewksbury junction, Stan began to feel slightly concerned. Betsy was not being fully responsive. As he applied pressure on the accelerator pedal, the response was not instant or as expected. Not wanting to cause any undue panic, Stan kept this breaking news to himself, thinking that the problem would sort itself out and go away.

With darkness enveloping the evening sky, the Zodiac crossed the bridge over the River Avon, still not performing one hundred percent efficiently. Stan felt impelled to share his feelings with his passengers.

"I think we may have another problem with Betsy," stated Stan. "Strencham Services is only a mile or so ahead, I want to come off the motorway and take a look under the bonnet."

"Not again!" wailed Christine. "You are definitely selling this wreck when we get home."

"Don't start," responded Stan rolling his eyes. "It's probably nothing."

As the Zodiac approached the junction for the services, the engine started to cough and splutter constantly. Stan was trying his hardest to maintain his low speed without loading up the engine.

To everyone's relief, Betsy made it off the motorway. Stan guided his car to the far side of the ample car park. It was quiet, no cars, vans, or lorries were occupying this area. Stan wanted space to take a good look under Betsy's bonnet.

Stan pulled up to a stop. Steam or smoke could visibly be seen coming from each side of the bonnet, accompanied by a sharp hissing sound.

"Go and get the fire extinguisher out of the caravan, Barry," commanded a worried Stan. "And get me a tea towel, the bonnet area is probably quite hot."

"Right you are," replied Barry as he leapt quickly out of the back seat.

Moments later, Barry returned with the tea towel and fire extinguisher. Holding the tea towel, Stan lifted the smoking bonnet. A large plume of smoke instantly rose from the bonnet area, closely followed by a set of orange flames. Stan grabbed the fire extinguisher from Barry, pulled out the retaining pin and pressed the lever. A jet of foam squirted over the engine bay, causing clouds of smoke and steam to belch into the evening air.

An onlooking lorry driver ran across clutching another fire extinguisher, joining Stan in firefighting duties. Christine, Barry, Jenifer and Penny backed off to a safe distance as the brave duo fought the engine fire.

Another lorry driver joined the gang, also carrying a fire extinguisher.

"I've called the Fire Brigade," announced the out of breath lorry driver. "Is there much fuel in the tank?"

"It's almost full," replied Stan frantically. "I've not long filled up."

As the third fire extinguisher was being sprayed over the smoking engine, it appeared that the flames had almost abated, and the fire was more under control.

Within a further ten minutes, a bright red fire engine with blue lights flashing and sirens blaring entered the service station car park. By now, quite a crowd had gather to watch the unfolding action.

Firemen seemed to jump out of every available door on the fire engine, running across to Betsy to get a prompt update.

One of the fireman arrived with a handline, spraying foam all over the Zodiac engine, making it look more like a Ford Meringue.

"Looks like it's out!" announced a tall fireman. "How did the fire start?"

"Absolutely no idea," replied a tearful Stan, looking at his pride and joy smoking like a steam train.

"Lucky nobody was hurt," continued the fireman. "That's the main thing. Also, lucky you could get off the motorway. It would have been a different outcome if you didn't get the assistance from these lorry drivers."

"Indeed," responded a distraught Stan.

"We will have to stay with the vehicle," added the fireman. "Just to make sure the fire is completely out."

Stan trudged wearily over to his family. He needed a big hug from his wife right now. Seeing the possible demise of his beloved classic was too big a pill to swallow. Sensing his anguish, Christine put her arms around her husband.

Jenifer returned to share her news. Understanding that Betsy was probably not going to get them home, she had been inside the services making phone calls.

"I tried to get hold of Margaret," explained Jenifer. "But she's not answering her phone."

"Why are you phoning Aunty Margaret?" asked Christine.

"To give us a lift home," responded an irritated Jenifer. "How are we going to get home in a car that has just decided to commit suicide."

"I see," replied Christine.

"Anyhow," continued Jenifer, "with Dave still in Cornwall, I was running out of options. So, I phoned Rob's dad. He has agreed to come out and give us a lift. He's on his way now."

"Excellent," responded a jubilant Christine. "That's kind of him."

Forty minutes later, the bottle green Ford Cortina arrived on scene. Graham greeted the destitute holidaymakers and guided them into his vehicle. Stan decided to remain behind to make sure Betsy came to no further harm.

Forty-five minutes later, Graham pulled up outside Christine's house.

"Thank you so much," said Christine. "You have been our saviour."

"Don't mention it," replied Graham. "It's the least I could do."

Christine, Barry, Jenifer and Penny piled out of the Cortina and traipsed up the path to the front door. Once inside, Christine made several calls to her sister to share the news of the great Strencham fire, and to ask Margaret to return Fiona home.

Forty minutes later, Margaret arrived with Fiona, full of questions regarding the missing car and caravan, that should have been parked up on the long driveway.

Inside the house, Christine and Jenifer went into great lengths trying to explain the events that unfolded the previous week, but Margaret was having none of it.

"You've just made that all up," said Margaret. "Maybe one or two things might have happened, but not all of them."

"It's true," explained Christine as the front room curtains were brightly illuminated by the tow truck pulling up on the drive.

Christine and Margaret rushed out to investigate the source of the activity.

On the drive was a large recovery truck. On the load bed was a sad looking Betsy still dripping liquids from the engine bay. Hitched up to the recovery truck was a mud splattered caravan, that looked like it had seen better days.

Stan climbed out of the passenger side of the recovery truck and walked towards the house smiling.

"Same time next year?" asked Stan as he put his arms around his wife on the doorstep.

"You must be joking," replied Christine, brushing away Stan's advances. "I'm going to Cornwall with Dave next year. At least I know we will get there in one piece!"

Disturbed by the commotion at the front door, Fiona had made her way to the front of the house from behind the garden shed. Looking at the wrecked car and caravan completely plastered in mud, Fiona could hardly believe her eyes.

"You must have had a good time. Wish I'd stayed after all!" said a smiling Fiona.

"Don't you start," snapped Christine. "You were part of the problem."

"Leave me out of this," responded Fiona defensively. "This is nothing to do with me."

"Never is," growled Christine. "Now, Stanley. Come inside and start reading the phone book. You need the phone number of a suitable scrap yard to take this pile of junk that's sitting here making a mess all over my drive."